GROWING RIPPLES

ROOTS OF CREATION BOOK 2

JASON HAMILTON

MYTHHQ

MYTH HQ, LLC

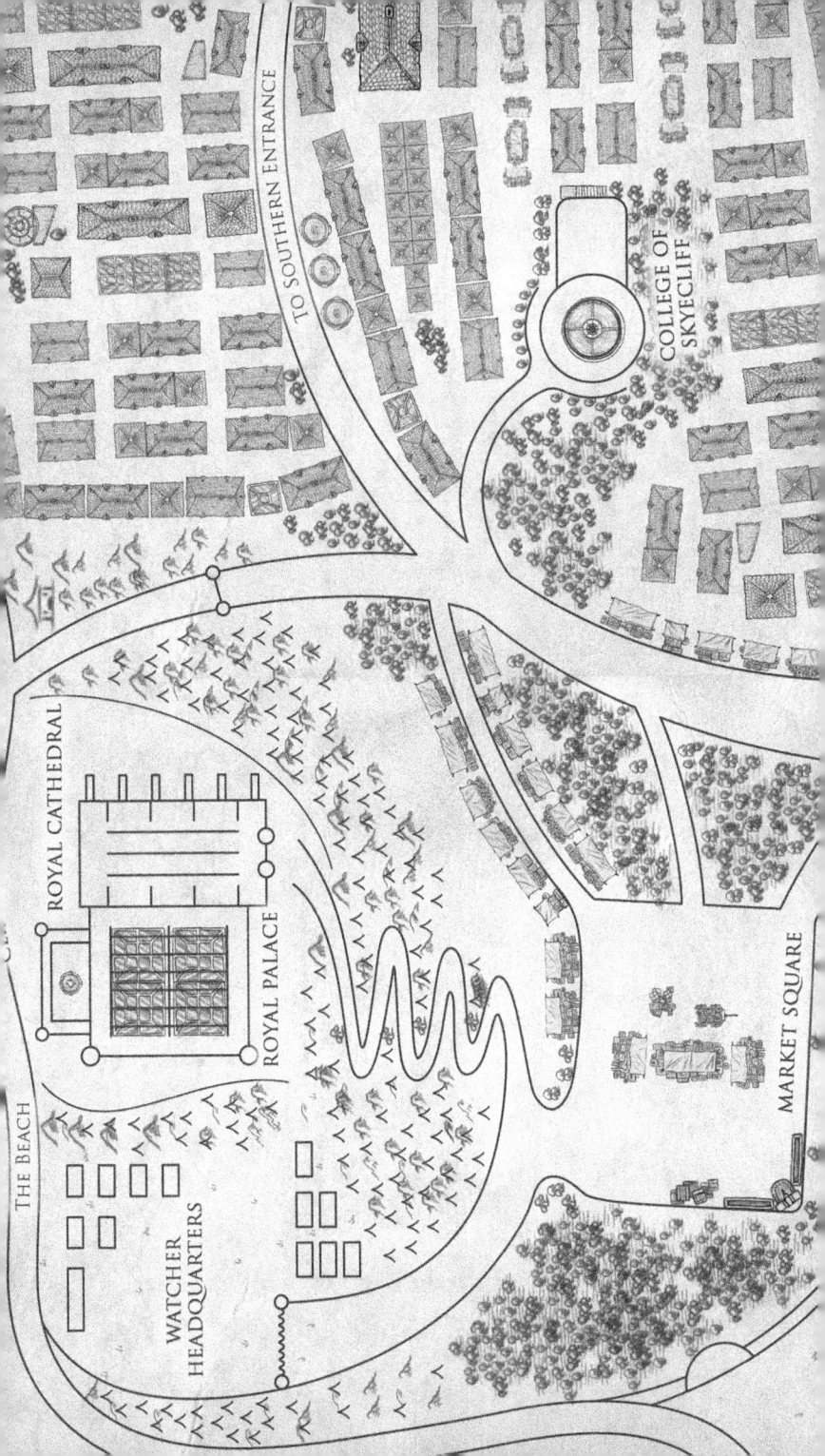

TO SOUTHERN ENTRANCE

COLLEGE OF SKYECLIFF

ROYAL CATHEDRAL

ROYAL PALACE

THE BEACH

WATCHER HEADQUARTERS

MARKET SQUARE

GET THE R⊙⊙TS OF CREATION PREQUEL!

A prequel short story to the Roots of Creation Series.

(contains some spoilers for Out of Shadow)

Heroes are never born...they are nurtured.

Before Jak became a hero, a horrible secret surrounded her birth. Witness the beginning of that secret as we follow her father while he searches for his wife, and finds more than he could possibly imagine.

Now he's faced with a choice. Follow orders, or turn against his comrades. What will he do when his wife's safety is on the line?

Get this **(and several more)** short stories for free when you join my fantasy group: https://storytellingdb.com/go/a rgovale

Cheers!

Jason

CONTENTS

CHAPTER 1

"**Y**OU KNOW WHAT'S INTERESTING?" Naem said stepping up behind Jak. "We haven't seen a single demon this entire trip. You don't suppose we killed them all?"

Jak resisted the urge to look around the rolling hills searching for one of the demons. Instead, she adjusted her spear and pack strapped to her back and kept walking. Naem was right though. Everyone knew it was difficult to travel in small groups. Demons were monsters that used to be human, but through the misuse of magic lost their sanity and became animalistic killers. But their travelling group was small, and no one had seen hide nor hare of a demon. True, they had killed several thousand of them just over a month ago. But Jak wasn't so certain they had seen the last of them.

"I don't think so." Her eyes were still fixed ahead of her at the horizon. Maybe just beyond that hill, she would see their destination...

Three weeks. That was how much time had passed since she and a few others had left Foothold. Left Jak's mother, a Shadow Fae, in the nearby mountains. Left all the men and women who survived that gruesome demon attack. Jak had lost a lot in that battle. Including her best friend, Marek. Now she was done with adventures. All she wanted for her future was to study magic.

"Yeah, I guess that would be wishful thinking." Naem continued, ignoring the fact that she wasn't meeting his gaze. "After what Kuldain said..." he trailed off.

Jak knew what he was talking about. Before he died, Kuldain had hinted at higher power, someone or something that gave the orders.

Jak heard a sniff and glanced over to see another of her travel companions, Estel, sulking as usual. Skellig had decided that Estel could benefit from the structure of Watcher High Command, much to Jak's annoyance. Though she had been oddly quiet through the journey. Jak liked to hope that the battle had changed her somewhat but didn't really expect it. More than likely she just didn't want to misbehave in front of their leader, Gabriel, the fourth and final member of their little group, and also the man who had first given her a brand. She stared at her left hand now, where the black lines ran on the back of her palm, past her wrist. She had found good uses for her magic, if not quite what it was meant for. Gifting was meant to imbue others with magical abilities. Use it wrongly and it could cause... violent reactions. So naturally she had used it to blow stuff up, including Kuldain, a Fae-hating Colonel who had turned out to be a demon himself.

Despite Naem's attempts to start a conversation, she kept her eyes glued to the path in front of her, and beyond. She hadn't said much to Naem during this whole trip, though it had been impossible to ignore him entirely. They had been close for a time, but after Marek's death... well. She had needed some time to think about everything. But that was not the only reason she avoided his gaze. She was looking for the city. As if reading her thoughts, Gabriel approached.

"We'll be there soon. I suggest we double our pace."

That was all Jak needed; instantly she felt her legs gain new strength, and she watched for any sign of the city beyond the hill.

Another two hills and she saw it. Skyecliff. *The greatest city this side of the mountains,* Jak thought. Her pace slowed to a stop, and she just... looked at it. The city was perched alongside an ocean cliff, with towers larger than Jak had thought possible extending into the air. She had thought the tower at Foothold was tall. It was nothing compared to what she saw now.

"It's quite a sight, isn't it?" Gabriel stepped to her side and placed one hand on her shoulder. "Sometimes I forget, but it is a marvelous city, despite its share of problems."

Jak almost asked what kind of problems such a magnificent work of human civilization could have, but Gabriel kept talking before she could say anything.

"You gave up a lot to come here, you showed great courage."

Jak shrugged, not taking her gaze off the city, "I just want to learn."

"Leaving your mother, especially given her... eh, changes. That can't have been easy."

Jak frowned. Why was he bringing this up now, while they were almost at their destination? It wasn't like they could turn back now.

"I'll see her again. Maybe after my studies, I can help her and the other Fae."

"Indeed," Gabriel said nodding slowly. "Well, you've already shown great promise so far. I'm still amazed that you managed to make a brand stick, even if it didn't work the way it was supposed to."

He was referring to the Flamedancer brand she had used to blow things up. If it had been used correctly, it would have imbued the object with fire magic.

"You're sure I won't get in trouble for that?" Jak asked for the hundredth time. "I know students aren't allowed to give brands without supervision."

Not to mention kill someone with them.

"Child, I may not be in charge at the college, but the one who is trusts me. I travel a lot, but I'm essentially the head teacher when I'm there. You have nothing to fear. Your circumstances were, shall we say, out of the ordinary."

That was an understatement. But it still didn't do much to ease her mind. She had done much more than use her gift without supervision. She had somehow managed to give Naem more than one brand, something no Gifter had ever achieved. She did it to save his life, but she had never been able to replicate the process. Naem now had Toughness and Healing, in addition to his original Grace. But Jak had yet to figure out how she had done it. She couldn't even get a single brand to stick for longer than a few moments before it malfunctioned, even with the training Gabriel had given her in the last few weeks. He told her to be patient and she was already far ahead of others at her level. But that didn't stop Jak from wanting more.

"Well, let's get a move on," she said and marched down the hill towards Skyecliff.

If she thought the towers had looked large before, it was nothing like what they looked like up close. As they finally entered the gates, she thought she might fall backward just from looking up at the city. She didn't even notice the guards lining the walls, or the small group of men Gabriel paused to speak with as they entered. All she could do was stare, first at the towers, then at the city around her.

It was nothing like what she had expected. There was something everywhere. She couldn't even see the sea from where they stood. All around her were buildings, roads, markets, inns, and more. Everywhere she looked, she saw something man-made. For a moment, she felt like all the activity pressing in around her was trapping her away from the rolling hills and snow-capped mountains she was used to. But there was a beauty in Skyecliff, too.

Looking up, she saw the Royal Palace. That was where the queen herself lived!

"Do you think we'll ever get to see the queen?" she asked Gabriel after he had finished speaking with the men at the gate.

Gabriel laughed. "I certainly hope not. Most people who see the queen these days are usually in some kind of trouble. She doesn't make too many public appearances anymore."

"Why is that?"

Gabriel shrugged. "Who knows? Keeps to herself these days, with only her most trusted advisors surrounding her. And personally, I wouldn't trust them any farther than I could spit. Too many of their own interests take priority."

Jak let Gabriel's words wash over her. It didn't sound like Gabriel had a high opinion of the queen. But... she was the queen, wasn't she? She was supposed to be the one that served the people most, providing safety and security for the kingdom. At least, that was what Jak had heard, growing up. She tried to think back if her father had said much about her. Nothing came to mind. She knew now, thanks to her mother, that Rael, her father, had been a Watcher before her birth. The Watchers worked under the queen's authority to take down supernatural threats. Naem was a Watcher too, and technically, so was Jak, though she had only been recruited after her father died and her village was attacked. Now that she was going to the college, continuing as a Watcher probably wouldn't happen.

"Which way to the college?" she asked.

Gabriel pointed, and they began to walk again until Jak noticed Naem was not with them. In all the hustle and bustle, she had forgotten about him completely. Turning, she looked back to see him standing near the gate, watching them go.

Backtracking, she caught up to him. "Aren't you coming?"

"I've got to report to the Watcher High Command. They'll want a complete rundown of what happened."

"How complete?" Jak asked narrowing her eyes. Certain things were best kept quiet.

"Okay, well maybe not a *complete* report." He rubbed his sleeve as he spoke, where his extra brands lay. "But honestly, some secrets won't stay quiet forever. I'll have to tell someone eventually."

Jak nodded. She didn't like that idea, but Naem was right. They couldn't keep it a secret forever.

"Okay, well... I guess I'll see you around."

Naem nodded back. "I hope so. Care to keep training together?"

She hesitated. They hadn't trained together since before the demon battle. But she could use the practice, and Naem had been so patient with her. Perhaps she could spare a little time.

"I'll see what my schedule is like at the college, but I'd like that."

Naem smiled, showing his white teeth. She hadn't seen him smile like that in days.

"Great! We'll talk later then. It shouldn't be too hard to find me." He pointed north, closer to the palace. "Watcher High Command is that way. Just ask around, you'll find it."

Jak smiled and turned to go, shoving down her annoyance that Estel got to follow Naem. It was an awkward goodbye, but there was nothing Jak could do about that. Besides, her mind quickly busied itself with other things as she joined Gabriel and they made their way to the college.

"He's a good young man," Gabriel said after a moment.

"Yes, he is," Jak said, almost to herself.

But there was no time to think about Naem now. She had too much else going on. She was about to embark on her training as a full Gifter. Maybe even become a full scholar. She'd get a chance to study history, art, magic, and military strategy. Any knowledge she wanted or had ever wanted to learn was available at the college. Or at least, that's what Gabriel had told her.

They rounded a corner, and there it was. Jak sucked in her breath and her eyes widened. The college was a large, circular building with pillars holding up the roof on all sides. Behind the structure was a large, square courtyard, lined with what Jak guessed were the living quarters. Jak gaped. It was absolutely enormous. You could have fit all of Foothold in there and there would still be room to spare.

Gabriel chuckled at the expression on Jak's face. "Come. It's time I introduced you to some people."

They stepped through a pair of giant oak doors, and Jak felt the cooling of the air as they entered the large stone edifice. It was darker in here, but the light of day still illuminated the room through rectangular openings in the walls. They were in a large open space with tables and desks lining the walls. Jak wasn't sure what this room was used for, but she guessed it might be where they ate. In the center of the room was a large spiral staircase that led to a room above. What could be up there?

A woman hurried to meet them. She had a face that looked like it was chiseled from marble, pale and aloof. "Gabriel, I'm so glad you're back. We have a situation."

The woman leaned in and whispered something in his ear. Jak tried to look nonchalant as she did her best to listen. But she heard nothing.

Whatever it was, however, caused Gabriel's typical cheery face to furrow. "Have the stables readied. I'll rest tonight and set out early tomorrow morning."

"What's going on?" Jak couldn't hold in her curiosity anymore. Gabriel was leaving again? But they had just arrived.

"And this is...?" The stern woman glanced at her briefly.

"Oh, I'm sorry. This is Jak, our newest Gifter. Jak, this is Mrs. Semwei. She's the headmistress here, and you'll listen to her as you would listen to me. She's in charge when it comes to the administration of this place."

Jak did her best to imitate a curtsy, though it was the first time she had ever needed to. Even the Lord Mayor of Riverbrook didn't really stand on that kind of ceremony. Yet something about Mrs. Semwei demanded respect.

The woman nodded at Jak but turned back to Gabriel. "I'll make sure she's thoroughly acquainted with the customs here. You needn't worry."

"Thank you, Semwei. If you'll excuse me." Gabriel nodded to Semwei and Jak in turn. "I'll be needing as much rest as I can get in the next few hours." He turned to Jak. "Something has come up with one of our student excavation sites along the coast, and I need to investigate. I'll be back shortly I expect. Maybe a day or two."

As he laid a comforting hand on her shoulder, Jak nodded but she didn't really like the idea. They had just arrived, and already her teacher was leaving. "When can I start my studies?" she asked as Gabriel turned to leave.

"Anytime you want, once Semwei shows you around. You don't need me to teach you everything. Find a few books in the library."

"You have a library?" Jak's eyes lit up.

Gabriel only chuckled before leaving out the back.

Semwei regarded her down that pointed nose, looking at the spear strapped to Jak's back. "Well, you're a scrawny one. We'll have to put some meat on those bones."

Jak shifted uncomfortably. What should she say? "Um, yes ma'am."

"Supper was two hours ago, but I suppose the cook can give you some leftovers for now. In the future, if you miss a meal, you do not eat. Understand?"

Jak nodded. She was pretty hungry now that she thought about it.

"Better hop to it. Bedtime begins promptly at ten o'clock. Listen for the bell tower from the Royal Cathedral. Do you go to church girl?"

Jak stammered at the unexpected question. "Um, not usually. I mean, our Lord Mayor sometimes read to us from the Annals of Adam, but other than that..."

"Well, you'll need to fix that if you want to fit in here. Church service is in two days on High Morning in the Royal Cathedral. All little girls need to learn how to become respectable women after all. I require all students to attend."

"Yes, ma'am." Jak had never really thought about church. But she had seen the Royal Cathedral on her way in, attached to the Royal Palace itself. It was one of the largest, most impressive structures in Skyecliff. It might be worth going just to step foot in that building.

"Very good." Semwei kept staring down her nose at Jak. "You'll find a spare room out the back. You'll pass the kitchen on the way. The library is up the stairs if you need it."

Jak turned to see the large central staircase curling up into the floor above. So that's where that led to. She almost forgot her hunger at the notion of seeing the library.

"Well put those skinny bones to work, girl. Get moving!"

"Yes, ma'am!" Jak said again, and she hurried to the back door.

She found the kitchens easily enough and explained the situation to the cook, who was much less stern than Mrs. Semwei. The woman was plump and red-faced, with kindly eyes. Jak feasted on cold dumplings that nevertheless were some of the best morsels she'd ever had. Much better than Watcher rations. She could get used to this.

After scarfing down her food and ignoring the cook's insistence that she eat more, she left and quickly found a spare room. She ran into a few other students reading by candlelight or lounging in their rooms. A few glanced at her, but most kept to themselves. Were they used to seeing new students arrive at the college?

Soon, Jak found a room that was empty. She gently laid down her pack and the long cloth-covered parcel that was her father's spear and sat on the bed. It was firm, but not uncomfortable. She had one wooden table with a few unlit candles on it. The sun was all but gone so she would need those candles soon. But first, she had one last stop to make.

Unburdened by all her things, she stepped back the way she came. She was surprised how empty the place felt. Surely there were more students than the few that she saw. The large open area at the entrance looked eerily dark in the fading light. But a cool, blue light emanated from the room above the staircase. Leaning one hand on the center column, she began her climb to the library.

What reached her eyes as she crested the upper floor nearly brought on a flood of tears.

She had never seen so many books! Rows and rows of old dusty volumes greeted her on all sides. The entire outer wall had shelves reaching as high as the domed ceiling. There had to be hundreds, no, thousands of books here.

Jak had to keep her legs from collapsing and sending her falling back down the spiral staircase. Everything she had ever known was contained in her one journal. She could just imagine how much more she could learn. Where to start?

She hadn't the faintest idea.

CHAPTER 2

"**G**ET UP, GIRL. GET up!"

For a moment, Jak had absolutely no idea where she was. All was dark around her, save for a small light that nevertheless blinded Jak as she looked at it. She blinked, disoriented.

"W-wha?"

"I am sorry to wake you at this unorthodox hour, but you have been summoned by a very special person."

It was Semwei, leaning over her bed in the small student quarters. Jak had retired there eventually, only after being forced out of the library at curfew. Even then, she had managed to take one book with her, which she read into the night. Jak peered out the door. No light came through, it must still be dark outside. Now, why... did Semwei say someone had summoned her?

"Broken brands, child. Didn't you hear me?"

Jak swung her legs off the bed sat up. "Who wants to see me?"

"Why, the queen of course."

Jak stood up faster than she thought possible, then immediately regretted it as blood fought to reach her head. She swayed. "The queen is here?"

"Of course not, child. The queen doesn't just waltz into the college to speak to the likes of you. She has sent an emissary." Semwei's lips formed a straight line. "He is waiting for you downstairs. I suggest you hurry."

"But why?"

"No questions, girl!" Semwei was losing patience. "Get dressed!"

Jak stumbled across the room to where her travel clothes lay abandoned, but when she picked them up, she looked at Semwei. "Ah... I don't really have something suitable."

"You needn't worry about that." Semwei folded her arms. "They will take care of you in the palace. Assuming you ever get there at the rate you're going."

Jak was starting to feel more awake now and hurried about putting some clothes over her night shift. The gravity of Semwei's revelation was beginning to sink in. The queen? Wanted to see her? How did the queen even know who she was, or care?

She finished putting on her travel clothes, sniffing the collar and wincing. Why couldn't the queen have summoned her after she had a chance to wash her clothes? She hadn't bathed in days. She had noticed the washroom earlier but bypassed it in favor of the library the night before. She had thought to wash in the morning, but now that was out of the question.

Semwei looked her up and down. "Hmm. Well, I suppose it will have to do. I'm sure the palace servants will make you more presentable."

Jak swallowed, feeling her nervousness rise with each second. Her head pounded from the sudden awakening. She couldn't have had more than a few hours of sleep. Semwei turned, and Jak followed her to the outer courtyard. Sure enough, the sky had not even begun to show signs of a rising sun. It must be incredibly early, yet Semwei acted as if all was normal. Did the woman even sleep?

Semwei led her to the large domed circle that sat on the entrance to the college. There, Jak saw a man waiting. He wore a red and black frilly doublet and britches. His hair was combed back, completely flat along his head. How did he get it to stick like that?

"This is the girl?" he said, looking her up and down.

"It is."

Jak's nervousness rose. Where was Gabriel? Had he already left to investigate the problem along the coast?

The man adopted a formal stance and... actually bowed to Jak. She wasn't sure what to do, so she curtsied back. Her second curtsy since arriving.

"Jak Draconis," the man said formally. "You have been summoned to appear before Her Majesty, the Queen Telma Lomalin, first of her name, ruler of land, ocean, and island, wearer of the Crown Relics, and defender of the downtrodden."

"Uh... okay." Jak didn't know what to say. "Do I just follow you?"

The man seemed not to notice her discomfort. "Indeed. A carriage waits outside." With that, he strode away, and after a glance at Semwei, Jak followed.

The carriage waited there, and Jak took a moment to take it in. It was far more lavish than anything she had seen before. Drawn by two beautiful black horses, the wood of the carriage was polished and gilded with gold and red paints. Another man sat in the driver's chair, while the man who had met Jak inside held open the door for her. Was she getting special treatment or was this how all the visitors to the queen were summoned?

She climbed the small step into the carriage and took a seat on one side. The messenger followed and sat across from her, not saying anything.

As the carriage started up, Jak held her arms to her sides, feeling the chill and being acutely aware of how much she smelled in the confining space. She should really have taken a bath instead of visiting the library last night. The messenger didn't seem to notice.

Jak couldn't see much outside, but she could feel the carriage begin a steep incline, and it wound back and forth on its way up. Not long after, they arrived in a small open area outside of the palace. When she exited the carriage, Jak had to stop and stare for a moment. The palace was even more magical up close, supported by huge buttresses, the building seemed to reach up into the heavens. The light was beginning to appear in the east now, and she glanced around at the rest of Skyecliff. The palace was far more elevated than it had appeared from the ground. She could see for miles in every direction, far beyond the city limits.

"The girl will please follow me." said the messenger.

Jak walked behind him, noticing how shabby she looked with each step. The main entrance led into a hallway lit with bright torches and filled with oddities like suits of armor, large tapestries, and even what looked to Jak like a minor Relic. Jak felt her anticipation grow, and the questions reappeared in her mind. Just why did the Queen want to see her?

The messenger led her to a small but decorated room. Jak noticed a large tub sitting in one end, partially hidden behind a wooden screen. Several women, about Jak's age, stood inside.

"The girl will undress and leave her soiled clothes with the maidens." The messenger turned to face Jak, indicating the other women in the room. "After which she will bathe and select new clothes."

Undress? Here? Jak clutched her arms again, feeling all eyes on her. The messenger, blessedly, left the room.

"My lady, if you would?" one of the maidens said.

My lady? Jak had never been referred to as a lady. After a bit more prodding from the others, she stripped and entered the bath as quickly as she could. To her surprise, the water was wonderfully warm. She could almost feel her muscles relaxing as they made contact with the liquid. But she tensed again, as almost immediately, three of the other girls approached the bath with sponges in hand. They didn't plan to... to wash her, did they?

It turned out that was exactly what they were there to do. Jak could do nothing to hide her burning red face as they washed her from head to toe. Following the bath, she was provided with not one, not two, but seven outfits to choose from. After finally picking the outfit with the least amount of frills on it, she felt her face burn again as the girls helped her dress.

The process took forever, and Jak could see the sun shining brightly through the window by the time they finished. And just as Jak thought they were done, she received a face full of powder. She coughed.

"What is...?"

But one of the maidens pressed a finger to Jak's mouth, to keep her from speaking, after which she applied a red stick to her lips. Then the girl indicated that Jak should rub her lips together, which she did, tasting something bitter. What exactly were they doing to her face?

Hours later, Jak had almost forgotten why she was there. The girls brought her a mirror, and Jak almost screamed in shock. She did not recognize the girl staring back at her. Her face was white, her lips were red, her hair was pulled back in one of the most ornate designs she had ever seen. And that wasn't to mention her clothes, which were far from practical, though better than some of the other options she could have selected. This one at least didn't puff out like a lost sheep who hadn't been sheered in months.

"Does the image please the lady?" said one of the girls holding the mirror.

"Uh... I suppose so." Jak really had no idea of what accounted for pleasing around here. But she smelled nice, so that was something at least.

The girl curtsied to her! Jak had never seen anyone pay her with such respect. "I will inform the Lord Chamberlain you are ready to see the queen."

Jak felt her stomach grow nauseous. But she said nothing. What could she say? 'Uh, please I'd rather not see the queen at all if you don't mind.' There was nothing that could be done at this point.

The young women continued to fuss over the details of her hair and makeup. Jak let them. Her thoughts were turned inward. What was the queen going to ask her? Or even more pressing what was she going to say? Did one even speak to queens? But of course, that was silly. People spoke to queens.

A moment later and the same man who had arrived to pick her up from the college stepped into the room. "Hmmm." He looked her over. "Not bad. Still looks a little thin."

Jak felt like hugging her arms to her sides again, but she resisted. So, what if she was skinny? But she didn't like it when the man's eyes looked her up and down, even if it was his job.

"Very well," the Lord Chamberlain said, "I shall escort you to the Royal Hall. Follow me please."

Jak followed, still too nervous to ask any questions.

They went down what seemed to be an endless set of hallways, each lined with valuable items and artifacts, as Jak had seen when they first entered. Yes, there were definitely some

Relics here. Actual Relics! Jak resisted the urge to pluck one off the wall and examine it up close.

Distracted, she almost bumped into the Chamberlain as he came to an abrupt halt. Jak peered behind him. Two enormous oak doors stood in front of them, lavishly decorated and carved with exquisite detail. Figures depicting some historical event, most likely, were carved into the wood. Jak could have spent a while just looking at this door.

"This is the entrance to the Royal Hall." the man said. "Her Majesty awaits. Regarding matters of etiquette. Do not speak unless spoken to. Do not meet Her Majesty's eyes until she has addressed you personally. Always meet her eyes thereafter when she is speaking to you. Do not ask questions. You are expected to curtsy upon entering and then again when before the throne. I understand there will be others in attendance. You are not to interact with them unless the queen gives her leave to do so. You will address her first as Your Majesty, and thereafter as My Lady. Do you understand?"

Jak did her best to remember everything but nodded. What would happen if she forgot one of the rules? Would the queen have her head cut off?

The oak doors creaked and slowly swung open, revealing the room beyond. It was enormous! Jak didn't think there was a single building in Riverbrook that would not have fit inside this single room. Jak almost forgot to curtsy as she entered, doing her best not to look directly at the figure who sat directly ahead.

CHAPTER 3

IF SHE THOUGHT HER own robes were overly lavish, it was nothing compared to what the queen was wearing. The woman's gown flowed beyond her feet, over the steps that led to the raised throne. How did the woman walk? Jak didn't look at the queen's face, as instructed, but she could tell that the woman had an extravagant headdress that filled the space around her head and shoulders.

Jak jumped as the Chamberlain spoke in a loud voice. "Announcing, Lady Jak Draconis of Her Majesty's province of Riverbrook. Brought here upon Her Majesty's request."

Jak stepped forward, still avoiding the Queen's eyes, and curtsied the second time when she felt she was close enough. Out of the corners of her eyes, she saw two others enter from the other side of the room. She restrained herself from looking to see who they were.

"My thanks, Lord Gent." The Queen spoke for the first time. Her voice was soft but held an authority Jak admired.

The Lord Chamberlain bowed and exited the way he had come. Jak thought her eyes might bore a hole in the ground with the way she intensely avoided looking up.

"Child." The queen spoke to her. "How has your visit to the Royal Palace been thus far?"

Okay, she was speaking to her. That meant she could look the queen in the eye. Jak raised her eyes to meet those of the queen. Her face was pale and covered in makeup like Jak's, but in far more generous amounts. Her headdress was indeed extravagant, fanning out like a territorial bird. Jak wondered idly how the woman managed to keep her head straight with all that resting on her head.

Just then, she remembered that the queen had asked her a question. "Uh, it's been wonderful....Your Majesty. I... had no idea I could be this clean."

She closed her eyes. Stupid!

A soft chuckle escaped the queen's lips. "I am glad we could help expose you to a modicum of civilization."

Jak wished very much they would cut the small talk. She almost asked why she was here but stopped herself just in time as she remembered she wasn't supposed to ask any questions.

"May I present two of my most trusted advisors. This is General Wilva Lonolok, of Watcher High Command."

Jak followed the Queen's gesture to her right, Jak's left, to see a stern woman with shaved hair and light armor. So, she was the highest authority among the Watchers. She would have to tell Naem about this later.

The queen gestured to her other side. "And this is the Royal High Priest who governs the Holy Church in the worship of its Relics. He has no name as everything must be sacrificed in the pursuit of true religion, but you may address him as Your Holiness."

Jak felt the need to curtsy again. "How do you do?"

She didn't like the way the other two were looking at her. General Wilva squinted her eyes at her warily, while the Royal Priest had an uncanny smile that made Jak wish she had several more layers of clothing on.

"Oh, she is quite adorable isn't she?" said the queen clapping her hands together.

"Yes, my lady," the Royal Priest folded his arms.

"Well then," the queen continued as if the Priest had not spoken. "Down to business. We have heard some strange reports coming from my fortress of Foothold. They all concern you."

"Uh..." Jak hesitated as the queen waited expectantly for her to answer. How much did the queen already know? "Yes, we had a fight with some demons. I helped."

"From what we've heard, you did far more than that. Please, tell me about the Fae."

Jak swallowed. So, the queen knew something about what had happened. Well, she had agreed to be an ambassador of sorts for the Fae. This was as good an opportunity as she was likely to get.

"They helped us take care of the demon threat. Without them, none of us would have remained alive."

"But don't you think it's a bit suspicious that they showed up while the demons began to organize? The first demon army we've ever seen, and our first major interaction with these Fae. Coincidence?"

Jak was prepared for that line of thought. She'd heard it before. "The Fae existed long before the demons began to organize themselves. I know some of the Fae came into being as many as seventeen years ago."

"What do you mean came into being? I don't suppose they just spring out of the ground." The queen laughed as if she had made a wonderful joke, but she was the only one who did so.

"No... uh... my lady. They used to be human."

Jak knew she had step carefully. No one knew that Jak's mother was a Shadow Fae, none but herself, Naem, Gabriel, and a few of the Fae themselves.

"So, you're saying that they are like the demons, mutated by magic?" It was the Royal Priest who asked this question. He looked like he had been waiting to ask it.

Jak shook her head, beginning to grow frustrated. She had heard this one all too often as well. "Not at all. In the case of the Shadow Fae, they had contact with a Holy Relic that changed them. In the case of the Bright Fae, their whole village suddenly turned into Fae with no warning."

The Queen nodded. "Yes, we've heard reports of two varieties of Fae at the battle. I'm told you led them?"

"Yes, my lady."

"Why? You're not even of age yet. What did they see in you?"

Jak opened her mouth but didn't know exactly what to say. She really wished she didn't have to keep her relation to the Fae a secret. "I'm not sure, my lady. I was in the right place at the right time."

That seemed to satisfy the queen. "And this Holy Relic you speak of, what was it?"

"It was an original copy of the Annals of Adam." Jak thought she saw the Royal Priest shift out of the corner of her vision.

The queen raised an eyebrow.

"Indeed! Well, then why didn't you bring it with you? Such a find would be the best news we've heard in a long time."

"It wasn't my place to take it. It is sacred to them, having been the reason for their transformation and all."

"Hmm, and have you any notion of how it performed such an unprecedented feat? Did the Fae do something to anger it perhaps, try to damage or manipulate it in some way?"

"No, my lady. As I heard it, it merely changed them when they drew near. And they aren't the only ones. Their numbers have increased as travelers came too close and turned them into Shadow Fae as well. Though not all turn into Fae."

The queen tapped her fingers together. "We shall have to put up a notice not to stray into those mountains if this transformation occurs as you say. Now I understand why you didn't bring us the book. You're sure it's the source of this magic?"

"Of that, I am very certain, my lady," Jak responded. She was beginning to grow more comfortable now. They just wanted to know about the Fae. Completely understandable. "I felt the power surrounding it myself. I can't exactly describe the sensation, but there was power there. And I got a chance to read some of it. Certain passages are different."

"Mmm? Like what?"

"Well, it's still somewhat vague. But it seemed to prophecy about the Fae themselves, and more than two varieties. There were more mentioned, and it talks about how they will all unite with humans into a great civilization."

This time she definitely saw the Priest shift uncomfortably. Was this not exciting news for him?

"I see," The queen lips flattened to a straight line. "Very well, girl. We have but one more matter to discuss with you. I will let my General take the lead on this one." She sounded colder now, and Jak felt the comfort she had begun to feel drain away.

General Wilva took a step forward. "You are familiar with Sergeant Naem?"

Oh dear, Jak thought. "Eh, yes. He and I became friends while on the journey."

"And the two of you, together with Major Skellig, conducted a mutiny against our own Colonel Kuldain, is that correct?"

Jak almost stammered as she tried to give a quick response. "He was a demon, uh, sir. We don't know how, but he had some sort of shapeshifting ability. In the end, he attacked all of us, and I... I was forced to kill him."

There was no way to sugar coat that last part. She had killed a Watcher Colonel, and they only had her word and that of the other Watchers who were present.

"We knew of this," Wilva said.

Jak glanced at the queen, who said nothing but merely watched Jak closely over her laced fingers.

"Am I to be punished?" Jak finally worked up the courage to ask.

Wilva regarded her for a few heartbeats. "No." She said at last, to Jak's immediate relief. "We've heard enough reports to substantiate what you said. If Kuldain was a demon, then he deserved what he got. As Watchers, it is our duty to seek out demons and magic abusers and eliminate them. You did only as you were charged. But that is not what we wanted to discuss."

Jak swallowed. If that wasn't the main issue, she had an idea of what was.

"I have come to learn that Sergeant Naem has received more than one stable brand. When I confronted him about this, he revealed that you gave them to him. To save his life."

All three of them were staring at Jak now, with calculated intensity. Jak understood. No one had ever produced a second stable brand, let alone a third. She had hoped to keep this quiet, but this was the queen she was talking to and a Watcher general. If anyone knew about the goings on in the kingdom, it was them.

"Yes. I did brand Naem with Toughness and Healing, in addition to his original brand of Grace."

"How did you do this?" The queen asked.

There was a stillness to her voice that worried Jak. She would have to tread carefully. A wrong answer would not help her.

"I did it with the help of a Bright Fae. They have an ability that I don't fully understand, to reveal the truth to themselves and to others. Naem was dying, and I was ready to use any method to save him. I thought, maybe, if the Fae was telling the truth, that maybe he could show me how to save Naem. And he did. It just wasn't what any of us were expecting."

"You realize that what you did has been attempted many times with no success?" This time it was the Royal Priest who spoke.

"I do. What I did was impossible."

"Have you replicated it since?"

Jak shook her head. "I can't even produce a single stable brand yet. Knowledge was given to me at that moment, but I lost it once the Fae stopped opening my eyes to the truth."

"Convenient," said the Priest.

Jak said nothing in response.

"You will speak of this to no one." The queen's tone held no room for question. "Until we understand what went on, you will never reveal what happened that day. Furthermore, you will keep what you know of the Fae peculiarities to yourself."

Peculiarities? But the Fae were good, and it was important that others know that. Jak almost opened her mouth to protest, but the fire in the queen's eyes shut her up.

"You will continue your studies at the college and learn what you can about Branding and about what happened that night with the young Sergeant. We will investigate the matter ourselves as well and will summon you again when we feel ready."

"Y... yes, my lady." She supposed that was okay.

The Watcher General shifted on her feet. "And as you are technically still a Watcher, you will make your reports directly to me. I will expect you to visit the Watcher compound at least once a week. I'm told the Sergeant oversaw training you in combat. He is skilled so you may continue your training with him."

"I don't know how much free time I will have from my studies."

"We are not asking, girl." The queen's voice was still stern.

What had happened to the sweet motherly tone she used earlier?

"You are a Watcher, so you will report to the Watchers. Consider it a command from your queen."

"Yes, my lady." Jak did not like this at all, but she couldn't see any way out of it for now. She needed time to think.

"Very well. That will be all. The Lord Chamberlain will arrange for your passage back to the college." The queen dismissed her with a wave of the hand.

As she turned, Jak caught one last look of the Royal Priest's face. The smile there did nothing to soothe her mood. Something was wrong here, but Jak could not figure out what.

She paced to the end of the hall, suddenly conscious of how loud her feet were on the stone floor. The doors opened with an enormous creek as she approached. How had they known she was coming? But that question quickly died as she saw who was on the other side of the big oak doors.

Naem stood there, almost as unrecognizable as Jak herself. He wore a laced doublet that extended all the way up to his neck, where a giant circle of lace created a halo around his face. He looked as uncomfortable as she felt, but upon seeing her, his face broke into a smile.

"Jak!" he said in a hushed tone. "I didn't expect to see you here, and in a dress. You don't look half bad!"

He glanced down at her ornate garments. Jak felt an unexpected feeling as she was torn between discomfort at wearing her dress, and pleasure that Naem seemed to like it.

"What are you doing here?" she asked him, pushing her other thoughts out of her head. The oak doors were still open, which meant they only had a moment.

"I was summoned by Watcher High Command. General Wilva found out about my brands." Naem's face grew solemn. "I'm sorry, I didn't know what else to say, so I told them the truth. The queen wants a report now."

Jak nodded. "It's okay, they already talked to me about it. And it would have come out eventually."

The Lord Chamberlain appeared behind Naem. "What are you waiting for get in there!"

Jak took a step to one side to let Naem in. But as he strode to pass her, she grabbed his arm. He paused, turning to look at her.

"Be careful," she whispered. "There's something not right here."

Naem gave the smallest nod to indicate he understood. Then he left her grasp and proceeded into the throne room. The oak doors boomed as they closed behind him.

"Now girl, I will arrange an escort for you," the Lord Chamberlain snapped his fingers, and two serving girls appeared as if out of nowhere.

Jak recognized them as two of the girls who had helped her bathe earlier. It took far less time for Jak to be extracted from her lavish clothes than it had to get in them. While she undressed one of the girls brought her old travel clothes. They had been washed and scented since Jak parted with them, and she could swear they felt far softer as she pulled them on. She almost felt it was worth an audience with the queen if she got such treatment every time. Almost.

The carriage trip also seemed to take less time, though this was more likely because Jak was lost in thought, rather than scared for her life. She had gone into the throne room with a preconception of what the queen would be like. Now, her assumptions stood on shaky ground. She wasn't exactly sure what made her uneasy. Perhaps it was the fact that the queen frequently referred to the Fae as peculiarities, rather than real people. It reminded her of the way Kuldain had thought of them as nothing but demons. Of course, Kuldain had been a demon himself, so his arguments against the Fae had likely been an act.

But she also felt uncomfortable knowing that the queen and her confidants knew of her miraculous branding ability, even if she didn't know how to replicate what she did to Naem. She had hoped to blend in at Skyecliff, to bury herself in her studies. The college had been her dream since she was very young, and now she felt uneasy living here.

She heard the horse hooves clatter as they slowed to a halt in front of the college. The door opened, and Jak stepped outside. She took a step forward, then another. For some reason, the college seemed more imposing than before, especially now that she could see it in full daylight. The carriage driver tipped his hat to her, then rode away towards the palace.

She was alone. Only random citizens walking to and fro on the street saw her there, a few curious to see who had stepped out of a royal carriage. But most averted their eyes and continued their merry way.

Jak didn't know why she felt apprehensive to enter the college again, but she squared her shoulders and marched inside.

As soon as her eyes adjusted to the lower light inside, she saw Gabriel taking great steps towards her from the opposite end of the circular hall. Good, he was still here!

"What did you say?" He asked as he neared. "Tell me exactly what they asked you word for word."

Jak almost stepped back. His face was furious, though his voice remained relatively calm. "Um... it's about what you'd expect."

And she told him everything that had just happened, about their conversations of the Fae and Kuldain, including the discussion of Naem and his extra brands. Gabriel listened with quiet intensity until she finished.

"And you're sure that was everything? They asked you no further questions?"

Jak shook her head. "Should I not have gone?"

Gabriel sighed and relaxed a bit. "No, one refuses a summons by the queen if they want to live. But I wish Semwei had warned me you were leaving. I would have given you some advice. She wanted me to get my rest. But I suppose there's nothing we can do about it now that it's done, and I'd say you did a good job answering their questions, though perhaps a bit more honest than I would have been."

"Why don't you trust the queen?" Jak asked, genuinely curious. Perhaps Gabriel could explain why Jak felt so uneasy.

"It's not the queen I distrust, but more her advisors. Wilva isn't all bad if just a little hot-headed and rash. But that other one, the Royal Priest with no name, he worries me. I assume Semwei made you promise to go to church?" Jak nodded, and Gabriel continued. "Well then, you'll probably see the problems when you listen to him preach. He has some radical ideas and is unfortunately persuasive in his techniques."

Jak remembered something then. "Weren't you supposed to go see something along the coast?"

Gabriel licked his lips. "I was, but once I learned that you were gone, I had to wait and make sure everything was okay. There's something unique about you, Jak, and while I don't plan to give you any special treatment while here at the college, I think you have a great destiny ahead of you."

"I don't want to be special."

Gabriel smiled. "Those that do rarely deserve it. But give it time. All you need to do is focus on your studies for now. Let me handle the queen and her politics. If she ever summons you again, I want you to make sure that I hear of it. Even if you have to make her wait. We must send a message that you are not at her beckon call."

Jak nodded, glad to have Gabriel around.

Gabriel clapped his hands together. "Well, now that you're here, I must be going. I'm afraid you've already missed breakfast and morning chores, which I'm sure Semwei will not appreciate, even if it was to meet with the queen. Go report to her and she'll tell you what to do next.

"Okay, I... hope you have a safe trip." Jak couldn't think of anything else to say.

She was not pleased that Gabriel had to leave. And she was beginning to feel her exhaustion returning as the early morning, combined with a late night and her recovery from their travels, took its toll on her body. Well, at least she smelled good now.

Gabriel took his leave, and Jak eventually found Semwei, who gave her some chores cleaning in the kitchen to make up for her tardiness. Unfortunately, it meant Jak missed her first round of classes for the day, but at the same time, Jak enjoyed the menial labor. It was the closest thing to normal that she had done in weeks.

CHAPTER 4

T HE NEXT DAY WAS High Morning, the day most people in Skyecliff went to church in the huge cathedral adjacent to the palace. Driven by her promise to Semwei, Jak rose with the other girls in her dormitory to make their way there.

Jak still hadn't formally met any of the other students at the college. A few gave her a glance as they prepped for church, but seemed more concerned with talking to each other, leaving Jak out of their conversations. Jak didn't mind this. She liked to listen in, rather than participate. This was how she learned most of the students liked going to church, not because of what was taught there, but because it was the only morning when they didn't have to perform chores.

Jak didn't really understand this. Sure, her knees were a bit sore from scrubbing the kitchen floor, but it had been relaxing work, helping Jak forget about everything else that had happened on her visit to the queen.

As they dressed in their school uniforms, something Jak had just received the day before, Jak thought she heard someone mention the queen. She turned to see several girls glancing in her direction, which they immediately stopped doing the moment she caught them staring. Great! They must have heard that she was summoned to see the queen on her first day in Skyecliff. If no one had talked to her before, they weren't going to now. Jak liked to remain aloof and not have to worry about others, but this was different. Who liked being the odd one out?

Grimacing, Jak focused her efforts on preparing herself for church, already convinced that she wasn't going to like the experience. Perhaps she could find a quiet corner in the back and slip out when no one was looking.

No carriage met her this time. Instead, she walked with the other girls and boys, led by Semwei, to the church. There were about fifty of them all together, probably most of the occupants of the school. Jak kept her face low the whole time, avoiding the awkward glances people kept sending her. Even the boys seemed to have heard about her by now. Did word really travel that fast?

As they approached the church, Jak noticed two men standing at the doors. Each gave a single glance to the group of approaching students, then nodded at Semwei, who waved at the others to follow her inside. Jak frowned. Did they have to have permission to enter? Were those men there to stop people from coming in? That didn't exactly seem like any of the churches Jak had heard about. The Holy Relics and their blessings were for all people.

But Jak's thoughts quickly faded as they entered the church itself. She stared around in awe. The building was the most beautiful and ornate building she had ever seen.

Even more so than the palace. Huge stone columns rose to meet the gilded ceiling. Each column bore glass mosaics that wrapped around and rose to the very top. Huge stained-glass windows rose on all sides, letting light in and painting the ground with multiple colors. Jak didn't recognize any of the events depicted in the glass, but they were beautiful as well.

She was glad she had the college uniform because she had no idea what else she would wear to a place like this. Everyone assembled wore something fancy and perfectly clean. She didn't see anyone who didn't obviously have money, unless it was her group of students. But even they had clean clothes, enough that they fit the tone of the room somewhat. Still, Jak had seen hundreds of people in the city already, and most of them looked like they couldn't afford what the patrons here were wearing. Perhaps there were other churches that they went to?

It looked like Jak wouldn't have her choice of seating as Semwei led them to a reserved space. Thankfully, it was in the back, so Jak didn't have to worry about passing all those people ahead of her. Maybe she could slip out quietly if she needed to. She managed to find an end spot, sitting next to a strawberry-blonde girl with a cheery face she didn't know.

"All rise!" A clear voice echoed through the cathedral, seeming to fill all the space at once. People obeyed, and wooden benches creaked as everyone stood.

Jak could see the man who spoke, a man wearing red robes at the head of the cathedral, next to some kind of altar. He continued.

"His Holiness, the Royal High Priest, keeper of the sacred Relics, our nameless advocate with the beyond, and advisor to Her Highness the Queen."

The man stepped back and gestured to one side. Jak looked to see a man dressed in over-the-top ornate robes, though not as decorated as those she had seen on the queen herself. He wore a flowing red robe, laced with silver and gold. His head bore a crown of sorts, though it was shaped like a perfect sphere, markings etched into it. It... it looked like a Relic.

When she finally looked at the man's face, she recognized him. It was the same High Priest she had met the day before, the counselor to the queen. She hadn't liked him much then, and she was no more impressed now that he wore all that ceremonial drapery.

The Royal Priest approached the altar, gave a brief nod to the man who had introduced him, then turned to face the audience.

"My dear friends and joint recipients in the blessings of our Holy Relics, welcome. You may be seated."

Muffled thuds sounded throughout the room as everyone obliged. The Priest extended his hands upward. "Let us pray."

Everyone started to chant with him.

"Oh, mighty Adam, our father's father, bestower of Relics, and the architect of magic, we thank thee. We thank thee that we have greater opportunity in life compared to our lessers, that we may use that opportunity for the betterment of all. We thank thee that we are thy holy children. Thou art holy, thou hast made us holy. We pray for thy blessing that we may never stoop to the level of our lessers, that we may remain holy..."

Jak couldn't believe what she was hearing. These people were actively saying they were better than other people. And it sounded like they were referring to the poor and other less-privileged members of the city.

Jak glanced around at the other students. Most weren't reciting the pledge, though only because they appeared not to know it from memory. Some, however, like the cheery-faced girl sitting next to her, kept their lips firmly sealed. Semwei, Jak noticed with satisfaction, was among those who said nothing. In fact, the stern mistress looked ever sterner. She clearly did not like this part of the ceremony. So why did Semwei make sure all the students went to church if she didn't agree with what was said? Perhaps there was more that Jak was missing.

She turned her attention back to the Royal Priest as the prayer ended. His arms lowered, and he met the eyes of people in the congregation. For the briefest of moments, Jak almost thought she saw his eyes linger on her.

"Thank you, my friends. I have here one of the Holy Relics." He plucked the orb off his head and set it in front of him. "I pray for your faith as we invoke its blessing."

Jak heard several mutters among the crowd as some of the members expressed their support in hushed tones. Jak, for once, was intrigued. Was the Priest going to activate a Relic right here and now? She wondered what it did?

White light poured from the Priest's left hand. His brand had activated. Jak couldn't quite tell what brand it was from her place near the back of the room, but it wasn't something she instantly recognized. And now that she thought about it, she wasn't sure she had seen his brand the day before.

Whatever it did, the Relic in front of them began to glow, first only out of the inscriptions it held, but then the whole sphere poured light in every direction.

Cries of joy erupted all around Jak. She looked from one to another. Everyone had a look of pure ecstasy on their faces. What was...

Then she felt it. Waves of pleasure rushed into her, a warmth so wonderful, so pure, that it had to be divine. She felt it course through her veins, filling every part of her with love and joy and...

An unexpected wave of revulsion replaced the pleasure. She doubled over, clutching at her sides as she felt actual pain. Where she had felt joy, she now felt anger, where there had been peace, she felt a growing sickening discomfort.

Unable to do anything about it, she vomited on the floor to one side. Her classmates yelped and did their best to remove themselves from the blast zone. Though many did not even notice, still caught up in the euphoric waves emanating from Relic.

Jak heaved again, feeling everything she had eaten for breakfast come spilling out of her mouth. She rose to her feet but bent over, facing the floor. When there was nothing left, she kept dry heaving, still feeling nothing but utter disgust. What happened to her?

As suddenly as it had come, the pain and revulsion died. So too, it seemed, did the pleasure received by the rest of the patrons. Only then did those around Jak notice the pool of sick on the ground. Mutters spread from where she crouched, still bent over from the ordeal.

"It would appear." The cold voice of the Royal Priest cut through the crowd. "That we have a doubter."

Jak turned to face him. There was uncertainty in his eyes, though that expression quickly vanished. Instead, he smiled and addressed Jak directly. "My child. Tell us your concerns so that we might best convince you of the truth."

Jak stood straight, wiping a drizzle of vomit from her mouth. Everyone in the building was looking at her. Her classmates had given her a wide berth, and even Semwei looked puzzled. Of all the places to make a scene...

"I... I don't think I had any doubts," she lied. "I just must have eaten something spoiled for breakfast. Just that."

"Oh child, it is far more complicated than that." The Priest was still smiling but in that unnerving sort of way that she had seen in him the day before. "This is the Relic of Bestowal. It grants each of us an experience that mirrors our commitment to the faith. If you had shown more investment in the words we say here, it would have healed your... spoiled breakfast."

Every instinct Jak had told her to turn and run out of the building. But a small part of her kept her feet frozen in place. Running would only make things worse. If she was forced into the spotlight, and there was nothing she could do about it, then maybe she could use the exposure to do some good. Breaking eye contact with the Priest, she looked around her.

"I think I understand why people come here," she said softly. "The Relic, it gives you pleasure. I felt it for a moment there, and I don't know why I grew sick. If the Royal Priest says it is because I doubt, then maybe that's true. But I'm confident I'm not the only one here who has issues with the words that have been said." She spared the briefest glance for Semwei, who narrowed her eyes at Jak.

"And what issues would that be?" said the Priest.

He licked his lips, as if eager for Jak's response. He knew her story, why was he so eager for her to elaborate in front of all these people? Jak felt it again, the urge to turn and run from this place.

"Putting yourselves above others and those that cannot be here."

"But surely you understand that our choices dictate what happen to us? We made wise choices, and therefore are here. They made foolish choices, and therefore cannot be here. It is the same as those who choose to be demons. They meddle in magics they cannot understand and bear the consequences.

Jak thought that through, and she could see heads nodding and mutters of agreement throughout some of the richer-looking patrons. "That's...not right at all. I've seen demons, and most of them aren't Gifters, they couldn't have mutated themselves without help."

"So, you're saying that rogue Gifters are to blame?" The Priest's smile widened. "Perhaps we should keep closer tabs on those we allow to carry the brand."

Jak swallowed. She had walked right into that one. She looked at the other students and Semwei. The older woman had her head down, a look of defeat on her face. Several of the others were shaking their heads. They were all Gifters, and Jak had just implied they were a threat.

"I... I didn't mean it like that."

"My friends," The Priest addressed the crowd. "Pay no heed to what this young one has to say. She is young, but furthermore, I know something concerning her story. She arrived only two days ago from Foothold." A murmur ran through the crowd. "Yes, you've heard the reports. A demon army, and other new varieties of demon that some are calling the Fae."

Jak felt her face grow hot. This was what he had wanted all along. To discredit her in the face of everyone here. She opened her mouth. "But they aren't..."

"Hush child," Semwei moved to her side and whispered quietly to her. "You can't make things better here."

"As a student of the college, you are all, of course, welcome." The Royal Priest extended his hands to Jak and the others. "We are grateful for the chance to raise our young ones, so they can avoid the mistakes of the fallen and come with us to partake of the blessings of the Holy Relics. We are here to help you, young Jak."

Jak looked at him. It was the first time he had used her name. That had been intentional, she realized as she saw the look on his face. Now everyone would hear about the young Gifter who rejected the blessing of the Holy Relic. Even those who weren't here and couldn't recognize her face would find out eventually who she was. Her initial impulses had been right, she should have left while she had the chance.

Without another word, she turned on her heal and made a beeline for the door. She didn't bother to look at anyone. They were all watching her, she knew. Nothing she could do about that now. She used the pedestrian entrance to exit the building, not even bothering to acknowledge the puzzled glances from the two beefy men standing guard outside. She hadn't liked this place from the beginning, and now she knew that she would never come back. Not if Semwei gave her all the chores in the college.

She eventually stopped at the base of the hill, overlooking the large market square, and feeling the cool wind on her face. Emotions welled up in her, and she felt her eyes burn. She needed to see Naem. He was the only one she could talk to in times like this. Making a right hand turn, she marched towards Watcher High Command.

It wasn't long before she arrived, and two Watcher guards stood at the entrance to a large complex. Through the door, Jak could see the barracks and training fields. It looked like Foothold, only nicer, and with more space.

"State your business," one of the Watcher guards said as she approached.

"I'm here to see Sergeant Naem? He's a Watcher."

"Does he know you're coming."

"Uh... yes. He's supposed to train me. I'm at the college, but I'm supposed to train with the Watchers. General Wilva said so." That wasn't exactly why she was here now, but they didn't need to know that.

One guard turned to the other and jerked his head behind him. The man nodded and retreated inside. Jak waited in silence, and the other guard said nothing as they stood there together.

A few minutes later, the guard reappeared. Naem was not with him. "I'm sorry, the Sergeant is on pressing business for the General. He is not here."

"Oh..." Jak felt her shoulders slump.

"I did confirm you're meant to visit throughout the week," he said and handed her a small letter. This will get you through the next time you come."

"Thank you." Jak accepted the letter. Well, that was something at least.

She traveled back to the college, glancing at the merchants and the beggars lining the streets. None of them gave her a second thought, but she figured that might change once word got out of what happened in the church. It was probably best if she just stuck to her studies. And right now, the library sounded like the best option for her. If she got back soon, she could beat the other students there, grab what she wanted, then retreat to her room. She could only be grateful that there weren't enough students to warrant giving her a roommate.

When she arrived at the college, only the staff were present. Semwei and the other students were nowhere to be seen. She stepped upstairs and borrowed a large book called *The Shape of Branding* from the library. Then she took it to her room and sat down to read.

She had had a chance to read through some of the books already, but as before, she realized that she still had so much to learn. The book was full of helpful advice on how to make a brand stick, which was the problem she still dealt with. Of course, she technically could make a brand stick, but then it would cease to function. In the case of the Flamedancer brand, it would cause the subject to explode. She needed to find a way to keep the brand stable.

Turning to the section on Flamedancer brands, she read and soaked up all she could. But it wasn't long before she was interrupted.

A knock sounded on her door. Jak grimaced. Hopefully, it wasn't one of the students come to gloat. She rose from her bed and opened the door.

It was Semwei, and she carried a plate of food. Her stern, pale face looked somewhat softer now. "I figured you wouldn't want to eat with everyone else today. So, I brought you some food." She held out the plate.

Jak accepted it gratefully. "I... I don't know what to say. I didn't want..."

"It's okay child." Semwei entered the room and sat down on Jak's bed, indicating Jak sit next to her. Jak saw no way to refuse so she did as requested. Semwei continued, "the Head Professor told me a few things about you. He didn't elaborate, but I got the feeling that you were something special."

"Ugh, why do people keep saying that?" Jak felt her frustration leave her in a huff. "I'm just a kid who had to learn the hard way how to survive. I didn't want any of this! All I wanted was to come here, learn how to be a Gifter, and return in the summers to visit my... father." She choked.

Semwei looked unsure of what to do at the moment. Ultimately, she extended an arm and wrapped it around Jak, albeit gingerly, like she half expected Jak to explode.

"I understand," she said after Jak had a moment to quiet her breathing. "And what that Priest said and did to you... no one deserves that."

"Why do you even go there? What could they possibly have to offer? Is it the Relic, the one that makes you feel good? Is that why you go?"

Semwei averted her eyes, and Jak almost thought she saw a hint of a shame there. "Perhaps," she said after a pregnant pause. "It wasn't always like this. The Church of the Holy Relics was once something true and pure. Now it is only a large branch off a dead tree. But some truth can still be found there, from time to time."

Jak considered that. Yes, she supposed it was really the Priest who was the problem. Jak didn't know the church well enough to understand their core doctrines. She knew a few things about the Annals of Adam, and she had no doubt that those words, at least as they had originally been given, came straight from their father's father. But that clearly had nothing to do with what the Priest taught now.

"I think I would rather look for the truth elsewhere."

Semwei nodded. "I would normally ensure that all of our students go. It's important to at least be aware of such things." Jak opened her mouth to protest, and Semwei put up a hand. "But... I am willing to make an exception after today. I don't know what happened when you felt the power of the Relic of Bestowal, but I'm sure you don't want to risk it happening again. But don't let that make you think that you can shirk off in other areas of the college. I expect you to do all your chores and attend all your classes. Is that understood?"

Jak nodded. At least Semwei was understanding if a bit uptight.

"Well then, I'll leave you to your studies. There's some learning to be had in that one." She indicated the book Jak had open on the bed. "I trust you to take full advantage of that fact."

Then she left, leaving Jak feeling at least a little better than before. She quickly did as instructed and took up her reading again. The Flamedancer brand, probably the brand Jak was most familiar with by now, even though she had yet to get it right. So, what exactly was the problem?

She scanned each page closely. One paragraph stood out to her. 'The Flamedancer brand requires a few unique behaviors during its branding. Unlike most brands, the Flamedancer requires a more fluid imagination, not unlike the flames it represents. Where some brands require the Gifter to imagine them with complete detail, the Flamedancer brand requires an extra step. First, imagine the brand in its entirety, then imagine it like a flame, dancing...'

This was new to Jak, who had never heard of any other conditions to specific brands. Perhaps that was the reason why she had never managed to make it stable. Did the other brands have extra conditions like this? And if so, why hadn't Gabriel mentioned them? Perhaps he was just planning on doing so later.

This could be the link she was looking for. Could she? She almost scrambled out of bed right then, but soon slumped back down. Students weren't allowed to practice branding outside of the classroom.

But the more she sat there, the more she realized that she couldn't put it off. She had to know. She had to practice.

Tiptoeing outside, she managed to avoid most of the others as she found a small tree and picked up a dead branch lying next to it. When back in her room, she broke it up into several pieces and readied some water and her blankets, just in case it didn't work again, and the small wood chips erupted in flame.

Taking the first chip, she laid it on the stone floor and touched it lightly with one finger. Closing her eyes, she ran through the motions. The first step was to speak true to oneself. She usually went with something mundane like 'I felt uncomfortable today.' which worked like a charm in this case. The brand on her left hand began to glow with a bright light.

Next came the visualization of the brand. She imagined it completely, noting the width of each line, the contours, the exact angles as lines met. Finally, she added one more thing, imagining the symbol waving in the air, like a flame. She opened her eyes as the brand clearly etched itself into the small piece of wood.

And then promptly burst into flame.

Jak hurried and stuffed her blanket on top of the open fire, pouring some water on top to make sure.

Relics, she had really hoped that would work.

She tried again, and then again. Each time, the little twig disintegrated as the entire thing was consumed in flame. Jak did a good job at putting out the flames, but her room was still beginning to fill with light smoke.

On the second to last piece, she took a moment to watch it burn, observing the flames as they danced. Chaotic. Hungry. Then she dowsed it with her wet blanket.

Just one more left.

She wasn't going to try this again tonight. Her room was already suspiciously smoky. If someone opened the door, she would have a hard time explaining what was going on, and she was beginning to cough. She would need to open the door soon and get some fresh air.

But first, she focused on the small wood chip, running through the process in her mind. This time, she felt like she had a better grasp on the...personality that fire exhibited. Like it had consciousness and a form.

The light from her brand flashed, then faded, the branding done.

Jak winced, waiting for the inevitable eruption.

Nothing happened.

She stared back at the woodchip. A Flamedancer brand was clearly visible there, black lines crisscrossing across the small wooden surface. It did not catch fire.

She whooped! Then instantly covered her mouth, remembering that she wasn't supposed to be branding on her own. She didn't want someone to poke their head in.

But she had done it! Her first stable brand. She had a strong desire at that moment to tell someone. That thought brought her spirits back down. Her father was dead, her mother was gone, Gabriel was away, and she had no friends here, and likely wouldn't have any after today.

For one night, though, she pushed all of that out of her mind. She had accomplished something wonderful, even if there was no one to acknowledge it.

She opened the door to her room just a crack, allowing the smoke to settle and leave. Then she nestled in bed for the night, though it took some time to fall asleep as she kept reading long after the sun went down.

She was barely aware that she had fallen asleep when a knock boomed on her wooden door.

CHAPTER 5

"Jak," a voice sounded came from outside her room. "It's Gabriel."

At first, Jak didn't fully realize what was going on. On another loud bang on her door, she rose and nearly stumbled to open it. She did so just by a crack, she was still in her nightwear after all.

Gabriel met her eyes from the other side. "Oh my, you do look tired. I apologize. But I need you to come with me."

"Wha' why?" Jak said through a yawn.

"I'll explain on the way, but it's important, Jak. You've got ten minutes."

While it still took a moment for everything to register, Jak was beginning to feel more alert. If Gabriel said something was important, then it must be. And the look on his face would seem to confirm that.

She got dressed as hurriedly as she could, not even sparing time to do more than pat down her hair. It was messy, and she could have used more time to wet it down and use her brush. But Gabriel had said ten minutes, and she didn't have the time.

Finally, she grabbed her travel cloak and pushed open her door. Gabriel had left, so she went outside to the main courtyard and then into the entrance dome. There Gabriel waited, along with one other. Jak grimaced as she approached. Please, no... not her.

Estel stood next to Gabriel, her typical sneer firmly in place. Jak waited for some sort of snobby remark about her hair. But oddly, Estel said nothing, though she gave Jak an amused look that clearly indicated she thought Jak looked ragged.

Estel, on the other hand, looked like a warrior. She had on her Watcher armor, which was polished and bright, even in the dim light. Her hair was pulled back in a bun. Jak tilted her head looking at her. If Estel shaved her head and added thirty years, she would have looked a lot like General Wilva.

"Good, you're here," said Gabriel, not really noticing the looks that Jak and Estel were giving each other. "We have a small walk ahead of us."

"Where are we going?" Jak couldn't help but ask. "And why is she here?"

"Estel is the only person besides yourself who is familiar with what happened at Foothold, particularly about the Fae."

"What about Naem?"

Estel spoke for the first time. "Naem is on a special assignment for the General. He won't be back for a few days I hear."

That was probably the most that Estel had ever said to Jak without some snide remark. Odd.

Jak turned back to Gabriel. "So, what do the Fae have to do with this?"

"It's better to show you, I think." Gabriel was stroking his thin beard. "Best if we leave now. We can't take the horses because it's a bit of rocky terrain. But it's not too far out of the city."

'Not too far' was not the best estimate. They travelled out through the south gate, which Jak had not been to yet, then kept on the road for some time before Gabriel took a sharp left turn which led them towards the coast. After that, their progress slowed considerably as they did their best to keep from tripping or spraining an ankle on the rocks. Occasionally, there were stretches of earth and grass, but for the most part, they walked along hard, and sometimes sharp, stone.

Estel was unusually nice to Jak. Well, nice compared to how she usually behaved, more like she just wasn't being horrid. Of course, she had been relatively nice to her on the trip from Foothold. Perhaps Gabriel's presence had something to do with it. She even asked Jak how things were going at the college, which Jak answered in as few words as possible. Surely Estel had heard about what happened to Jak at the cathedral. The whole city must have heard of that by now. But Estel made no mention of it.

Soon, Jak thought she could smell salt on the wind. By now, the morning was well underway, and the sun shone in their faces.

Gabriel paused for a moment. "We're almost there. I need to warn you that what you see must be kept between the three of us. And I suppose you can tell your other Watcher friend. But no one else must know what has happened here."

Jak wet her lips. What could have happened to make Gabriel sound so serious?

Estel voiced Jak's thoughts. "What exactly are you talking about, sir?"

"Before I show you, I need a verbal yes that you will tell no one, not even your superiors." That last remark was meant for Estel.

After a moment's hesitation, Estel nodded. "Yes, sir."

Gabriel turned to Jak.

"Yes, of course," she said, feeling the apprehension grow.

"Very well, they're just over this rise." Gabriel turned and led them up and over the hill.

On the other side, Jak could make out the ocean. She had only seen it before at a distance when standing near the palace. But now she marveled at how... big it looked. She could see nothing by water in all directions, and if she looked north, she could make out the city of Skyecliff, sitting proudly on the raised peninsula.

But in the opposite direction, just ahead of them, there was a small inlet, and Jak could make out a few tents set up there. A camp. Perhaps this had been where Gabriel was leading them. The tents indicated people. Was there something important that Gabriel wanted them to look at? Something to do with the Fae? Jak began to feel her apprehension change to the excitement.

A man exited a tent as they approached, a young man, probably only a few years older than Jak. "Gabriel, you're back!" He eyed the two girls. "I thought we agreed to tell as few people as possible."

"We did, but these two have experience that I believe will prove useful. I trust them both."

Jak wasn't sure he should be trusting Estel. The girl was friendlier, and it made Jak uncomfortable. But nevertheless, she was glad to hear that Gabriel trusted her. But trusted her for what? That was the question.

"Girls," Gabriel continued. "This is Danen, he was the lead on a small excavation we were doing here. Someone found evidence of an ancient structure buried in a cave at the base of this inlet."

Jak looked and could just make out the cave Gabriel was speaking about. A small stream came out of it and made its way towards the sea. They had seen no sign of a stream or river up until now, so it must come from under the ground.

"You sure you want them to come close... after... what happened?" asked Danen, looking nervous.

"I do not believe there will be any threat," Gabriel said with a wave of his hand. I have closed the offending item in a magic inhibitor box. It shouldn't cause us any problems now."

Magic inhibitor box? Jak had never heard of such a thing. Was that some kind of Relic? And just what had they put in there, and why was it dangerous?

She glanced at Estel, who was shifting her feet nervously. "Uh... professor?" Jak ran a hand through her tangled hair. "What exactly..."

"Don't worry, child, there is no direct threat to you. I would not have brought you here if it weren't completely safe."

Estel relaxed a bit, but Jak still felt nervous. Whatever had happened here, it had Danen on edge. He looked from Estel to Jak, and back at Gabriel.

"Come, I'll take you to meet them."

Danen led them down the bank and into the cave itself, but not before lighting a torch and bringing it with them. It was dark, far darker than Jak would have suspected. But once her eyes adjusted to the torchlight, it wasn't so bad. For a split second, Jak was reminded of the last time she had entered a strange cave. Though there had been no water then, and no torch to light the way. Yet something felt familiar as they walked alongside the small stream. They hadn't gone far when they reached a small pool. The water here looked deeper, but Jak couldn't make out much. Danen set his torch down on a raised boulder.

"You can come out. Gabriel's here, and he's brought help."

It took Jak a moment to realize that Danen wasn't talking to them. There were people in these caves!

A splash in the small pool almost made her jump. To her satisfaction, Estel jumped and hurried away from the edge of the water.

In the torchlight, Jak could see faces in the water. There were at least four of them, and they all swimming in the small underground lake. It had to be freezing in there what were they doing?

Gabriel straightened and spoke. "May I introduce the rest of the expedition. This is Haffi, Pearl, Nigem, and Cerai. They, together with Danen, comprised the entire group sent to study this area and bring back their findings."

Jak's brow furrowed. So why were these people swimming? It didn't make much sense to her.

As if voicing Jak's doubts, Estel asked, "so what exactly is the problem?" She looked annoyed, probably from being scared by the approaching students.

"Look closer," Danen offered.

"Here," said one of the students, Cerai. She looked scared, though of what Jak could not tell. "I'll show you."

She leaned away from the edge as if to float on her back, and Jak felt her eyes go wide. She heard a gasp from Estel behind her, who had clearly seen it too.

Sticking out of the water, where Cerai's legs should have been, was a beautiful and enormous fin. Even in the dim light of the cavern, Jak could make out multiple colors shimmering off the scales. It continued up to Cerai's hips, where enormous muscles resided where the thighs should have been.

The other students took Cerai's lead and leaned back to show their tails. All had a similar build, but each one looked unique. At least they all had a different colored shimmer, and the pattern on the tail didn't match either. It was like looking at four different butterfly wings, each one unique, but each one just as beautiful. Jak found her mouth open in a gaping smile.

"What did you do?" A harsh voice spoke from behind Jak. She turned to see Estel standing there, her back against the stone wall. She looked horrified. Jak turned back to the... affected students.

"We didn't do anything," Cerai said. "This just happened to us."

Estel sniffed in disbelief and was about to say something when Gabriel cut her off. "Let them speak."

Jak remained silent as Cerai continued. "We were investigating this area. Someone had found a structure a little further in, so we were combing this part for any signs of ancient life. As we were diving, we found what had to be a Relic."

A Relic! Of course, just like what happened to her mother. They found an original copy of the Annals of Adam, and suddenly they changed to become the Shadow Fae. Had these students found another copy of the book here? Jak found she couldn't stop herself from asking.

"Was it a book?"

Cerai looked at her, confused. "No, it was just a piece of gold."

"So how did you know it was a Relic?" Estel asked, arms folded.

"Because parts of it were...suspended in mid-air. It had several rings held within larger rings, but they did not touch, they simply stayed together. They looked like..."

"Ripples." One of the other students offered, "They looked like ripples on clear water."

"Yes, that's exactly what they looked like." Cerai went on. "Anyway, no sooner had we found the Relic when some of us began to feel a little strange. For one, we had a strong desire to enter the water again. Then we felt pain in our legs. So, we found ourselves in the water and...it hurt, a lot. But after the pain subsided, we tried to leave the water, and... discovered what had happened."

"That's incredible," Jak said in a near whisper. Cerai and the others looked at her strangely, not expecting that response.

"This is Jak," Gabriel explained. "And the other is Estel. They've had business with others who had... similar transformations. Jak, tell them what you told me about the Shadow Fae and their Relic."

So Jak did so, though she left out the part about her mother being a Shadow Fae like she usually did. But she explained about the Annals of Adam, about how it somehow changed humans into Shadow Fae. She told them about the Bright Fae, and their miraculous transformation, though Jak admitted that there hadn't been a Relic involved that time, and they didn't know why. When she finished, everyone was listening intently.

"So that explains why nothing happened to me," said Danen. "If not everyone was affected by the other Relic, maybe this one only affects certain people as well."

Jak nodded. "There doesn't appear to be any logic behind who changes and who doesn't. But we can be certain that it's a natural transformation."

"Assuming all involved are telling the truth." Estel still had her hands crossed, and she was leaning against the stone wall with an expression Jak did not like.

Jak glared at her. "That's Kuldain talking. There's no evidence of any misuse of magic here."

"Now wait one second!" Cerai's face flushed in the firelight. "We never did anything..."

"No one is accusing you, Cerai," Gabriel said in a calming voice. "But... unfortunately some will not believe us on that matter." He shot a cautious glance at Estel.

"That is why we need to keep this matter quiet," Danen added. "As you can see, they aren't exactly mobile outside of the confines of this cave. We could take them to the ocean, but I don't know how the saltwater could affect their, ah, current condition."

"But this is natural," Jak felt her temper rise. "It even said in the Annals of Adam, the original one, that there would be races returning to the Earth, protectors of its elements. It mentions light and darkness, which I guess are the Bright and Shadow Fae, but it also made a list of other elements." She met Cerai's gaze. "So I guess you could call yourselves Water Fae, or something like that."

"Where is the Relic now?" Estel turned to face Gabriel. "I wouldn't want it affecting anyone else."

You mean you don't want to turn into a Fae and have people like you accuse you of witchcraft, Jak thought. But she kept her mouth shut. Eventually, people would come around once this became widespread enough. When a friend and family members joined the Fae, surely there would be less talk of magical sorcery.

"I've repressed its magic," Gabriel replied. "With a Void brand on the box, we're carrying it in. We're taking it with us."

A Void brand? Jak had never heard of such a thing. Apparently, Gabriel still had a lot to teach her.

"Do you really think that's wise?" Estel regarded Gabriel with a cold stare.

"Of course I do, child, why would I take it with us if I wasn't sure it was safe?" Gabriel's tone had an edge on it now, as if to remind Estel who held authority here. Estel got the hint, and said no more, her lips forced into a thin line.

Jak was still interested. "May I see it?"

Gabriel shook his head. "I'm afraid not. For now, it must be kept safe inside the container we've prepared."

Jak felt her shoulders slump but did not argue.

Cerai spoke again. "You've already helped us out a lot telling us about the other Fae."

Jak smiled. "Of course! I almost wish I could have a tail like that."

"It's inconvenient," said another of the students, or Water Fae as Jak was beginning to think of them. "Not a silly girl's fantasy."

Cerai glared at the other student, but Jak hung her head. He was right of course. This was a massive change for them, and Jak treated it like nothing. "I'm sorry, I..."

"You have nothing to be sorry about," Cerai responded. "We're grateful—" she shot a look at the others. "—for any news you can give us."

"Can we do anything else for you? Bring you some food perhaps?" Jak racked her brain for anything else they could do.

"We've already arranged for that," Gabriel explained. "Danen and I are taking it in turns to bring supplies from the city. In the meantime, we'll have to figure out what to do in the long term. We're keeping it quiet for now, but sooner or later someone will let the word out that...Water Fae, as you call them, exist. Who knows what their reaction will be? So we must ensure that they are safe before that happens.

Jak nodded. "Just tell me what you need me to do."

Gabriel chuckled. "Right now, I need you to focus on your studies young one. This is a matter for those of us with much more experience."

Jak frowned. He was right of course. He was the more experienced one, even if Jak knew more about the Fae. But she supposed that was why Gabriel had asked her here in the first place. She wanted to know what would happen to the Water Fae, but that didn't mean she couldn't keep a low profile and just keep studying.

She thought back on the night before, when she had performed her first stable brand. Moments like that were what she lived for. She'd prefer to just do more of that. More learning. Yes, better to leave these bigger matters to people who knew what to do.

They left the cave and got ready to head back into the city, though not before Jak noticed Gabriel tuck something in his pack that hadn't been there before. No doubt it was the Relic that had caused all this. She wished she could see it now. She didn't feel any power radiating from it, not like she had with the Annals of Adam, but that was probably due to the Void brand that Gabriel had placed on its container. And speaking of that, Jak couldn't wait to get back to the library and research this new brand that she had never heard of.

The trek back seemed even longer to Jak than it had got to the cave in the first place. Estel was quiet, but Jak could see the girl giving her venomous looks now and then. She clearly wasn't happy with what they had just seen. Gabriel had made them promise to keep their mouths shut, but Jak had a suspicion Estel would probably break that promise eventually.

But ultimately, it didn't matter to Jak. She could contribute best simply to learning all she could. Who knows, maybe she could learn something that would be useful to Gabriel and these new Water Fae. Jak felt a smile grow on her lips. A third variety of Fae... how exciting was that? Jak idly wondered how many more they might encounter. She desperately wished she could get her hands on that original copy of the Annals of Adam. She knew there had to be more about these races appearing.

Finally, they arrived at the college. Estel said her farewells, sparing a single sneer for Jak as she left. Jak shrugged it off. She was on her way to the library.

Inside the main doors, she and Gabriel ran into Semwei.

"Goodness, Gabriel. You can't just take the students willy-nilly like that. They've got responsibilities you know. This one has barely seen the inside of a classroom yet."

Jak narrowed her eyes at Semwei. The woman gave no sign of her compassionate side that Jak had seen the day before. Gabriel cleared his throat. "I am indeed sorry, Madame Semwei, but it was a matter of some urgency. She is yours for the rest of the day."

Semwei pursed her lips. "I hope you're not wrapping her into your little side projects. She's dealing with enough as it is."

Why were they talking about her like she wasn't there? Gabriel raised a hand to assure Semwei.

"Nothing so dramatic, my dear."

"Very well," Semwei turned to face Jak. "You child, I want you reporting to the cook for your chores."

"But morning chores are over!" Jak felt her face flush. She wanted, no, needed to get to the library. She had no time for chores.

"The morning chores are not over until they are done. And as you have been away all morning, they are still unfinished. You'll miss your first lessons of the day, but that should teach you that we're serious about discipline around her. Now hop to it."

Semwei's tone held no room for argument, though Jak seriously considered it anyway. Gabriel had come to take her away, it wasn't her fault that she hadn't been around for the morning chores. In the end, she turned on her heel and marched towards the kitchens. She would show Semwei. She would finish her chores, attend her classes, do everything she was supposed to do. Then she would visit the library and spend the rest of the day, and every day after that, trying to learn more about branding. And maybe, just maybe, she might find something about the Fae that could prove useful to Gabriel and the others.

CHAPTER 6

T HAT EVENING, SHE AWOKE with a start from her seat in the library. Someone had lit the candles, as it was dark outside. But it couldn't be too late yet, because no one had woken her to inform her about the curfew.

She lifted the huge tome sitting on her lap to try and get a better view in the candlelight. How much time had she wasted while asleep? She couldn't even remember falling asleep. One minute she had been reading, the next...well she supposed it made sense, seeing as she had almost no sleep the night before, then had traveled outside of the city and back, performed her chores, and went about her day as if nothing had happened. Of course, she was tired.

But something had woken her up so what was it? She peered around the room of dusty volumes.

"That's a tough one you've got there." A voice spoke from one side.

She turned her head to see. In the dim light, she could make out a man sitting in the chair a few feet away. He was about Naem's age, but he looked different. At least, different from most people Jak knew. The skin on his face looked almost stretched, and his eyes were slanted. His hair was black but his face...well his face held a smile that put Jak at ease before she even realized what was happening.

"Excuse me?"

"Your book," The man indicated the large tome Jak held. "*A Comprehensive History of Holy Scripture.* Not exactly what most people would call light reading."

"Were you spying on me while I was sleeping?"

The man held his hands out in a gesture of surrender. "I'm merely observant."

There was that smile again. Jak couldn't quite tell what it was about it that seemed to disarm her.

"Did you want to read this one?" Jak asked.

"Oh no, I've read it. Twice. It's mostly modern propaganda, promoting a rather specific view on the Annals of Adam. I didn't think it held anything of lasting value."

"You don't believe in the Annals of Adam?"

"Oh, it's an inspired book. But for a long time, it was in the hands of gatekeepers who fed only the things that benefitted them to the general public. Now, it's mostly accessible to all of us, but the damage has already been done."

Jak leaned in. There was something very interesting about this man's view. "What exactly would that be?"

He sat up in his seat. "Imagine if you had a book that was passed down from generation to generation. Eventually, you would need to make copies, and then copies of those copies. And what if, as you were making the copies, you decided to eliminate pieces that didn't line up with what you thought was right, essentially molding the book to your own viewpoint."

"But that's horrible. Why would anyone do that?"

The smile wavered on the man's face. "It's just a thought, sorry. I can get carried away."

"No," Jak realized suddenly that the man was right. Why else would the original copy of the Annals of Adam have whole sections that were not to be found in other editions? "It makes sense, I just... you'd have to be pretty corrupt to do something like that intentionally."

The man laughed. "Indeed. Well, I'm glad we've had a chance to talk about theological politics. I can think of no better way to introduce oneself." He smiled again, then rose and put his hand to his chest in a traditional greeting. "I'm Seph. And to whom do I have the pleasure?"

"Uh, Jak." She almost forgot what to say, putting her own hand to her chest. That smile though. "My name is Jak. I..." she broke off and stared at his left hand. "You don't have a brand!"

Her voice was so shocked that Seph began to laugh. "No, I decided several years ago I would not have one."

"But... but... everyone has a brand!"

"Not everyone, only those who can afford it, and a few others like myself."

Seph's face darkened just a bit, but Jak barely noticed. She brought her hand to her chest a second time, showing off her Gifter brand.

"Maybe one day I could give you one. I'm a new student here."

"I gathered as much, given the Gifter brand and the fact I haven't seen you here before. And if I ever change my mind, I'd be honored for you to perform the Branding."

Jak felt herself blush but instead calmed her face. "So, do you always wait around watching young girls like myself in the library?"

Seph's mouth quirked. "Like I said, I'm just observant. Plus you..." He cut off for a moment as if deciding what to say. "You intrigued me with your choice of reading. I thought I could at least stick around until you woke up. You made me wait for over an hour." He winked at her.

"Well, I'm so sorry to waste your time," Jak said through rolled eyes.

"Oh, it wasn't a waste. I finished the book I was reading." He held it out for her to see. *A Catalog of Ancient Relics, Volume Three.*

"You're reading a catalog? And you thought what I read was dry?" Jak didn't exactly know why she said that. She had planned to start reading through that same catalog eventually. Who didn't want to know more about the Relics?

"I try to learn all I can say about Relics, they're the closest thing we have to true scripture, unmarred by several generations of corrupt theologians."

"You really don't like religion, do you?"

"Ah, now that is most definitely not true." He said with a knowing smile. He looked like he was hiding something. "I just know that many precious things were removed from the state religion over time."

So, they were back to this subject. Something tickled Jak's mind. "Could you tell me exactly how you know that? Do you have any evidence?"

"Hmm... of a sort," he said, thoughtfully. "Not necessarily something I get into with total strangers." He flashed a smile at her again.

"We've introduced ourselves, we're not strangers anymore."

"I'm sorry," he broke his eye contact. "I'm just not accustomed..."

"Well, I can prove what you say."

His grin vanished, and he looked back up at her sharply. "Come again?"

Hang it all, Jak. Why did you say that? "Ah, yes. I... may have come across an original copy of the Annals of Adam while I was in the Hollow Peaks."

"The Hollow Peaks, whatever were you doing there?"

Jak withdrew. "You know, I shouldn't have said anything. We only just met and..."

"Well, it's like you said, we introduced ourselves which means we're not strangers."

She hesitated. "I don't know..."

"Please, Jak." His voice dropped to a whisper, and he leaned closer to where she sat. "This may be more important than you know."

Kind of dramatic of him. But at that moment, staring into his eyes as they bore into hers, she found herself trusting this strange man.

So, she started at the beginning. This was now the third time that she had related her experience with the Annals of Adam and the Fae since entering the city. The first time, she had felt interrogated, the second time she had felt mistrusted. This time, however, something was different. Seph hung onto every word of her story, and they had to stop several times for him to ask a clarifying question. He seemed particularly interested in the differences that she read between the Annals of Adam that they all knew, and the copy that the Shadow Fae kept in the Hollow Peaks. He really believed her, she could sense it. She didn't exactly know why.

Once he began asking her specific questions about the Fae's powers, often guessing facts about them correctly, she decided she had said enough. "Okay, I've told you a lot, it's now your turn. Why are you so interested in the Fae and the Annals?"

Seph paused to consider that for a moment. He considered Jak, and she got a distinct impression that he was deciding whether to trust her. Finally, he seemed to come to a decision.

"Well, you see. I've already heard a lot of these things. In another book."

He fished in a back pocket and took out a worn, small volume. It was brown and rough around the edges, but Seph placed it carefully, almost lovingly, in Jak's hands. It bore one word on the cover, a name: 'Illadar.'

"What is Illadar?" Jak asked, leafing through the book. "And what do you mean that you've already heard what I told you?

"I discovered this book in my country, many leagues east of here. The details are not important. Illadar, as it says on the cover, is the name of a place. The book is one large prophecy you could say, of a place where a chosen few will gather and form a great nation, perhaps many nations. It will be a place of sanctuary for many... races. And if what you've told me is accurate, your Shadow and Bright Fae will be among them."

Jak looked down at the book in her hands with new interest. "How...how did you come by such a book. Why isn't everyone talking about it?" She looked back at Seph. "Who are you? Really. You look like an outsider, but your accent is perfect. Start at the beginning."

"Well, I'm part of a small church, not affiliated with the Church of the Holy Relics, or anyone in their organization." Seph crossed his arms. He didn't seem hesitant anymore like he had already made up his mind about what to tell Jak. "We meet on High Morning, like the rest, but we believe a few things that... shall we say, don't line up with what people are taught from a young age to believe. That book that you're holding there, it's the key..."

"What is going on here!" Jak whirled as Semwei entered the room, her face flushed. "Have you any idea how late it is girl? It's high past curfew."

Jak quickly hid the book around her back and stood straight. "Yes, Madame Semwei. I'm sorry, I lost track of time."

"Did you not notice that none of the other students were here?" She looked at Seph. "Oh, and you've been talking to that one, have you?"

"Lovely to see you, Madame Semwei, as always." Seph's smile was back, and he was on his feet, bowing to the head-mistress with a flourish.

Semwei stared down her nose at him. "I don't want you filling the heads of my students with your nonsense."

"I wouldn't dream of it, my lady. And I apologize for the late hour. I take full responsibility for keeping Jak awake."

"Hmm... very well. The library is closed, see yourself out." Semwei tilted her head at the staircase.

"At once." Seph kept smiling and turned to say goodbye to Jak. She still had the book hidden behind her back. Seph met her eyes and mouthed, 'keep it.' Then he turned on his heel, placed a wide-brimmed hat on his head, and marched down the stairs.

"Well!" Jak jumped as Semwei barked at her. "Get to bed child. You'll be rising with the rest of them on time tomorrow, and I don't want you thinking that you'll receive any special treatment. You'll respect the curfew, or I will have your backside paddled until you can't sit for a week. Understand?"

"Yes, madam." Jak leapt into motion, barely managing to keep Seph's book out of view as she hurried down the stairs.

Once she found her room, she closed the door hard and leaned against it. Semwei had a way of making you feel like you were being chased by a demon. Jak was breathing hard and almost wanted to open her door a crack, just to see if

Semwei had followed. It was almost like the woman had forgotten what happened to Jak at the church, and the moment they had shared.

She collapsed on the bed, feeling her exhaustion return, despite the nap she had taken earlier. But there was one thing she had to check before she went to bed.

Lighting a candle, she ran her fingers across the leather embossing on Seph's book. Illadar. It was a beautiful name, and from what Seph had said, a hopeful concept, though she doubted that any such paradise was anything more than superstition. Still...

She opened the book and began reading on the first page.

"Hello," it began. "To whomever reads this, my name is Abel. As I write this, I am on the run from my brother, who I believe means to hurt me. He's been this way ever since my father chose me to pass on the birthright, giving me ownership of the artifacts we have created. The discoveries my father has made through science and... something more, they are precious to us. But my brother is hot-tempered and seeks power for himself. It didn't take my father long to realize that he would not make a great leader. And so, he passed the responsibility to me, the younger brother. While I fear for my life at this moment, both from my brother, and my other brothers, sisters, and nephews who follow him, I have a responsibility to posterity. May you find these words comforting in a promising future."

Jak felt a mixture of feelings. If this was true, this sounded like one of their ancestors, perhaps one of their earliest ancestors, the ones who created the Relics. But it seemed too good to be true, which made her doubt its veracity. Her father used to tell her: "If you want it to be true, it probably isn't."

Yet, she could not stop reading. This Abel, whoever he was, she had never heard of him before from any other scripture. But as she read she realized just how everything she read seemed to fit. It spoke about future races, in similar language to what she had read in the Annals of Adam. It talked about the elusive Illadar, a spiritual sanctuary that would allow all races to dwell in harmony together. It was all a bit much to take in, and she found herself going back and re-reading large portions of the text.

It was a long time before weariness overtook her, and she fell asleep, the book still clutched in one hand.

CHAPTER 7

S HE ROSE THE NEXT day and immediately wondered if the previous night had been a dream. But no, there was the Illadar book lying on the corner of her bed. She almost felt the need to leaf back through it and confirm that she had read what she thought she read. But then the bell tolled, signaling breakfast. Jak hesitated. She wouldn't really have time to read the book again until the evening.

She shrugged off that thought and stuffed the book into her pouch. Maybe she'd find a bit of downtime.

Breakfast was the usual oatmeal with a slice of bread. Not the most amazing meal, but they had some honey to sweeten the oatmeal, and that helped. Jak managed to sneak a peek at the book while eating, carefully keeping it out of sight from other students. But doing so almost cost her her meal, as she wasn't quite done when Semwei entered and announced it was time for morning chores.

She stuffed the book in her pouch again and scarfed down the rest of the oatmeal on her way out. This morning, her assignment was to scrub pots, not the worst job in the world. She set to work and quickly lost herself in thought.

Apart from accurately describing the Shadow and Bright Fae, the book also mentioned many other varieties of Fae, something she'd seen hinted at in the original copy of the Annals of Adam, but this other book seemed to have much more detail on the subject. What really concerned Jak, was that there was a description of a Water-related variety of Fae, which was spot on. Large fins instead of legs, and most likely brought about by the power of a Relic. It was either a really good guess at what a Water Fae would look like or evidence that the book was, at least in part, real. There was no way that Seph knew about the Water Fae, and the book was too old and worn to have been transcribed after their transformation.

After finishing the pots and doing her best to wash the grime and charcoal from her hands, she heard the bell ring. Time for their first core class. Physicality.

This was the first time she'd been in this class, as before she had always been occupied in the mornings. She lined up with the rest of the students, though she noticed many glancing in her direction. Apparently, no one had forgotten the incident at the church.

"Hey there," one called at her. "You think you can keep breakfast in this time?"

A chorus of snickering came from the speaker and his friends. Jak ignored them. She could take a little physical exercise and not lose her breakfast, couldn't she?

Their instructor was a large man who looked like he might have been part of the city militia once. He didn't introduce himself. He had probably already done so when Jak wasn't here.

"Listen up. Today, in addition to your laps, we'll be doing some pushups to build up your upper body strength. One thing you'll learn about physicality is that you must give place for every muscle in your body, not just the ones in your legs."

He had an accent Jak recognized from some of the lower classes in the city. His face bore some scars and seemed to be missing a part of his left ear. This man had probably lived a hard life.

He set them running laps around the courtyard, something Jak didn't mind at first but began to feel winded after the fifth lap. By the fifteenth, she was gasping for air and barely managing to put one foot in front of the other. She wasn't the only one. Others were gasping beside her, though others were still passing them up.

Blessedly, the instructor blew his whistle and they all ground to a halt. Jak leaned on her knees, seriously wondering if she could keep her breakfast down like the other student had teased.

"That's enough of that! Now for the pushups."

Students all around Jak groaned, and she felt the same way. But she hobbled back to the head of the square where the instructor began walking them through a proper pushup, noting the positioning of the hands, the posture, etc. Jak only half listened as she was still busy catching her breath. She hadn't felt this worn out since Naem had made her walk for miles using combat forms instead of normal steps. Her legs were in great shape, but it had been a while since she'd had that level of workout.

She noticed, with some chagrin that not all the students looked tired. She recognized one girl who seemed almost eager to start the push-ups. It was the same strawberry-blonde girl she'd sat next to at the cathedral. The girl caught her staring, but rather than smirk or look away like Jak expected, she smiled and waved. Confused, Jak raised a hand to wave back.

But just at that moment, their teacher ordered them to get down on all fours and begin. Jak's upper body was not nearly as strong as her legs, and it only took a few push-ups before she realized just how much this was going to hurt. But she grit her teeth and kept going until her arms literally collapsed beneath her. She looked around as she lay on the floor. Most were still going, though she noticed with a small amount of satisfaction that she hadn't been the first to collapse. Nevertheless, not training with Naem for the past few weeks had already taken its toll.

Following Physicality, they had a small break to wash and get ready for their next class, Mathematics. By now, Jak had all but forgotten about the Illadar book, and she was still kneading her arms and legs as she entered a large chamber where they were supposed to have the class. Jak found a seat near the back, not wanting to draw attention, though the eyes of students still followed her, then glanced away when she met their gaze.

"Hey there!" The strawberry-blonde girl sat in the seat next to her. Her voice was cheery, and the girl was not at all worried Jak might vomit on her or something. "I thought you could use some company. Have you been to the Mathmatics classes before? I don't think I've seen you. It's basically just stuff that the professors think we need to know. I don't see why they teach it honestly since I can't see how we would use it in real life. It's not nearly as fun as the Branding classes. I saw you at one of those, but not at the others. Why is that? I'm Amelia by the way."

She stuck out her hand to Jak, who took it slowly. This girl seemed to enjoy talking, but now she was staring at Jak, expectantly.

"Uh...Yeah, I've had things come up." Jak said.

"I've seen you come in late with my grandpa Gabriel. He says..."

"Wait, Gabriel is your grandfather?" Jak hadn't realized Gabriel had kids.

"Oh yes, anyway, he said that he can't talk about anything and that I can't ask you about it either. But I guess I just did. Sorry! But seriously, can you tell me?"

"I'm sorry but I can't."

"I'll bet he's giving you private lessons. He won't tell me anything about you, but I've heard rumors, I know something big happened out there."

Other students were glancing in their direction; Amelia was not exactly discreet.

"Yeah, sure, something like that."

Amelia nearly squealed. "I knew it! You must be important, I can tell, especially after..." She broke off, probably
realizing for the first time how uncomfortable Jak looked.
And that talking about that moment in the church would
probably not help things.

"That doesn't bother you?" Jak said. "What happened to
me there?"

"Oh no, of course not. I just think it makes you more interesting."

"Great, now I'm an oddity on display." Jak couldn't help
but notice all the eyes turning in their direction.

"Oh, I didn't mean it like that, I just..."

But at that moment the teacher entered the room and
began to speak. This teacher was an elderly woman, who
looked almost as stern as Semwei, though not as young.

"Welcome class. We will continue today with our discussion of geometry, particularly the triangle and its many
unique qualities..."

The woman began to drone, and Jak felt herself become
distracted. Amelia was still cheery, looking like she wanted
to say more to Jak, but conversely paying attention to everything the teacher was saying. She would take notes and smile
at Jak when she caught her looking.

As the woman continued in her monotone voice, Jak idly
fished in her pouch for Seph's book. Glancing at the teacher
and those around her, she opened it up under her desk and
continued where she had left off.

"But as to the creation of Illadar, it has not yet been revealed to me how or when that will take place. But I am

sure that such will not be possible without an Oren, a being like myself and my brother who can bestow multiple gifts on a person or object. It is how we made the artifacts we've assembled, and it is how Illadar will come into being."

Jak almost snapped the book shut. Amelia glanced at her and frowned with concern, mouthing "are you okay?" while everyone else kept listening to the lesson. Jak nodded at Amelia, who went back to listening. But the truth was, Jak was not okay. She had just read something she had never expected.

Apparently, this Abel, the author of Seph's book knew how to give multiple brands. And his brother too. That could explain the Relics, most of which held a lot of markings on them, some of which were definitely recognizable brands. But Jak had thought those were just inscriptions, not real brands. Because, well, more than one brand would have rendered the Relic useless. But perhaps not.

What really bothered Jak, however, was this mention of an Oren, a person who could bestow more than one brand. Until several months ago, she would have thought such a person was a fantasy. Until she had done it herself.

Naem had more than one brand, and Jak had been the one to give them to him. At the time, she had thought it a magical fluke of some kind, some complex process revealed to her at the moment by the Bright Fae's ability to reveal the truth.

But what if it wasn't a complex process that anyone could learn? What if it just had something to do with the person who did the branding?

She didn't like that thought at all. If there was one thing she didn't want, it was to stand out from the crowd more than she already did. All she had ever wanted, ever since she was a young child, was to be here at the College of Skyecliff studying to be a Gifter and a scholar. And no one would get in the way of that dream if she could help it. Not even the words of a silly book.

But she had bestowed a second and third brand to Naem, there was no getting around that. Perhaps more people could do the same, someone else who could help locate or create this Illadar place. Perhaps multiple people.

That thought made Jak feel a little better.

"Young girl, can you tell me what happens when you multiply each side of the triangle by itself then add the results of the two shorter sides?"

It took a moment before Jak realized that everyone was staring at her? The teacher had drawn a triangle on the board and waited expectantly for Jak to answer the question.

She looked at the board, barely remembering something about triangles from her schooling in Riverbrook. But with all eyes on her, she could barely think.

"Um... I don't know, ma'am. I'm sorry."

"That's what I thought. Perhaps you will pay attention next time."

"Yes, ma'am. I will."

As the woman continued speaking in that monotone voice, the rest of the class turned to focus, paying much more attention than before. Apparently, none of them wanted to be the next one called out on their distractions. Jak, her face still hot, joined them in taking all the notes she could. It was difficult to work, this woman was hard to pay attention to, but she wouldn't risk a repeat of what happened. Why was it that people always seemed to draw the attention of the entire group onto her? When the class ended, the freckled girl, Amelia, caught up with Jak as she exited the classroom.

"Boy, that was embarrassing wasn't it? I wish they hadn't singled you out like that, I would have died if it had been me. But I guess you were reading a book, can I see it? What were you reading?

Jak stopped in the middle of the hallway. "Listen, um…"

"Amelia."

"Yes, Amelia. Do you always talk this fast?"

"Pretty much, my mother says I won't make any friends because I ask too many questions. Do you think I ask too many questions? Oh wait, that's a question. Did that bother you? Oh, Relics…

Jak couldn't help but laugh. "No, I don't think it's annoying. Takes a bit of getting used to though."

"I'll take that! So, are you a Gifter then? What am I talking about, of course, you are. Just trying to make conversation. So, does this mean we're friends?" She shrugged and grinned as if asking for forgiveness.

Jak offered her hand. "I think I said this already, but I'm Jak, and sure, I'd love to have a friend. I don't really have any here." She thought of Naem as she said it, but she hadn't seen him since they arrived, and she had no idea where he could be.

Amelia almost clapped her hands with joy, but to her credit, stopped herself before it got that obvious. "We have our Branding lesson next, want to come?"

"Um... I think I have to, it's on my schedule."

"Oh right, of course. Well, let's go!"

Jak did her best to stay on pace with Amelia as she all but ran to the next classroom. This was the biggest room in the complex, save for the entrance dome and the library above. It probably sat two hundred people or so, though only a handful filled the seats now. It wasn't the first time Jak wondered why there weren't more Gifters here. This was the only place where they taught Gifting. Anyone who chose Gifting as their brand had to come here by necessity. And yet, Jak had only counted maybe fifty or so in total, and some of those weren't even Gifters, they were just here to learn other disciplines. But none of them were here for this lesson. This time, the lesson was reserved only for the Gifters.

Another elderly woman took the stage and cleared her throat, indicating that everyone should quiet down.

"My grandfather is supposed to teach this one when he's here," Amelia whispered to Jak as they sat. "But he's been back for several days now and hasn't taught it once. Not sure what he's up to."

Jak stayed silent. She knew what was keeping the old mage, of course, but she could tell no one. Instead, she listened as the teacher began to speak.

"I see a few new faces today. Welcome, I am Professor Gona, and today we'll continue our discussion of the mental process behind the Gifting of simpler brands." The woman began. There was a cloth on the table in front of her, and something underneath that formed a small lump. The teacher removed the cloth to show some wood chips sitting there. "You may even get a chance to try a brand for the first time."

Excited mutters moved through the crowd. Amelia turned to Jak with the most excited look on her face that Jak almost choked. "We get to try a brand! I've never tried before."

"You haven't?" Jak was genuinely surprised. She had forgotten how most students took years before they could master even the more basic brands.

The professor cleared her throat again, and the room grew silent once more.

"These wood chips have had a knife cut through them, enough to slice through a portion of the wood, but not all the way through. Our task today will be to establish a healing brand in the wood. If done correctly, the healing brand will allow the wood to heal itself from the knife mark. If done perfectly, the chip will form into a live sapling which can then be planted. Like so..."

The professor's Gifter brand lit up as she imbued the chip she was holding with a healing brand. Everyone in the room stood in awe as the knife mark seemed to sew itself together. After waiting another moment, Jak noticed a few green buds emerging from the stick of wood. She had never known a healing brand could actually revive a piece of wood like that. Soon, the chip flourished with life, and Jak joined the other students in applauding as the professor laid the sapling down on the table.

"Now, before any of you ask questions, no, a Healing brand cannot restore life once it has been taken. But plant life is resilient. It gets its energy from the Earth, and our world cannot die. But try this on a dead animal, and you will see no results. Try it on a dead human, and you will see worse results."

A hush fell on the room as they all realized what the professor meant. Demons. So did that mean that some demons could be formed from people who were already dead? If true, that would explain why Jak had fought so many of them at Foothold. Perhaps someone was collecting the dead and turning them into demons. The image alone haunted her.

The old woman went on as if she had said nothing out of the ordinary. "Now, we've all practiced the act of activating your brand, and most of you are adept at that so far. But actually, using your Gift to bestow brands on others, that takes more work. Each brand is unique, see. Some require a different thought process to successfully make it work."

Jak nodded to herself. That went along with what she's learned about the Flamedancer brand. You had to imagine it dancing.

"The healing brand is among the simplest to bestow, and it is relatively harmless if you get it wrong on an object. Unlike the Flamedancer brand which could explode in your hand."

A few students chuckled as if she had made a joke. Jak didn't laugh. She knew all too well how a faulty Flamedancer brand worked. And to be honest, it wasn't always inconvenient. Sometimes you wanted a good explosion.

"To proceed, all you have to do is envision the Healing brand perfectly, each line exactly as I will show you."

The woman then proceeded to outline in exact detail what the Healing brand should look like. Jak paid attention to every word, noting each specific contour and angle of the brand. For once, she thought she had a shot of getting something right for once, and she didn't want to mess it up.

"Now then," the professor said as she finished her explanations. "Who wants to start?"

Amelia's hand shot up beside Jak. No surprises there. The professor smiled and bid Amelia come up to the stage. She looked nervous but excited. Taking one of the chips from the table, Amelia stared at it with intense concentration. The brand on her hand activated with a ray of light, and Jak thought she could see something pass into the wood chip. When Amelia's brand faded, she held it up so everyone could see the black lines etched into the chip.

Everyone applauded, and Amelia nearly danced up and down. But the professor swiped the chip out of Amelia's hand and studied it closely.

"Hmm, looks like you got the angle just wrong here," she said, pointing at something Jak couldn't see. "Notice it hasn't begun healing yet."

Amelia's face fell, but the professor patted her on the back.

"Don't worry girl, most don't make it their first try, you'll have plenty of time to practice."

The girl stalked back to her seat, and Jak gave her a half smile and a shrug, which Amelia returned. It didn't take long for her smile to come back.

Next, several of the others tried their hand, each determined to be the first to stick a proper Healing brand. Finally, one of them managed to heal the crack in the wood. The young man cheered, and many of the other students joined in, waving their fists in the air.

The professor examined the wood closely. "Hmm, well done. You've managed to stick the brand. But you'll notice right here, there's a slight deviation in the contour that is keeping it from being a perfect Healing brand. Work on that, and you'll have a mature sapling next time."

Jak hadn't really thought there could be some brands that work better than others, depending on the skill of the Gifter. She had thought they either work or they don't. Lucky Gabriel had been the one to Gift her brand, and not someone else who only partially knew what they were doing.

"You girl, you haven't come up yet, why don't you take a stab at it?" The old woman gestured to Jak to come forward.

Jak swallowed but found herself standing and approaching the front of the class. The professor's face was kindly, but all Jak could feel were the eyes of everyone in the room watching her. They knew who she was by now, even if they hadn't been present at the cathedral to witness the scene there. Now it would seem they were all on the edges of their seats, to see what the supposed "doubter" could do.

She picked up a wood chip off the table and shut out everything around her, closing her eyes and focusing only on the piece of wood in her hand. The professor was right. This wood chip still had a spark of life in it, lent by the Earth itself.

Activating her brand was no trouble at all, and Jak could vaguely make out the light through her closed eyelids. But instead, she concentrated on the wood chip, imagining every line with absolute perfection. She had grown up practicing this, she had literally practiced with a Flamedancer brand, something the professor said was much harder to do. Surely, she could pull off the easier Healing brand.

The light faded, and Jak thought she could hear whispers among the onlookers. For a moment, she kept her eyes shut, still feeling the life within the wood. As she concentrated, she almost thought she could feel that life increase.

Opening her eyes, she looked down at the chip in her hand. The cut from the knife was completely gone, and small green buds were beginning to emerge from the sides of the chip. At its center was a perfect Healing brand.

"Oh, my..." the professor seemed genuinely surprised. "I don't think I've ever seen a student perform a perfect Healing brand on the first try. Well done girl! I don't think I caught your name."

"Um... Jak." She tried to say it softly so the rest of the students wouldn't hear. Though they probably already knew by now. And if they didn't, they would figure it out after today.

But as Jak retreated to her desk, she couldn't help but smile a bit, especially when she saw the look on Amelia's face. She had done it. She was the only student to pull off a perfect brand. Granted, she'd had a practice that the rest in the room didn't. But still, it felt good to be the best at something for once.

"That was incredible!" Amelia said, as the class was dismissed and they began packing up their books. "How did you do it?"

Jak shrugged. "I've imagined how to give brands since I was a kid. I guess I just learned the shape right."

"Yeah but still, to get a perfect brand on your first try! And you weren't even here for the other beginner classes."

"Your grandfather gave me a few lessons on the way here." Jak figured that was a good way to explain her sudden adeptness at Branding, even if that was only part of the truth.

"Oh, that must have been amazing. I haven't even had a lesson with him yet."

Jak frowned at her as they began walking out of the classroom. "Really? But you're his granddaughter."

"I know right! You'd think he could have taught me something. But I've barely even seen him since he got here. I mean, I know he's not supposed to play favorites or anything, but it would be nice... anyway. Can you do it again?"

Jak was taken aback. "I'm not sure we're supposed to be branding outside of class."

"Oh please!" You would have thought Amelia's life depended on Jak the way she begged her now. "I just want to see it, and maybe you could help me get better. Oh! That would be so much fun!"

Jak chuckled. Amelia, for all her quirkiness, had a contagious enthusiasm. "Alright, I'll see if I can help. But only at night once classes are over."

"Oh boy!" Amelia rubbed her hands together in glee. "And in exchange, I shall help you understand triangles better."

Jak laughed, the first time she had done so in days. "Deal."

Sure, there were problems in the city, and then there was everything happening with the new Water Fae students. She had all but forgotten Seph's book. But ultimately, those were someone else's problems to deal with. For now, Jak could focus on her studies and enjoy having a new friend.

Perhaps this place wasn't going to be so bad after all.

CHAPTER 8

T HE NEXT FEW DAYS weren't all that bad. Sure, people still gave her weird looks in the hallways or during meals, but Jak was beginning to get used to that. Having one friend at least made things much easier to endure.

She and Amelia spent several nights practicing and practicing their brands. It took a while, but eventually, Amelia was able to perform a successful healing brand, though it still didn't sprout like Jak's had.

The teachers were more than a little impressed, and one even took Jak out of the dining hall during breakfast to ask if he could see Jak's healing brand. She turned the small, seemingly dead stick he handed her into a blooming sapling.

If Jax were honest, she wished they would stay away and just let her study in peace. It seemed everyone wanted to see her perform a brand. Each time they would marvel as if it were her first time to do it, every time. It was beginning to get old.

Returning from her class in Physicality, she washed and arrived in the dining hall for lunch. Amelia wasn't with her today. She tended to take a lot longer to bathe. Jak, who was used to bathing in a freezing brooke, took a lot less time.

The first face she saw as she entered the dining hall nearly caused her legs to buckle beneath her.

"Naem!" she almost shouted as she worked to steady herself.

The young Watcher stood waiting for her, fully decked out in his armor, newly polished and looking splendid.

Without realizing what she was doing, she rushed to him and wrapped her arms around his broad shoulders, not truly realizing until that moment how much she missed him.

"Hey!" He laughed as she barreled into him. "I missed you too."

She broke the hug and placed both hands on her hips. "Where have you been?"

Taken aback by her sudden change in attitude, he stammered. "Uh... here and there. On assignment. Where have you, uh, been?" He rubbed the back of his neck with his hand as he realized how ridiculous that question was.

Jak smiled. "You'll have to tell me what you've been doing over the last few weeks. Want to sit?"

He nodded, and Jak heard the clink of his armor as he sat on the flat bench across from her on the dining room table. Jak forgot entirely about getting lunch, though she couldn't help but notice the other students staring at them from all sides, probably wondering what a Watcher was doing looking so friendly with the "doubter."

"Heard there was trouble at the cathedral," Naem said, noting the student's behavior as well.

"I don't really want to talk about that."

"Fair enough."

"But where have you been really?" Jak asked again. "I was supposed to train with you. Your General Wilva even said so when I met with her."

"I've been caught up in a few errands for the General," he said. "Can't really talk about all of it, though it's nothing important. Mostly playing armed guard for some merchants and providing security for the ones dealing in foreign imports. Nothing special."

"And they couldn't get someone from the Skyecliff militia to do it? A Watcher seems a bit like overkill."

Naem nodded. "Mostly I agree, but some of the things people try to smuggle in can be dangerous. I've even seen at least one Relic since I started. Plus, I think they're overstaffed here. After what Kuldain did, word has gotten around, and Wilva is calling in as many Watchers as she can."

"Do you think we'll see Major Skellig then?"

Naem shook his head. "No, I think the General wants her to stay put since that is where most of the trouble originated. She's even sending reinforcements and a new Colonel to replace her."

"Replace Skellig! But she was amazing! She should be Colonel."

"I agree, I'm just repeating what I heard. But anyway, what's happened with you?"

"Well, I've managed to make a Healing brand stick." She leaned in close and whispered. "And a Flamedancer brand, though the teachers don't know about that yet. It's supposed to be one of the hardest."

Naem chuckled. "I mean, what happened at the cathedral? Are you okay?"

"Oh, that." Jak paused, and then shrugged. "I guess I'm alright. They haven't made me go back, so nothing has happened since, and I haven't seen that Royal Priest again. He gave me the creeps. Just like Kuldain used to."

"You don't suppose he's a demon in disguise too?"

Jak thought that through. "Could be. It would explain a lot. And if you're a demon, what better position of power than the nation's religious leader and advisor to the queen."

Naem smiled and nudged her across the table. "Want to look into it together? Maybe catch him in his demon tracks?"

His smile faltered as Jak immediately shook her head. "Something like that will come out eventually, and we've got a massive number of Watchers here. They'll take care of him. All we'd do is get in the way."

"That doesn't sound like any fun." Naem deflated from his recent excitement, slouching a bit more in his seat.

"Well, we both have better things to do. I'm best suited here, learning." Suddenly, Jak remembered the other exciting thing to happen to her since she arrived. "Oh! Naem, you'll never guess what Gabriel has been up to."

Then she told him everything that had happened since that day when she travelled down the coast to see the student excavators. She told him about their transformation and the Relic behind all of it.

"So you're telling me, Gabriel has a Relic that transforms people into fish, right here in the college!" Naem sounded incredulous.

"Hey, Jak!" Jak jumped as Amelia jumped into space next to her. "Who's this? He's handsome. What's this about a Relic?"

"It's nothing, Amelia." Jak did her best to shrug it off. "This is Naem. Naem, this is Amelia."

"Oh, you're *that* Naem. The one Jak has been telling me about. She says she thinks your name is funny. But I think it's about as appropriate as one could possibly have. Glad to meet you!"

Amelia thrust out her hand, which Naem took with some trepidation. "Nice to meet you too…"

Once shaken, Amelia withdrew her hand. "So seriously, what's this about a Relic."

Jak cursed herself and Naem for not being more careful. What had they been doing talking about these things in the open? Anyone could have been listening. "I told you, it's nothing. Just talk."

"No, I distinctly heard him say that my grandfather has a Relic that turns people into fish. I haven't seen many fish about. Well, no more than usual. Suddenly she stared at her plate in horror. "There's fish in my lunch! You don't suppose…"

"Calm down, Amelia." Jak grabbed her friend's arm and pulled her back down. Naem looked like he was using all his willpower to keep from laughing. Jak scowled at him. This was his fault after all. "We live in a coastal city, they put fish in everything."

Amelia sat, though she seemed thoroughly flustered by her own wild imagination.

"I'm sorry, but I can't tell you what we were talking about," Jak said.

"Why not?" Naem asked out of the blue.

Jak stared at him, trying to tell him through her wide eyes that now was not the time to debate this. Naem ignored her. "I mean, she said she's Gabriel's granddaughter, right? And she's your friend, knowing what happens around you, she'll probably find out anyway."

"I don't—" Jak hushed herself. Why was Naem trusting Amelia so quickly? He had only just met her, and already he said she should know about the Fae. Did Naem know something she didn't? "Gabriel told me that you were the only one I could tell."

"Well, you have to tell me now." Amelia's face looked hurt. "You can't just say a thing like that and not tell a girl."

Jak finally gave in. "Okay, but not here. We've said too much already."

They left and retreated to an empty hallway. Once they were sure no one was about, Amelia whispered. "Okay, so what's going on?"

Jak filled her in, reluctantly at first, but she focused mainly on the new Water Fae and the Relic that had caused it. Naem stood with his arms crossed at the end of the hallway, watching for anyone who might wander into their conversation.

By the end of Jak's explanation, Amelia's eyes were wider than Jak had ever seen them. And that was saying something. "So you're saying that there are more Fae, besides the ones you met in the Hollow Peaks?"

Jak nodded. "I would imagine they could come from anywhere with the right catalyst, like the Relic they found."

"And grandfather Gabriel has that Relic right now?"

"Yeah, it's probably in his quarters."

"Could we see it?" Amelia's eyes glistened with excitement. Naem seemed interested as well, taking one step closer to the conversation.

"I don't think that would be a good idea," Jak explained. "He's hiding it in a box that keeps it from affecting people. I saw the box, you can't see inside."

"Ah, come on, Jak." Naem put a hand on her shoulder. "That wouldn't have stopped you before. This is a genuine, powerful Relic we have here. Can't we just take a peak."

"I don't think..."

"I know how to get to his quarters!" Amelia all but ignored Jak's protests. "Come on this way."

Jak went along with them but regretted every step. "Hold up, someone will see us, and we'll get into so much trouble."

But Amelia and Naem didn't seem to hear her. They rounded a corner and almost collided with none other than Estel.

Jak blinked. What was Estel doing here? This wasn't the Watcher camp. And as Jak took her in, she realized that Estel was hurt. She clutched at one side with one hand, and the other covered a part of her neck that seemed red underneath.

"Estel?" Naem seemed equally confused. "What are you doing here?"

"Eh, nothing. Just visiting a friend."

Estel hurried past them, not even bothering to give Jak her signature glare. Something weird was going on.

"Um, guys?" Amelia said. "She was coming from my grandfather's room."

"Are you sure?" Jak faced Amelia, locking eyes.

"Positive, there's nothing else in that direction. This hallway leads exclusively to the Head Professor's room."

Jak swallowed. "Estel didn't look like she was in the best shape. Let's see what she was up to."

They followed the passageway until it led to a large door set in a stone frame. What they found made Jak's heart skip a beat.

The door was partially smashed in like someone had tried to knock it down with their boot. But the door was still attached to its hinges. If Estel had tried to break in, she wouldn't have been able to get through the door without smashing it completely.

Naem approached the door. "Why is it only partially..."

"Wait, stand back!" Jak grabbed Naem by his shoulder strap and pulled him backward, just as a jet of fire erupted right where his chest had been a moment before.

They all stood there, wide-eyed until the fire died down.

"It's warded." Jak clarified. "I just saw the brand on the stones right before you entered them. There are other wards here too, besides fire. Estel might have set them off."

Naem was staring at the marks on the stone. "You're saying he's keeping people from entering his own room?"

"I'll bet there's a way to deactivate them. Gabriel would know, but he's not here, obviously."

"We should tell Semwei," Amelia offered.

Jak agreed. They would have to come up with an explanation for being somewhere they shouldn't, but this was too important to keep from the Headmistress.

"And I think we should try to see where Estel went," Jak added.

Naem nodded and turned to Amelia. "Could you tell your Headmistress about this if we follow the girl?"

"Um, me? By myself?" Amelia had never been too comfortable around Semwei.

"You'll do fine, Amelia." Jak tried her best to comfort the girl. "You're just reporting a disturbance. You can say you were going to see if your grandfather was home."

Amelia didn't look all that convinced, but a look of determination settled on her face. "Okay, good luck to you."

They retreated down the way they had come, then Amelia split off to go find Semwei. Jak and Naem ran up another hallway where they had last seen Estel.

"You don't suppose she took the Relic with her?" Jak asked Naem as they ran.

"No, the door was still mostly shut, and it didn't look like she was carrying anything."

That was something at least. But still, they needed to see where Estel was going, and perhaps discover why she was there in the first place.

The passage they ran through eventually led to the courtyard. "This way," Jak said. "She probably made for the exit." They ran as fast as they could to close the distance, eventually making their way out the exit to the crowded street beyond.

Jak peered at the rise in the street, leading up to the main square and the castle. Dozens of people lined the streets, but through a stroke of luck, Jak caught a glimpse of someone stumbling away from them at the top of the hill.

"There!" she pointed.

Naem followed her gaze and started forward. Jak followed, finally arriving at the top of the street.

From there, they had a much clearer vantage point. Not far ahead, they saw Estel taking uneven steps away from the college. She looked like she could be headed towards Watcher High Command, though the market square and the Palace were in the same direction.

Now that they had a clear view of the culprit, Jak and Naem kept their distance. It didn't help that Estel kept glancing behind her as if searching for followers.

So they kept to the busy areas of the street, pretending to be interested in the merchant's shops. But Jak barely lets her eyes break away from Estel. They followed her until they entered the main market square, which was so busy they almost lost her. But Estel was limping, and that made it easier to find her again.

"Look!" Naem said after a few more minutes. "She's not going to the Watcher camp."

Jak saw that he was right. Estel was climbing the switchbacks that led to the palace and the cathedral. Those were the only two destinations in that direction. They followed as far as they could, but the gates to the ornate buildings were guarded by several of the city's militia. They might have made it through with a good excuse, but they had none. So instead, they watched Estel disappear above them.

"There aren't too many people she could have gone to see up there. Probably the queen or the Royal Priest." Jak felt her brow furrow with worry. "You think she's going to tell them about the Relic?"

"I think it's likely she already told them," Naem said, still looking up where they had last seen Estel. "I'd say they probably sent her to get it, or even more likely to use Estel as a way of testing Gabriel's defenses."

"Meaning, they probably knew that Estel would fail."

Naem nodded, but he looked troubled. "That doesn't explain everything though. I mean, Gabriel could just hide the Relic somewhere else, so maybe Estel wasn't supposed to try and take it yet."

They stood there, thinking it through before Jak said. "We should probably head back soon."

"Oh, you can go. I actually have to go back to Watcher High Command for duty. Are you going to drop by sometime?" His face looked hopeful.

Jak smiled, glad to have Naem back. "I wouldn't miss it."

Naem smiled back. "I'm glad to hear it."

"I mean, I literally can't miss it because General Wilva orders me to be there, so..."

Naem laughed. "Okay I get it, well I look forward to seeing you all the same."

Heat rose in Jak's cheeks. "Me too." was all she managed to say before Naem turned away.

They split as Jak returned to the college and Naem left to join the other Watchers. Jak didn't like the worry that replaced the butterflies in her stomach. Who was Estel reporting to, and what were they planning? She really wished Gabriel was around, but he spent most of his time now away from the college, coming back only for short breaks to relax and restock. Who knew when he would be back.

Hopefully, he would come before whoever was pulling strings in the palace made up their minds on what to do next.

CHAPTER 9

S EMWEI, TO HER CREDIT, did not take the intrusion into Gabriel's room lightly. She set up regular rotating schedules for one of the teachers to constantly watch the area until Gabriel returned. Jak and Amelia both volunteered to help out, but Semwei refused, warning them that Gabriel's wards were "too dangerous for those with less experience."

Jak was pretty sure she knew enough about wards to navigate them safely, as long as she didn't try to enter the room itself. But honestly, she was grateful for the rejection. It just gave her more time to learn and practice.

She was getting better too. Brands came naturally to her now, and she had successfully stuck five separate brands during her classes. Teachers now invited her to try some of the more advance brands, and Professor Gona nearly lost her mind when Jak successfully pulled off a Flamedancer brand.

"Never in all my life seen someone... usually takes years of work." And she went on muttering to herself like that for a while until she realized that the rest of the class was waiting for her to continue teaching.

The students, except Amelia, grew more and more bitter towards Jak. It seemed they not only thought of her as a doubter, but it also annoyed them that she surpassed all of them in their classes. It was especially bad on High Morning when all the students would return from the cathedral while Jak stayed at the college. No doubt they experienced the euphoric effects of that Relic the Royal Priest kept. By now, Jak was sure that the Relic held no other value than to make people feel good, leaving them open to manipulation by the Priest.

But while Semwei had relaxed her requirements for the students to attend, most returned anyway, probably eager to experience the same pleasures again. Every time the students would return and treat Jak like she was the only problem in their lives, tripping her while she tried to get food at the dining hall, knocking books out of her hands, even going so far as to slip a load of mice through her door while she was sleeping.

Semwei and the teachers defended Jak if they ever caught someone treating her poorly, but the students were wise enough to find moments when no one was looking.

All in all, Jak didn't feel much animosity towards the others. She still had her friends in Amelia and Naem and used her friendship with the young Watcher as an excuse to get out as often as she could. Though she had to wear a cloak because even the villagers appeared to have heard of a young raven-haired girl with a red streak in her hair. What they had heard, Jak wasn't sure. Some of the richer citizens looked at her much as the students did, but some of the beggars and merchants appeared to have a different attitude. Some would tip their hats or smile as she passed by.

Oddly enough, this made her even more uncomfortable. Gone were her hopes of just blending in and focusing on her schoolwork.

She was on her way to the Watchers now, doing her best to hide beneath a hood and cloak that Amelia lent her. It was a little short for Jak, but it did the trick.

When she arrived at the market square, the first thing she noticed was a familiar figure purchasing a bit of cheese from a local merchant. The figure turned and saw her too.

"Well, I was beginning to think we'd never see each other again." Seph's face broke into that smile of his.

Jak smiled back. "You haven't returned to the library."

"Oh, I've been there once or twice, but never saw you around. Have you read anything from the book I gave you?"

"Ah, yes." Jak had almost forgotten about the book. She'd read most of it since it wasn't a very long book, but her studies had distracted her. And that one passage about the so-called "Oren" had troubled her. She hadn't read much after that. "I haven't finished it yet, but what I read was interesting. I'm headed to the Watcher camp to train with a friend, you can follow if you want." She began walking ahead towards the Watcher camp, waving Seph along.

"Do you believe it?" Seph's face was completely serious as he fell in step beside her. He wanted her to believe.

"I'm not sure. You seem to have the definitions of the Fae right. They match up with what I've seen." She didn't tell him about the Water Fae, and how their descriptions in the book had matched exactly, even though they had only been around for a matter of weeks. "But some parts seem a bit far-fetched. Like the bit about the Orens, people who could give multiple brands?"

"It's true, Jak. If you don't believe it, believe me. There were once people who became heroes among the people because they could give and hold multiple brands."

"So where are these people today, how come no one has ever been able to give or receive more than one brand in, for all we know, centuries?" She didn't even want to think about Naem and his brands. The brands she had given him.

Seph spread his hands to indicate he didn't know. "There could be any number of reasons. Perhaps it was a specific bloodline, or perhaps other circumstances were surrounding their birth that we just don't know about now. But Abel and his brother..."

"Yes, who is this Abel?"

"He was the son of Adam, eventually killed by his brother, who I'm sure you read about."

Jak nodded. "How do you know he was killed? It's not like he could have written that down."

Seph's smile returned. "I just know."

Something didn't quite match up about Seph, but she found herself intrigued. There was just one problem that she didn't like, the prophecy of an Oren coming to save these races. She certainly wasn't capable of any such thing. She had only given Naem his multiple brands under unique circumstances. She couldn't replicate it.

Though honestly, had she ever even tried?

"I actually wanted to find you to tell you something," Seph said as they approached the Watcher camp. "The people who follow me, we meet on High Morning for a brief... I guess you could call it a sermon. I would like to invite you."

Jak thought it through. "I haven't exactly had the best experience with churches."

"Yes, I heard about that. But I think you'll find we're a lot different than the traditional cathedral experience."

"No pleasure Relics?" Jak asked, the hint of a smile on her face.

Seph chuckled. "No pleasure Relics. We believe every man and woman should choose for themselves what to believe, and not be influenced in such a way."

"Well, I'm with you there." Jak looked ahead and realized they were almost there. "I'll think it through," she said, turning to face him.

"Great, I look forward to it. We meet at the coast, down where the Palace cliff meets the water."

"Hey, Jak!" Jak turned to see Naem trotting towards them. "Who's your friend."

Seph held out his hand. "My name is Seph. Pleased to meet you."

Naem took Seph's hand in a firm shake. "I'm Naem. You a friend of Jak's?"

"Yes, you could probably say that." Seph glanced at Jak with that special smile of his.

Naem frowned, and so did Jak. Seph was going to give Naem the wrong idea if he wasn't careful where he threw that smile around.

But Seph's smile faded suddenly as he held Naem's arm. He looked from Jak to Naem, and back again, then inexplicably his eyes turned to look at Naem's other arm, where Naem had covered his brands with a long sleeve. Did he...?

No sooner had his smile wavered, then it was back again. "Well, I'll let the two of you get on with things. Hope to see you again soon!" The last part was for Jak, as he turned and marched back down the hill.

"He seems... interesting," Naem said, still staring at Seph.

"He is," Jak replied. "I think he's good person though, which is more than can be said for some.

"Well then, are you ready to start practicing?" Naem changed the subject.

"I'm ready," Jak said with a grin. They had met several times so far, and it was beginning to feel familiar to Jak, like old times. Training with Naem was one of the few comforts she was afforded now. "More sparing?"

"I actually thought we would try something a little different. We've done a lot of training to combat against demons and those with non-combat brands. But what about, say, a Flamedancer?"

"Why would I ever fight a Flamedancer?" Jak laughed, confused. "Most of them are Watchers or in the militia. At worst the only people they get to fight are drunks in the street."

"Hmm...you'd be surprised." Naem looked thoughtful. "Regardless, it pays to be prepared. So, any ideas?" He led Jak to the open grass between the Watcher tents and command buildings.

"Um, well, not get in their way?" She half chuckled, but Naem nodded.

"Easier said than done, but that's essentially the long and short of it. Flamedancers can only shoot fire in a single direction, and they can't make anything spontaneously combust. They have to be in range and line of sight with their target."

"So, stay away and hit them with a ranged attack?"

Naem nodded. "Or find a way to be unpredictable to get inside their defenses."

Jak tapped a finger to her lips. "But I thought Flamedancers could influence flame beyond their hands?"

"Only if the fire already exists. They can manipulate it from a short distance, like put it out or redirect it. That's the reason that Flamedancers are often called to put out fires. But they can't attack too well with those methods."

"So, what's this have to do with today's training?"

"Well," Naem grinned. "You're already learning archery, but you're not going to have a bow with you all the time."

"These days I don't carry *any* weapon with me all the time."

Naem ignored her. "So, we're going to practice the javelin. Comes in useful if you need to take a Flamedancer out from a distance. And at other times too." He winked at her.

Jak hid her smile. Naem had saved her life on more than one occasion by hurling his spear into an approaching enemy. The second time it happened, it had actually annoyed Jak at the time, who was deprived of taking out the demon herself. But she was glad, now, that Naem had saved her the trouble. Back then, she wouldn't have lasted two seconds against the demon. Now...well now was different.

"Well then, let's get started."

Naem set up a target at one end of the Watcher complex, far out of range of the barracks. Did he not trust her to hit her mark?

But to Jak's chagrin, Naem was right to give them a lot of space. Her first attempts fell far out of range, and she sent Naem a murderous gaze when she caught him snickering. Of course, when Naem gave her a demonstration, to try and teach her how to improve her form, he hit the center circle dead on. But he had the gift of Grace aiding his hand-eye coordination. That wasn't exactly fair.

After an hour of practice, Jak was starting to get better. At least she hit the target now, most of the time. Her arm was beginning to feel flimsy. Occasionally, Naem would adjust her posture just slightly, and Jak could feel his hands linger as they guided her arms. What was worse, she found she didn't want to complain.

"Well, not bad for your first try," Naem said after they began wrapping it up. "Care for a bit of sparing to end the day?"

Jak felt her muscles protest but nodded anyway. She liked sparing with Naem.

Naem went and got two quarterstaffs, and they faced each other. Jak was the first to make a move, launching herself at Naem using every technique she had ever learned. And of course, Naem blocked her onslaught with ease, gently side-stepping and whacking her across the shoulder.

Jak yelped with the sharp pain and rubbed her shoulder.

"That should teach you to be so aggressive." Naem grinned. "Let your enemy come to you."

"If we both use that technique we'll get nothing done," Jak goaded.

Naem's smile widened. "True enough."

He darted forward, and Jak caught his first blow, then the second, with her quarterstaff. She was on the defensive, and she needed to get out of it, but at least she was holding her own.

That is until several strikes later Jak felt another sharp pain along her arm as Naem's staff left a large red welt there.

"You don't have to hit so hard." Jak protested, but Naem ignored her, coming again and again.

They continued for a while, Jak growing ever more focused as they fought. Soon, the number of times she got hit grew fewer and fewer, and she found herself building up enough confidence to take the offensive once or twice, causing Naem to take a few steps backward.

Parry, swing the staff downward, bring the other end up, parry again. Jak felt her muscles lean into the routines, responding automatically when needed.

Thwack! Jak's staff landed a blow, squarely in Naem's side. He broke their engagement, more out of surprise than pain.

"Oh, you got me!" He clutched his side and covering up his surprise with mock pain.

"You have Toughness and Healing now, you can take it." Jak whacked him again, this time on the thigh. She held no sympathy, feeling multiple bruises forming on her body. It was only fair.

"Good job, though!" Naem said, positioning his quarterstaff to stand upright. "That's the first time you've legitimately landed a blow."

Jak grinned. "I was going easy on you the whole time."

"Were you now?"

Suddenly he lunged forward, taking her completely by surprise. Her feet were knocked out from under her, and she found herself tumbling to the earth. She caught Naem's quarterstaff on her way down and pulled hard. Jak laughed as Naem tumbled after her, doing his best to roll out of the way.

Naem joined her laughing, and they lay there, side by side for a moment as the laughter subsided. Jak rolled to one side to face him, and he did the same. They stayed that way for a long time. Then Naem leaned forward and planted a kiss on her lips. Jak let it happen, kissing him back, needing this. It was the first time they had kissed since Foothold... since Marek died...

Jak pulled back, breaking the kiss. "I... I'm sorry. I can't do this right now," she said quickly as she stood up and brushed the loose grass off her clothes.

Naem stared at her, a confused look on his face. He remained on the ground, propped up on his elbows as Jak rose. "When will it be okay?" He asked.

"I don't know, I'm still dealing with a lot right now."

Naem rose. "I have a lot going on too, and that's why I want this. Having you with me, it makes things better. Don't you feel the same way?"

"I don't know, I think so. But..."

"So why do you keep resisting? I've given you some space, I realize you needed that. After everything, you've lost. But we need to move on from that, find joy in new places. In each other."

Jak felt her face begin to flush. "I know, I know that. It's just...I can't yet."

"Is it that other man? The one you arrived with?"

"What, no?" Jak let out a short laugh at this.

"He was obviously interested in you," Naem said still serious. "And you saw the way he looked at me." His voice was beginning to rise, and Jak didn't like it.

"It's not like that at all."

"Well then, why? Don't you like me?"

Why was Naem getting so upset? "Of course, I like you." Jak offered. "I just have a lot to figure out, and you're not exactly helping by putting pressure on me."

"Oh, so I'm the bad guy here."

"What? No! No one is a bad guy."

"Well, it sure sounds that way!" Naem was almost shouting.

Other Watchers began staring in their direction.

"I just don't want anyone else to get hurt, okay!" Now she was yelling, finally saying what had been in her heart all along. Naem blessedly calmed down. Jak felt a tear run down her cheek. This was not how tonight was supposed to go. She wiped it away with a sleeve and turned to march out of the camp.

"Wait, Jak." Naem followed after her. "I'm sorry, I shouldn't have gotten mad."

"You think I owe you something?" Jak said over her shoulder as she walked away. "My best friend, my father, half the people I knew growing up, they're all dead. And then to find out that Kuldain led the demons that attacked my village and killed all those people to get to me, for reasons I don't even understand yet. Even my mother was hurt because of me. I can't have you get hurt too. Don't you see? It's not that I don't care about you. It's that I care too much!"

She felt a hand on her shoulder, and she paused for just a moment.

"You don't owe me anything," Naem said from behind her. "I'll admit I felt that you did, a moment ago. But I think I understand now."

Jak didn't look back around. "All I want is to lay low, complete my studies, and live a quiet life away from everything. Perhaps then, we could make something of this." She reached up to touch his hand that held her shoulder. "But I don't think it's safe enough to be my friend until then, so I think we should spend some time apart for now."

Naem didn't say another word as she stomped out of the Watcher camp, wiping the tears as she went. The tears progressed to full sobs as she put more and more distance between her and Naem. People turned to look at her, but few saw anything more than a hooded girl crying as she all but ran back to the college.

She didn't see Amelia or any of the teachers as she shot to her room to be alone, only barely managing to hold in her tears so the other students wouldn't notice. But she could hold them back no longer once inside her room. She collapsed on her bed and let it all out into her pillow.

She loved Naem, she really did. He was the only person who seemed to be able to draw out the more confident side of her, the only one around whom she was really happy. But everything that had happened with everyone else she loved made the relationship complicated. She was sure that she already put Naem's life in danger by giving him extra brands. If word of that got out, Naem wouldn't last long against the mobs that would come for him. Jak was already an oddity in Skyecliff, and she would do what she could to keep everyone else from whatever trouble awaited her.

But maybe, just maybe, if she could focus on not standing out, the queen, her priest, and all the rest would forget about her. Then maybe she and Naem could be together.

All the possibilities, from the worst to the best, played over and over again in her mind for hours until sleep mercifully took her.

CHAPTER 10

T HE NEXT MORNING WAS High Morning, meaning every student in the college jumped at the chance to not do chores and instead dress in their nicest school uniform for church. Everyone except Jak that is. She stayed in her room while everyone else got ready, not wanting to be seen.

So, she was surprised when she heard a knock on her door.

"Who is it?" She asked, brow furrowed.

"It's me, Amelia," came the peppy voice.

Jak rose and opened the door. Amelia stood there, dressed in her uniform, and bouncing on the balls of her feet in excitement. Jak looked around. "Haven't the others gone already?"

"Yep," Amelia said. "I didn't go with them. Semwei said I could stay, so I did."

"Then why are you dressed?"

"Because we're going to go to that handsome man's church."

It took a moment for Jak to understand who she was talking about. "You mean Seph? How did you know about that?"

"Oh, he came by last night, didn't I tell you? Of course, I didn't, I haven't seen you until right now. Well, yes, he came by and recognized me as your friend. Isn't that nice? He told me to tell you that he'd like to see you." Amelia paused to wink at Jak, twice.

Jak rolled her eyes. "I'm not sure he's my type." She walked away from the door and sat on her bed again, picking up the book she had been reading.

Amelia followed her. "Of course, he is. Someone with eyes and a smile like his can by anyone's type. Come on, Jak. Just this once, please! I think it could be fun!"

Jak looked up from her book. "Why do you want to go to his church?"

"Because I've heard horrible things about it."

"And... that's a good thing?"

"Oh yes! You see, I've only heard bad things from those snobby rich people that go to the cathedral for church. I overheard one of them arguing with a shoemaker I know who attends Seph's church. And if they don't like it, it must be good, right?"

"I guess." Jak appreciated the logic. Anything that displeased the Royal Priest and his followers were worth looking into. She closed her book and looked Amelia in the eye. "Well, what are you waiting for? Get out of my room so I can change."

"Oh good!" Amelia clapped her hands once and scrambled for the door. "I'll be waiting right here."

True to her word, Amelia was standing right outside the door when Jak opened it again, this time dressed in her school uniform. She wasn't sure what they wore to Seph's church, but she figured dressing nicely was always a good idea. Plus this way she matched Amelia, so if they stood out from the crowd, they would do so together. On her way out, she made sure to pocket Seph's book. Perhaps she could lend it back to him.

It took them longer than Jak anticipated to find the winding road that led down to the cliff base. Jak had never been there before and regretted missing it as soon as they arrived. The ocean was beautiful, and the cliffs were stunning. Looking up, she almost fell over backward as she tried to get a view of the cathedral and palace, which perched on top of the cliff, hundreds of feet above them.

Once at sea level, it didn't take them long to find a small group of people gathered at the cliff's base. But it was hardly what Jak would call a church. There were maybe three dozen people gathered there, all standing, with no building or structure of any kind. Jak wondered what they did when it rained.

Standing on a box was Seph, who spoke loud enough for everyone to hear. In one hand, he held a book, which Jak realized was probably another copy of the same book that he had given her.

Seph paused as they approached, looking them both in the eye. A few others glanced in their direction, but most kept their eyes on their preacher. Amelia blushed, and Jak almost chuckled. She had grown so used to people staring at her that she forgot that Amelia didn't really know what it was like.

But Seph only smiled and continued with his speech. "Are we some random intelligences brought here by chance? Do our father's fathers, who are all long dead and gone, still influence our lives? I say, they do not. We revere them as our forefathers, but they were nothing but mortal men and woman, no different from us today. There is nothing that makes them more important, or that gives them a greater place in the hereafter. Each of us is capable of the same great things that they accomplished."

Many heads were nodding in agreement. Jak surveyed the crowd and found that most of them were listening intently.

"But the Book of Illadar teaches us that there is a guiding Hand over all of us, a God who shapes this world and worlds above us. The sun and the moon and the stars, all were fashioned by this guiding Hand. I read now from the words of Abel," He raised the book, pointing to a specific passage. "'Indeed, I know that my mother and father knew it. They have taught that they would have perished on Earth, were it not for the Guiding Hand and his angels. And I add my testimony that the Hand exists, and I have seen his angels with my own eyes. They have taught me much and have revealed the future to my mind.'"

Seph looked back at the congregation. "That future, my friends, is Illadar."

The crowd seemed to swell at the name, and Jak felt an odd rush of elation.

Seph continued. "And I would add my own witness, that these angels Abel speaks of, are real. I have seen them. It was one of them who told me where to find the Book of Illadar, and who taught me many things concerning our future, and the part we were to play in it."

Strangely, Jak realized that she didn't doubt Seph on his radical claims. It was new information to her, the idea of a God, a Hand guiding the forces of their world. She must not have reached that part of the book yet. But something tickled the back of her mind, a moment from when Yewin, the Bright Fae, had revealed the truth to her. That moment enabled her to brand Naem with his extra brands, but there had been other information revealed to her at that moment, most of which had disappeared as soon as the link was broken. But she thought she could remember something now. Or at least, something about a Guiding Hand, and angels that served it felt familiar to Jak.

"It would appear, my friends, we have some visitors today, one of which is a friend of mine, a special witness to the fulfillment of prophecy."

Oh no. Jake looked up at Seph, barely shaking her head in his direction. She did not need more eyes on her.

Seph raised a hand in her direction and smiled. "I apologize, Jak if I put you on the spot, but I hoped you might share some of your experience with the Fae."

At the mention of Fae, excited whispers spread through the crowd. All turned to look at Jak, who instantly wished she could melt into the cliff face. Amelia stood next to her, wide-eyed and excited. She gave Jak a little push, and Jak found herself walking forward, against her better judgement. Hadn't the queen told her not to talk about the Fae with people? If they found out she had told this group...

As she neared, Seph stepped down from his box, his arm still outstretched to Jak. She took his hand as he guided her onto the box.

She stood, totally and completely petrified. The cold ocean air whipped at her hair.

There weren't nearly as many people here as there had been in the cathedral, or even in her classes at the college. But something about the way they looked to her made her feel even more nervous than she had in front of those other crowds. These people actually wanted to hear what she had to say, and they would believe her. That lent her a responsibility that she didn't necessarily want.

But she stood, looking from Seph, to Amelia, and back again. Amelia gave her an encouraging nod, and Seph merely smiled, waiting patiently for her to speak.

"Um... hello, everyone. My name is Jak. And I guess what Seph wants me to talk about is my experience at Foothold."

Excited whispers moved through the crowd again. Jak swallowed, gathered her courage, and continued. "Your Book of Illadar speaks of twelve races. Us, and eleven others. If I had seen this book a year ago, I would have thought it a fantasy. But I have met the Fae, at least two varieties, and they are very much real. They are not merely a new spawn of a demon, like some may have you to believe. They are not unlike us in intelligence and emotion."

Jak was finding the words came to her easily, and she realized her voice sounded far more confident than she would have ever imagined. It almost felt like the words leaving her mouth were not hers but instead belonged to someone else speaking through her.

"Some of you may have heard of a demon attack in Foothold. I've heard many rumors. Some say the Fae joined the demons in the attack. Others say that the Fae helped fight the demons. Others say they weren't even there at all. Well, I was there. I can confirm that the Fae participated in the battle, and without them, every human in that stronghold would have died. The Fae saved our lives."

"Which of the twelve did you see?" Seph asked. He knew the answer but asked on behalf of the crowd.

"One was like a shadow, living in darkness. The other was bright, shining like the sun in the morning. They each had abilities that fit their appearance, but neither were like demons." Jak didn't really know what more to say about them. But the crowd was eating up every word. Expressions of joy lit some of their faces.

"It's like the book said." One person spoke up, an older man who looked like he might be a beggar. "Doesn't it, master Seph? Doesn't it say the Fae of darkness and light will come first."

"And they shall cast a shadow on the errors of old and illuminate the path ahead." Seph nodded in confirmation. Turning to Jak, he offered his hand again. "Thank you, Jak. You've been a great help."

She accepted his hand and stepped off the box. He rose to take her place.

"My friends," he said, his voice solemn. "This marks the beginning of prophecy, fulfilled. We live in a wonderful era, and many among us will live to see everything promised in the Book of Illadar. A hero will rise, the first Oren in modern history, and he or she will make us stronger, and will build for us Illadar, where we might find peace among the Fae and us."

It was all a bit touchy-feely for Jak, but having read Seph's book, as well as the original copy of the Annals of Adam, she couldn't deny that some convincing arguments supported what Seph said. Without a doubt, they lived in a time of change. And Jak found herself hoping that Seph was right, that someone would build them a paradise for all to live in, including the Fae. But just the thought of this Oren troubled her as it always had. Could it be her? She had branded Naem with two extra brands, but it was a one-time thing, a fluke. Perhaps something about her connection to the Bright Fae at that moment had made it possible. She couldn't replicate it, could she? And even if she could, that didn't mean she was the hero Seph spoke of. There could be others.

She was so lost in her thoughts that she barely heard the sound of horse hooves approaching. But when Seph broke off his sermon, she looked around to see what the man was looking at.

Four Watchers in full uniform sat on horseback, their armor gleaming in the morning light. Jak recognized one of them as a man who she had talked to earlier when she went looking for Naem in the Watcher camp. The second, Jak noticed immediately was Estel, looking smug as always. She didn't recognize the other two.

Seph hesitated only for a moment before smiling at the newcomers and spreading his arms in welcome. "Hello my friends, do you wish to listen as well?"

"By order of Her Majesty, the queen, this congregation is no longer authorized to meet, either in public or in private." The lead Watcher repeated from a piece of parchment he held in one hand.

Disbelief swept through the crowd, as faces grew angry. Jak looked at Seph in shock, but he only calmly regarded the Watcher as he continued.

"All persons are required to return to their homes and not meet together in a group exceeding two individuals. Should you continue to gather here, or anywhere in Her Majesty's kingdom, you will be subject to punishment no less than fifteen lashings in the public square for each perpetrator." The Watcher rolled up the parchment and stuck it back in his tunic. "And I'm afraid we've been asked to give ten lashings to this man, today." He pointed at Seph.

CHAPTER 11

"**N**o!" Jak said, but her protest was lost among others from the crowd. All four of the Watchers raised their spears in warning as angry faces drew closer.

"Peace!" Seph said loudly. The noise quieted and all turned to look at him. Seph faced the Watcher. "May I see it?" He indicated the notice the Watcher had read.

The Watcher dismounted and brought the writ to Seph, who looked it over carefully. Seph nodded. "It bears the queen's seal, I will gladly accompany you to the market square."

Protests erupted again but quieted as Seph raised one hand. "We must abide by the laws until such time as we are delivered from them. Lead the way, soldier."

"Ah, see." The Watcher looked genuinely uncomfortable. "We weren't explicitly instructed to punish you publicly. Right here will be fine if you wish."

"Very well." Seph began stripping his shirt off.

"What are you doing?" Jak stepped forward. The Watcher turned to regard her, and Jak saw recognition in his eyes.

"It's okay, Jak. I always knew persecution would come with the territory."

"But the queen can't whip you just because you preach something she disagrees with."

"I'm afraid she can, and she's done far worse things to me." A look of revulsion crossed his face for only a moment. "This is temporary, but Illadar will last forever. Remember that." He raised his voice to address the rest of the crowd. "My friends, I'm sure these gentlemen would be more comfortable if you left. Do not worry, I will be fine."

The others hesitantly moved away, obeying their leader despite urges to do otherwise. Even Amelia began moving with the crowd.

Jak kept her feet planted. "This is not right." she said, wanting nothing more than to pick up some pebbles from the beach, brand them, and send them exploding at the Watchers.

Seph leaned against the cliff face, his back exposed. "There will always be something not right with the world." he muttered, almost soft enough that Jak could not hear. "I can only hope that my suffering will be a learning experience for others." He glanced at Jak, then at the Watcher holding a whip, who dropped his head. "Do what you came here to do."

The whip cracked out, and Jak felt herself flinch with each sound. Seph made no sound at first, though after the fifth lashing he cried out and collapsed against the stone. Each lashing after that brought a soft grunt. Stragglers from the congregation stood far off, their heads bowed. Jak kept her feet rooted to the spot. She knew that these Watchers were just doing their jobs, but she found herself hating them, hating that she had ever called herself a Watcher, or ever wanted to be a part of them. How could they carry out a sentence that was so obviously unfair?

A glance at Estel made Jak's blood grow hot. The girl was fascinated as she watched Seph's punishment. Her mouth was open and her tongue licked her teeth as if entranced by what she saw.

The girl caught Jak's furious gaze and smiled. Right then, the only thing keeping Jak from launching herself at Estel was Seph's request that she stay out of it. But Estel's time would come. Jak was sure about that.

When the Watcher finished, Jak moved forward to help Seph up. A few others who remained helped her do so. One woman, with smooth, tanned cheeks and light brown hair that seemed to blend in with her skin, helped Jak support Seph. "I'll take him to my house. I know a few things about healing herbs. He should be safe there."

"Seph," Jak whispered before the woman could take him away. "You don't have any brands. I could give you a Healing brand and it would help with this."

"No, Jak." His words were more forceful than Jak would have expected. "I will not take a brand, not even from you."

With that, he managed to stand on his feet and walk beside the smooth-faced woman, wincing with each step, but standing tall.

"Come on," The lead Watcher waved at his comrades. "We're done here." His face clearly showed that he was not happy with what he had done. But Jak didn't care if he felt any remorse.

"I hope you're happy." She said to them as they mounted their horses. "Especially you, Estel."

Estel turned in her saddle to face Jak. "You always do associate with the wrong sort." She said, glee evident in her eyes. "Be careful, or it will get you into trouble."

"You will pay for this." Jak growled. She had never hated someone so much than she did in that moment.

"Don't count on it." Estel said. "These are only the first steps the queen is making to purify the kingdom of troublemakers."

"What do you mean?" Jak felt fear rise in her throat.

Estel leaned down in her saddle towards Jak . "Let's just say your fishy friends won't be around much longer."

"Estel," Jak felt her face grow pale. "You promised Gabriel. No one was to know."

"Gabriel hardly has more authority than the queen." And with that she turned in the saddle and rode off, leaving Jak alone with the remaining stragglers on the beach.

Amelia approached Jak. "Are you okay? That didn't go at all like I thought it would. I'm sorry if..."

"The Water Fae are in trouble."

"Who?"

"The student excavators I told you about. The ones who transformed. I think the queen knows about them and plans to hurt them or... or maybe kill them."

Amelia's face grew pale. "What can we do?"

"I...I don't know. Let me think."

She racked her brain, feeling the pressure muddle her thinking. "Well, we should start by going to see if Gabriel is around. He'll know what to do."

"And if he's not?"

"I don't know, okay!" Jak shouted. Amelia recoiled from Jak's raised voice. Jak instantly regretted it. "Hey, I'm sorry I didn't mean to shout. This is all just a bit much all at once."

"I understand," Amelia sounded far more empathetic than usual. "Come on, let's get back to the college."

Jak followed Amelia this time, letting her friend lead. She was too caught up trying to figure out what to do. This was exactly why she avoided situations like these. If she couldn't keep a straight head then others would suffer as a result.

A half-hour later, they arrived back at the college. Semwei and the rest of the students were already back from their trip to the cathedral, and Jak quickly sought out the Headmistress as they entered.

"Headmistress!" Amelia called out as they neared her. Jak was glad Amelia was doing the talking. She wasn't sure she could say anything coherent at the moment.

"What is it, you two?" Semwei said, concern slowly forming on her face as she saw how distressed Jak appeared.

"Is my grandfather around?" Amelia asked, trying and failing to sound casual.

"I'm afraid not, girl. He was here this morning, but set off again with some supplies for the students excavating along the coast."

He had been here this morning! Jak nearly groaned. She had wanted to talk to him for a while, and he hadn't even taken the time to say hi before turning around and going back the way he came. Though perhaps Semwei had told him about Estel trying to steal the Relic.

"Did you tell him about someone trying to break in?" She asked. Semwei turned to regard her.

"Yes I did, and this time he took the...ahem...object in question with him so no one could attempt to steal it while he was gone."

Instead of comforting Jak, this news only made her worry more. Turning to Amelia, she silently indicated they should leave. Amelia nodded and the two left Semwei without even saying goodbye, and didn't stop until they were in Jak's room.

"I think maybe Gabriel's in trouble too."

"What makes you say that." Amelia asked, concern for her grandfather evident on her face.

"It's too much of a coincidence. Think about it. The queen chooses now to silence Seph and his followers, on the same day that Gabriel takes the Relic out of his defenses, and to top it off, Estel hints that the Water Fae might be in danger. The queen is making all her moves at once!"

"But hold up a second, why would she even want to do that? What does it gain?"

"I don't know, but you saw what they did to Seph, the queen isn't fooling around. And besides, I think it might be all her advisor's doing, the Royal Priest."

Then she told Amelia about the suspicion she and Naem had that the Royal Priest could be a demon in hiding, much as Kuldain had been. Amelia listened with mouth open. "So you're saying a demon could be causing all of this?"

"It would make sense. Why else would the queen want to eliminate the Fae? And when I met with both of them, he made me very uncomfortable. He honestly *felt* like Kuldain. But right now, that's not important."

"Why not?"

"Because we need to focus on helping the Fae first, then we can worry about the Royal Priest. We need to leave the college tonight, find them, and make sure they get out of there as soon as possible."

"How are we supposed to get there in time?" Amelia's face was hard to read for once. Jak realized that there were probably two conflicting emotions in Amelia's head right now: excitement for the adventure, but worry for Gabriel and the others.

Saying all her thoughts out loud was helping Jak. She was beginning to see the path before them much clearer. "I think I know someone who can help."

They arrived at the Watcher camp not long after. Jak showed the guard her letter that let her pass. Amelia waited outside.

Once inside, it thankfully did not take long to locate Naem. He was at the training grounds, running through a few light exercises. Upon seeing her, he stopped and walked to meet her. There was an excited look on his face.

Of course, she remembered. Just yesterday she had suggested they spend some time away from each other. Well so much for that.

"Hey, Jak. I'm so glad you're here." Naem bore a hopeful expression as he trotted to meet her.

"I wish I could come under better circumstances, but I need your help." she said as soon as she was close enough.

"Anything, what's up?"

Jak explained the situation from the beginning, but glanced over some of the details, as they were in a hurry.

"I need some horses," she finished. "I thought you could get us some. For me and Amelia."

"I could, but they won't just let me give them to you." Naem said, his hand characteristically rubbing the back of his neck. "I'll have to go with you."

It wasn't perfect but Jak had no time to argue. "Alright," she said. "We'll wait for you outside."

It took far too long in Jak's opinion before Naem emerged from the Watcher camp leading three horses behind him. Jak barely managed a thank you before she mounted her horse and took off as fast as she dared in the city. Naem quickly followed while Amelia took some time to catch up. She was used to riding a horse, but hadn't done so in a while. Jak, on the other hand, had grown up with two horses. She knew exactly how to ride.

"Wait up, Jak!" Naem called from behind, but Jak would not slow down now. They exited Skyecliff through the south gate and once free of the hustle and bustle of the city, Jak increased her horse's pace. Naem and Amelia eventually managed to keep pace behind her, but only when she was forced to stop and rest the horse once its breathing grew too heavy.

They rode for about an hour. Jak wasn't sure if she was glad that they passed no one on the way there, apart from a few merchants. Hopefully that meant that anyone who meant harm to the Water Fae, or Gabriel, had not yet returned from doing so.

The sun was setting by the time they arrived at the inlet. Naem and Amelia closed the distance between them and Jak as she slowed and dismounted. The inlet was quiet save for the sound of the ocean in the distance. Without the sound of her horse's hooves, Jak thought she could have heard a pin drop. All was still.

She led Amelia and Naem inside the cave, following the stream that came from inside. Jak grabbed a fallen stick from a nearby tree and quickly gave it a Flamedancer brand. She gave it a slight variation of the brand that she had learned, which caused the stick to glow with a fiery pattern, yet not catch fire itself. She heard Amelia make a sound of admiration behind her, but she was too determined to look back yet.

Then Jak heard something. A muffled sound that she couldn't quite make out. She waved her torch ahead of her. Something was lying on the ground ahead, right next to the pool where the Water Fae lived.

As she approached she realized it was Gabriel. His head was bleeding, and his pack lay spilled out on the ground. As they approached, he looked up and met Jak's gaze.

"They're gone." He said. "They took them away, them and the Relic." His voice wavered, clearly disoriented from the blow to his head. But his words chilled Jak to the core. She looked to the pool of water and saw no one. No Fae, no students.

The queen's men had arrived first.

CHAPTER 12

I T TOOK MORE TIME to return than it had to get there. This time they were bringing Gabriel with them, and the man was not in the best of shape. He was still partly delirious from the blow to his head and kept nearly slipping off the horse. Eventually, they had to tie him to Naem on his horse, and Jak and Amelia took positions in front and back to make sure nothing worse happened.

Jak's mind was blank. All she could do was simply stare at the path in front of her. She said nothing when Naem or Amelia tried to talk to her. For the longest time, she felt Gabriel was her savior, and that he would solve all her problems and leave her with the sole responsibility of learning. But it looked like not even he could handle everything that was being thrown at them.

The Water Fae were gone, probably being tortured or worse in the queen's palace... if they were even alive at all. No, she had to believe they were still alive, otherwise, they would have been slaughtered where they were, instead of carted off.

Jak was pretty sure, now, that the merchants they had passed on the way were actually the queen's guards in disguise. They had been carrying large wagons full of items to trade. Perhaps the Fae had been hidden inside. Why Jak had not thought to search any large containers on the way there...well it was too late now.

When they arrived back at the college, Semwei forgot how angry she was at Jak and Amelia for sneaking away as soon as she saw Gabriel. Without a word to Jak and Amelia, she took charge and ordered another student to bring a doctor. Then she helped the three of them carry Gabriel to his quarters. Apparently, Gabriel had lowered the defenses on his room the last time he was here, when he took the Relic with him because now they could enter unopposed and lay him on the bed.

"Th..thank..." Gabriel said, his eyes still unable to focus.

"You girl," Semwei said to Amelia. "Go and get some cool water and a towel."

Amelia didn't argue, and immediately left the room.

That was when Jak realized how interesting Gabriel's room was on the inside. The walls were covered with a huge map, several drawings, and bits of paper with words written on them. Small threads connected some of these papers with places on the map, or with other drawings or inscriptions. The map wasn't just of Skyecliff but of the entire nation, from one coast to the other. Jak could see Tradehall and Foothold, even Riverbrook had a place.

What was Gabriel researching?

"And you girl," Semwei caught her staring at the room. "I think it's best if you give Gabriel a little space. Why don't you head off to bed? Your Watcher friend should leave as well."

Her tone was kind, but Jak felt sorrow sink into her. The last thing she wanted was to be alone now. If alone, her thoughts of failure would only overwhelm her.

But Naem agreed and began to exit the room. When Jak did not follow, he returned and took her hand to lead her out. She followed without protest. They exited the room just as the doctor showed up, his eyes still blinking from waking so early. Good, at least someone could take care of Gabriel. There was nothing Jak could do.

They walked towards the exit. Naem finally spoke. "I'm sorry about all this. I know he meant a lot to you. At least we can be certain the Water Fae is not dead. Not if they were taken like that."

"Wherever they are," Jak spoke for the first time all night. "It can't be good."

"Who knows," Naem tried to add some cheer to his voice. "Perhaps we're overthinking things. Perhaps they just want to keep the Fae protected from anyone finding them by chance, maybe they just want to learn more. We shouldn't judge them."

Jak looked at him amazed. "You know very well that the chances of that are slim."

"But we can't just assume their actions are hostile. Maybe they want to help."

Jak folded her arms. Naem hadn't been there to see what happened to Seph, he wouldn't know that the queen ordered it herself, personally. With that on her mind, Jak couldn't just assume that the queen or any of her followers meant any good to happen to the Fae. But to her, at that moment, that didn't excuse Naem.

"I think you'd better go now," she said finally.

Naem's face grew still, and he looked like he was about to say something. Jak avoided his gaze. Eventually, without another word, Naem retreated to the lashing poll and retrieved the three horses, leading them back to the Watcher camp. Jak watched him go until he disappeared over the hill. Then it began to rain in the darkness.

At first, Jak was ready to go back inside. But something else moved her. She took a step forward, then another, away from the college. Soon, her walk broke into a run, and she realized where her subconscious wanted her to go. She ran to the market square, mostly empty at this time of night, and found the switchbacks that led her to the cold spires of the cathedral. Her breathing was heavy from the run, her hair was wet and matted against her face, but she still managed to face down the two guards that stood outside the cathedral.

"I need to see the Royal Priest." Her voice was cold but strong. Stronger than Jak felt.

"He doesn't see just anyone. Certainly not someone in your condition."

"I'm a student at the college, we're allowed in."

One guard glanced at the other. "Hey, isn't she the one, the Priest, wanted to see if she ever would come? See the hair?"

Even in the darkness, Jak's red streak of hair was clearly visible. She turned her head to make it more visible. "Why does he want to see me?"

"Don't know, but you can go in Miss. Provided we search you, of course."

Jak held out her arms as they checked for weapons. Once done, they nodded and allowed her in. Jak wasn't sure why they bothered. She was a Gifter, which made her a living weapon. She didn't need swords or spears to be a danger to someone. All she had to do was touch them, brand them, and they would die or turn into a demon. Not that she would of course, but the simple fact that she could made her wonder why the guards didn't consider her a weapon.

The unlit cathedral was completely dark, save for a few candles at the other end of the hall. Jak managed to avoid running into any of the pews, and her footsteps echoed loudly throughout the chamber.

"I was wondering when I would see you again," came a voice as she approached the candle light. There, the Royal Priest sat at a table, writing a letter. He removed his hood and faced Jak squarely. "Your little show caused quite the talk. People still ask me about it, whether you're a danger to their children." He bared his teeth. "You want to know what I tell them?"

"Where are they?" Jak said, ignoring his words.

"Who?" The Priest's face held no confusion. He merely kept smiling.

"Don't play dumb with me," Jak growled. "You know who I'm talking about."

"I suppose you mean the poor, unfortunate students hidden away by your leader, Gabriel. Once the queen got word of their situation, she immediately ordered them to come here, for their own protection."

"What protection? They were fine where they were!"

"They were prisoners, locked away where no one could help them."

Jak felt her face grow hot. "They weren't in any danger!"

"That remains to be seen. And it really is none of your business. Suffice it to say, we will do all we can to reverse this condition imposed on them by your teacher."

"What? Gabriel had nothing to do with this. He was with me when it happened."

The Priest shrugged. "I hope you won't take it personally if I don't believe you. Your position in this is hardly unbiased. And after what happened here all those weeks ago. Well, you can understand if I don't trust you."

Jak shook her head. It was all coming apart. How was she supposed to get anything from this man if he kept pretending that he was the good guy here and that she was the dangerous one?

"You know the Fae aren't dangerous. They have not been cursed. I've seen the prophecies."

"You're referring to your friend's little book? Hardly prophecy."

"Not there, you know I've seen an original copy of the Annals of Adam. It mentions the Fae."

"My dear, anyone can modify scripture to suit their own needs."

Jak growled in frustration. "Stop turning everything against me!"

A light filled the space around them, a white light, different from that of the warm candles. Jak glanced down to see that she had, without even realizing it, activated her Gifter brand.

The Royal Priest's eyes flickered in the new light. "If you brand me, you'll never make it out of the city before someone finds you and executes you for heresy and treason." His face was completely calm, not at all frightened of Jak. Jak glanced at his hands once again, both laying flat on the table. Like before, the back of the palm was hidden in a glove. She couldn't see what brand he carried. It must have been something powerful for him not to be afraid of her.

She let her brand deactivate, and the light faded. She glared at the Royal Priest. "You've got it all figured out, haven't you? You have an answer for everything."

"Our father's fathers illuminate my path of understanding. Do not worry about your friends. If there is hope for them, we will find it."

"And if there isn't."

"Then I advise you to never again support the work of black magic." His voice was still calm but held an edge this time. "Either these people have perverted magic, broken our most important law, or someone else has done it to them. Either way, someone will eventually pay the price."

Jak had heard similar words before, coming from Kuldain. At that time, the demon in disguise had sought to discredit the Fae, to breed hatred among his soldiers. It had almost worked, and in some cases, like Estel, it had.

Once again, her suspicions rose in her thoughts. And right now, they were more than suspicions. Surely, this man had to be a demon in disguise, just like Kuldain, but even more cunning. That smile he always kept, like he was always one step ahead of Jak, and the way he had an answer for every argument she could summon. He was prepared for everything and almost certainly held the attention of the queen in his hand.

"I know what you are." She whispered, barely audible.

She met the Royal Priest's gaze and saw only his knowing smile. "You see what you think, girl, nothing more. That has been evident from the moment I met you."

"Someone will come for you." She said. "When it becomes plain to everyone else what you are."

The Royal Priest didn't skip a beat. "It appears I will not get through to you. This meeting is over."

For once, Jak agreed. She turned on her heel and stalked out of the cathedral, not bothering to say a word to the guards at the door.

When she returned to the college, Semwei was waiting just inside the dome.

"How's Gabriel?" Jak asked.

"He will recover," Semwei said through pursed lips. "But we need to talk."

"I'm not in the mood to talk right now." Jak turned to walk to her room.

"You will stay right where you are!" Semwei put one foot down, her fists at her sides, glaring at Jak like she had never done before. "Now I may have granted you some leniency before. After everything, Gabriel has told me, and what happened on the High Morning after you arrived, I know that special circumstances had to be taken."

"I never asked to be special!" Jak shouted. She knew Semwei had done nothing to her, but she didn't care. She was just so mad at everything now.

"Then you won't mind if I treat you no different than any other student who runs away when she belongs here. Twice in one night. You will spend the next week away from your classes and spend the day helping the cook and the caretaker in addition to your chores."

"What!?" Jak's classes were the only thing she truly loved about this college.

"Furthermore, you will not leave the college without my express permission, or it will become a month. And when you return to your classes, your teachers will tell you how to make up the classes that you missed."

Jak glared at the woman. How could she be this harsh to Jak when she surely knew the gravity of the situation? Without Jak, Gabriel might have died. And she was being punished for it!

Without another word, Jak turned on her heel and stalked off. Semwei didn't stop her this time.

The rest of the students were all asleep, and Jak didn't see Amelia anywhere. All for the best. The last person she wanted to see was her all-too-peppy friend.

She slammed the door to her room and sat on her bed, clutching her head with her hands and finally letting the tears come. After everything that happened, everyone was blaming her. From Semwei to Naem to the Royal Priest, they all blamed her for something. She was just trying to help. It all confirmed one thing to her, she was no hero. Whatever sort of redemption Seph sought for his followers, and for the Fae, it wasn't going to come from her.

As if automatically, she picked up a woodchip from her nightstand, one of many that she picked up to practice with. She gave it a Healing brand, done perfectly like before, where it sprouted and grew until it became healthy enough to be planted as a sapling.

Now was the time to confirm once and for all that she either was an Oren or was not. Focusing as hard as she could, she summoned her magic again, imbuing the sapling with a second brand, a Flamedancer brand.

For a moment, the sapling sat in her hand, unchanged save for the lines of the Flamedancer brand that settled into the wood, next to the Healing brand.

Before it began to wither.

Within seconds, the green buds that had formed on the sapling fell away, the wood lost all moisture, and it crumbled to dust in her hands, overwhelmed by the two brands.

She lay back in her bed. Well, that settled it. She was no Oren, no hero. Whatever had happened when she gave Naem her brands must have been a fluke. A one time thing.

This was not her fight.

And it never had been.

CHAPTER 13

THE DAYS BLURRED TOGETHER after that. Jak did her week of chores without further complaint. Other students would pause to watch her, some of them snickering to see the odd one suffer. They had no idea what had happened to her. Few even knew that Gabriel was hurt, but word soon got around, and her peers began to put two and two together. Trouble was, most of them thought Jak was somehow responsible for Gabriel's injury, rather than the one who rescued him.

Amelia tried to help by squashing the rumors. But most people didn't listen to her, knowing she was Jak's friend. That was also why Jak did her best to avoid Amelia when she could. Her friendship with Jak only made things worse for Amelia. Jak's penance made it easier to avoid Amelia since one was stuck in class and the other in the kitchens, but that didn't stop Amelia from tracking Jak down and trying to talk. Eventually, once it became clear to Amelia that Jak didn't want to talk, she stopped trying. So Jak was left to herself.

Once her week of chores was over, Jak resumed her studies and worked harder than ever before. She may not have succeeded in using more than one brand on a subject, but she was still determined to know all there was to know about branding. It was her only source of bitter comfort, seeing the looks on the other student's faces as she continued to pass them up in their studies. She was even doing fine in the other areas of study at the college. Physicality came as no problem, coupled with all the training she had done with the Watchers. And her Mentality classes weren't too hard once Jak applied herself.

Naem had not yet come back, and probably for the best, Jak thought. She would have turned him away anyway, much as she had Amelia. It was best for him.

These days, she spent most of her time in the library, going from book to book, making notes in her journal, and reading for as long as they allowed, then sneaking a book to her room and continuing there.

"*Variations on Strength Branding in Modern Relics,*" a voice spoke to her one evening while she read. "Now that's about as dull as it gets." Jak looked up to see Seph standing there, smile firmly in place.

"Seph!" She leaped from her chair and wrapped her arms around him. He winced, and she quickly pulled away. "Oh, I'm sorry. Your back. I shouldn't have."

"It's fine," he said, chuckling. "It's healing nicely. I'll be good as new within a few days."

"I'm so sorry they did that to you."

"A little suffering for the right cause can do more good than bad." He sounded like he was quoting something, but Jak couldn't place it. "And from what I hear, I'm the least of your problems."

Jak huffed. "Did Amelia send you?"

Seph smiled. "No pulling the wool over your eyes. Yes, she's worried about you. Says you haven't spoken with her in over a week."

"I have nothing to say."

"Well, I find that hard to believe. You've suffered a loss. The Fae you protected are gone, your teacher suffered as a result, and you're blaming yourself."

"How did you know about the Fae?" Jak went back to her seat. Seph joined her in another chair, careful not to let his back rub against it.

"Amelia again, but I'm glad she told me. It only confirmed my suspicions that you have an important part to play in all of this."

Jak scowled. "You've seen what trouble comes when I try to do something about it."

"Trouble would have come whether you were here or not. But you are here, and you can take action."

"But I made it worse." Jak felt her eyes burn. She wasn't angry at Seph, but perhaps speaking to him was unveiling the rest of her emotions.

"Did you? Let's see. You had nothing to do with the Water Fae appearing in the first place. You've had little or no sway over the actions of the queen and her advisors. Without you, Gabriel likely would not have made it back. The only failure I see is a failure to keep your friends close when all they want to do is help." He said the last line with emphasis.

"I'm not your hero, Seph," she said, ignoring his rebuke. "I thought I might be, I once branded...someone with more than one brand. It was a unique moment, and there was Fae magic involved. But I tried to do it again, more recently. It doesn't work."

Seph took the new information in with admirable calm. "You know," he said, changing the subject. "I believe we're all born on Earth with a purpose of some kind. We all come with a destiny to be a hero, whether that's to save the lives of others, or to be someone's hero for cooking their favorite pastry."

Jak shook her head. "I don't think I can believe that. It takes away our choice."

"Oh, everyone still has a choice. They can choose to accept their destiny or reject it. Personally, I feel that the world would be a near-perfect place if everyone accepted their destiny. Sadly, most do not, and only a few achieve the greatness they're capable of."

Jak paused, "What does this have to do with my failure?"

Seph smiled and took her hand. "Jak, you're a wonderful person. I hope you will forgive my frankness. But might I suggest that you have yet to accept your destiny."

"How do you even know what my destiny is?"

"I don't, but I suspect you do, and you're fighting it."

Jak hung her head. Something about Seph's words rang true. "So you're saying I can't perform more than a single brand on a subject because I haven't embraced my destiny?"

"No Jak, I'm saying you can't succeed because you don't want to."

Was Seph right? She had been in a bitter place the last time she tried to double brand the wood chip. Curiosity ate at her. "So, I can't form a second brand because I don't want the responsibility that implies?"

"No one ever wants to be a hero, Jak," Seph said, almost in a whisper now. "But sometimes other people are counting on us."

Jak looked into his eyes. There was a fire there, a passion that Jak admired. Seph truly believed in what he was doing, but not only that. He truly believed in her.

"I... will think about what you said." She moved her hands away, breaking Seph's touch.

"Of course." Seph didn't skip a beat. "I will let you be." He strode to the staircase, took one last look at her, and quickly disappeared.

He was gone so suddenly that Jak almost wanted to call him back, but she remained in her chair. She didn't feel as angry as she used to, but she still needed time to think. Her thoughts troubled her, but something felt different than before. Talking with Seph soothed her like nothing else had. There simply was no getting angry at that man.

Standing, she put her book away and walked down the large stone steps into the main dome. From there, she found herself taking long strides to Gabriel's quarters. The old man had recovered now but never asked to see Jak. Now, she wanted to know why.

Checking to make sure there were no dangerous wards about, Jak knocked loudly on Gabriel's door.

"Who is it?" Gabriel's muffled voice came through the door.

"It's Jak." She said in a clear tone.

A pause, and then the door squeaked on its hinges as Gabriel opened it wide. He stood there, his face a mixture of pity and respect. "Come in," he said after a moment.

Jak entered. Inside, she saw the same worn map that covered one wall, with the same pieces of string linking various papers to spots on the map.

"I... came to see how you were doing," Jak said.

"Oh, I've been fine for a few days now." There was a pause as Jak's unspoken question hung in the air. Gabriel cleared his throat. "I've been meaning to see you, to thank you for what you did. I'm sorry if Semwei's punishment for leaving the college seemed a little... harsh."

"You did nothing to change it," Jak said, surprised to find her voice was calm.

"No, that was not my prerogative. She is the headmistress, and I am only the head instructor. It would not look good if we kept countermanding each other's orders."

"It's okay. I've dealt with it." Jak took the chair next to Gabriel's desk. "But I wish you would have come to see me."

"Yes, I'm sorry. But I honestly didn't know what to say. I've tried to keep you sheltered here, where you can focus on learning instead of the Fae or demons or cruel men. It seems I failed."

Jak nodded. "I wouldn't blame you. I tried to do the same thing for myself, and it didn't help."

"Well, I'm sorry all the same. I'm just glad that the queen's guards didn't hurt you too."

"I'm kind of surprised they did not," Jak said, honestly. "They hurt Seph, do you know him?"

"He's that preacher that people have been making a big fuss about? Yes, I know him."

"He was flogged the same day that we rescued you. On the queen's orders."

"Really? Well, now that is interesting." Gabriel tapped his fingers together.

"Why?" Jak asked.

"Well, you see. He was once the adopted son of the queen."

"What?" Jak's mouth hung open. She would never have guessed Seph had any ties to royalty.

"Oh yes. I remember some years ago, he came to the palace from the eastern nations, in exchange for the queen's only daughter who left to marry a prince there. And as I recall they had some sort of falling out. The boy left the palace with nothing and has survived on his own ever since. I don't know much more than that."

Jak ran a hand through her hair. Why hadn't he told her any of this?

Gabriel stroked his beard. "Let me guess, you're wondering if there's any truth to what he teaches."

"I guess so. Some of it makes sense."

"A lot of it makes sense," Gabriel confirmed. "More than you know." He glanced at the map displayed on the wall. "Do you want to know what this is?" he asked. When Jak nodded, he continued. "This is my biggest research project. My life's work. And once upon a time, it was your mother's work too."

"What?" Jak looked more closely at the map.

"Yes, this is everything we know about the Pillars of Eternity."

Jak sat back in her chair, her eyes widening with understanding. The Pillars of Eternity, three Relics that were supposed to be the most powerful of all, each one capable of unspeakable magic. Though from what Jak knew, details were scarce about what they actually did. It was the search for a Pillar of Eternity that led her mother and her expedition into the Hollow Peaks, where they instead found the Annals of Adam, the Relic that changed them into the Shadow Fae.

"Yes, I see you recognize the name," Gabriel said. "Little is known about them, but everything we know is contained in here." he tapped his head. "I've made it my life's work to study them, and do you know what they're for?"

Jak shook her head.

"I found this in an old book almost forgotten in a dusty storage room in Tradehall." He stood and picked up a small piece of parchment where Gabriel had copied a single word. He handed it to Jak.

'Worldbringers' it read. Jak looked up at Gabriel. "I don't understand."

"The book referred to the Pillars of Eternity as worldbringers. It specifically mentioned a hero that would use the Pillars of Eternity to create a world of peace. At the time, I thought it was figurative. And it still could be. But you can imagine my surprise when I learned of a prophecy quite similar in your friend's book."

Jak swallowed. "Illadar, it's a world of peace."

I've kept track of that boy's teachings since before I met you. We have both lived to see parts of it spring right off the pages into the real world. I imagine it won't be long before we see more. It's too much of a coincidence, Jak."

"Why are you telling me this?"

Gabriel sighed, "Because as much as I hate to admit it, I believe you are an essential part of this. How I don't know yet."

The words of her dying father suddenly awoke in Jak's mind. *He fears you.* She hadn't thought about the phrase in a long time now, had all but forgotten it. She still had no idea who *he* was, but she suspected it was someone who controlled or otherwise led the demons, not unlike Kuldain had done but at an even greater scale. Someone who even Kuldain answered to. Could it be this Royal Priest, or did even he answer to someone?

"I... I don't know if I have the strength to be the hero the Fae, and these people, need." She said, opening up to Gabriel. "Aren't there others better suited to this?"

"No one is born a hero," Gabriel said quietly. "Heroes are forged, and the forge is always painful for the blade, yet without it, the blade could not exist."

"Do you think I'm what Seph thinks I am?" she asked. "Am I the one to create this paradise of his?"

"I don't know," Gabriel's eyes were sober. "I don't know what part you will have to play. But I know we are on the brink of something big, I'm not sure any of us realize how big. But I am sure of one thing." He paused, and Jak turned to meet his eyes. "I'm sure that you are a force of good. And I trust you to do what is necessary to help the Fae or anyone else in need."

A few days ago, these words would have frightened Jak, made her want to hide and bury herself in her studies more. But for some reason, all they did was calm her.

"Thank you, Gabriel. I think you've helped me come to a decision."

"Now don't go doing anything foolish just because I said you *might* be a hero."

Jak smiled and lied. "I wouldn't dream of it."

She was ready, she thought. Ready to take action, even if it was 'foolish' as Gabriel said. But first, she had to know one thing.

Saying her goodbyes, she retreated from Gabriel's room into the student quarters, eventually ending up outside her own room. Once inside, she shut and locked the door. In the corner of the room lay a long object wrapped in wool and covered in a light coating of dust. She hadn't touched it since she arrived at the college, but it was one of the possessions that meant the most to her. She crossed the room to pick it up, unwrapping the cords that kept the wool in place.

Her father's spear gleamed in the candlelight as she removed its covering. It was no ordinary spear. The shaft was gilded and carved with fine detail. Its blade barely needed sharpening. It was an old Watcher spear, from the time when her father had been one, long before Jak could remember. And it was hers now.

Wood chips weren't enough, she realized. She needed to brand an object that meant something to her, something she could not lose. Feeling a bit more confident than she expected, she infused her spear with a Healing brand, not a perfect Healing brand, she didn't want it to bloom into a living sapling, but enough so that any minor damage it took would slowly heal.

She took a deep breath. If Seph was right, she had to be confident in her destiny as a hero. She had to accept what it meant if she could successfully stick the second brand to her spear.

A part of her hesitated. Hadn't she just tried this days ago? It hadn't worked then. But what if it had, would she have been any more likely to embrace her destiny as an Oren? Would she have tried to be the hero that Seph said would come? Probably not.

Something was different now. With the Water, Fae caught up in the queen's palace somewhere, and with people like Seph being persecuted for what they believed, she knew that she couldn't just expect someone else to be the hero. If she was in a position to help, well then, she had to do it.

She closed her eyes and focused. In her mind, she summoned another brand, Toughness. When Naem had been hurt, these were the two brands she had given him. It felt appropriate that she would try to use the same brands now.

Light poured out of her Gifter brand, though Jak kept her eyes shut, trying her best to concentrate. Toughness was similar to Healing, in that it required little more than just imagining the brand in its solid state. There was no need to imagine it dancing like fire, or any of the other necessary perceptions needed for other brands. So, she imagined each line in the complex, triangle shape of the Toughness brand, and willed it to become part of her spear.

The light faded from her hand, and it took a moment before Jak dared to open her eyes. Finally, she did.

The spear was still whole in her hands. It had not disintegrated like the wood chip had over a week before.

Feeling excitement build in her, she grabbed a small knife she kept by her nightstand and scratched just a small sliver off the spear. It resisted, and Jak had to apply as much pressure as she dared before a tiny splinter flew off. Then she looked at it carefully.

The spear, almost immediately, healed itself. The wood grew in the space left behind by the splinter. It had worked! The healing power of her brand was still working! And given the resistance she had felt in trying to chip away at the spear, it would seem the Toughness brand worked as well.

Jak cheered, not caring if anyone heard her. She had done it! She had successfully performed a double branding. She now held what most scholars would call a true Relic, one that contained multiple abilities. No soldier in the entire kingdom held a spear as powerful as what Jak held in her hands. But that was not the true benefit of what Jak had done. Inside, she knew what she had denied for months. She was special, and it was up to her to do something about it.

She had work to do.

CHAPTER 14

T HE NEXT DAY, JAK quickly sought out Amelia during their Physicality class. The girl hesitated when she saw Jak approach.

"Hey," Jak said.

"Hey," Amelia replied, looking uncertain.

"Listen, I'm really sorry for avoiding you. It was a horrible thing for a friend to do. I hope you can forgive me."

"Did Seph talk to you?" Amelia asked.

Jak smiled. "He did, and it helped. You were smart to get him to come to talk to me."

Amelia half smiled. "I hope he knocked some sense into that head of yours."

"You know very well no one can knock anything into this thick skull."

"It's so thick, you should really have that checked."

Jak's smile widened, and she embraced Amelia with everything she had. "I'm so sorry. I'll make it up to you."

"You had better," Amelia said, breaking the embrace with a wink.

"When classes are over," Jak lowered her voice to a conspiratorial whisper. "I have something you're going to want to see."

Whatever hesitation Amelia felt, it was gone in a flash, and it was all they could both do to keep themselves from faking illness and asking to be excused. It was a long day of classes, but they finally got through it, and Jak led Amelia to her room.

Pulling out her father's spear, she let Amelia stare at it for a while.

"So that's what you've had in the corner, I never did ask. Oh, and it's branded..." she broke off. Jak smiled as Amelia's eyes widened. She looked up at Jak, then back at the spear, then back at Jak again. "It's...did you...how did..." She couldn't put a coherent sentence together.

Jak found herself laughing. "Careful, you might choke!"

"You did this?" Amelia barely got the words out.

Jak nodded. "It can be done."

"But how, you realize that no one has ever managed to perform a second, stable brand. Like, ever! People have been trying for decades, more like centuries probably. Tell me what you did differently." Amelia broke off her words and wrung her hands together as she waited for a response.

Jak grimaced, "Yeah, I'm not sure it has anything to do with the technique. But more with the person who actually gives the brands."

Amelia's mouth formed an "o" of understanding. "So, you're saying only you can do it? Well, that's not exactly fair." Her face scrunched up in annoyance.

"I'm sorry," Jak said, putting an arm on Amelia's shoulder. "I wish I could teach other people how to do it, but I'm not sure I can. But I honestly don't know much more about how this works than you do."

"I don't understand though," Amelia tapped her lips with one finger. "Did you just decide to try it and it worked? What even gave you the idea?"

Jak found herself grimacing again. "There's actually something I haven't told you."

Then she began to tell Amelia about Naem, and the time when he almost died, the time when Jak had somehow branded him with Toughness and Healing to save his life. As she went on, Amelia's eyes grew wider and wider. When Jak finished, she was all but speechless. "All along, Naem had more than one brand. All this time! I... wow!" For once, Amelia seemed at a loss for words.

Jak continued. "He's not the only one. Remember Kuldain? Well, he somehow had multiple brands as well, and they worked. I'm pretty sure some of them were brands we've never seen before, though I only got a glimpse of them."

Amelia's brow knitted. "So, you're saying..."

"That if only a few people can Gift multiple brands, then I'm not the only one. Someone out there is doing the same thing."

"But what if Kuldain just branded himself?"

Jak shook her head. "I don't think so. He implied that he answered to someone higher than him. I don't know who, but I have an idea."

Amelia said nothing but listened closely.

"I think the Royal Priest is behind everything. Think about it, he's the most powerful man in the nation, he has access to basically every Relic we know about, he keeps his own brand secret, he's taken the Fae away to do Adam knows what with them. Plus, he's in the best position to manipulate the queen. It all makes sense!"

Amelia nodded her head. "There's definitely something going on. If he's not the boss person that Kuldain talked about, maybe he's in league with them."

"Definitely!" Jak was glad Amelia saw the same irregularities. "I'll bet he's a demon like Kuldain, or something worse."

Amelia looked almost excited, but then her face fell. "But what can we do about it? We're just students, and I know Gabriel and Semwei have some pull with the queen, but even they can't touch the Priest. Especially if he is what you say he is."

Jak nodded. "I know, I've been thinking it through a lot. I didn't like the thought before, but I think I have some kind of destiny to help the Fae."

"What makes you think that?"

"Well, all this. My experiences, being able to give multiple brands. Even my dad, right before he died, told me that someone fears me. Like he already knew I was special. I've was putting it off before, but I don't think I can any longer."

"This is so cool!" Amelia repositioned herself on Jak's bed. "I'm friends with an actual legendary hero!"

Jak slapped her on the shoulder. "Whatever happens I do *not* want you saying something like that again."

"Right, we don't want this going to your head. Could end badly. Apologies oh worthless, lazy, inconsiderate—yikes!" She rolled away as Jak aimed another punch at her arm.

They both broke into giggles for a moment before Amelia put on her serious face again. "Okay, so you still haven't told me what we're going to do about this."

Jak nodded. "I need to arrange a meeting with Naem and Seph. You can come if you want, though you'd probably be safer staying out of it."

"Are you kidding? I wouldn't miss it for the world!"

And so, a few hours later, Jak and Amelia found themselves down at the coast. Seph was already there, clearly having received the message that Jak sent through one of his followers that she regularly saw in the streets outside of the college.

"Jak, and Lady Amelia. I'm so glad to see you both."

Amelia tried to hide her giggles at Seph's cordiality, but Jak heard them anyway. "Thanks for agreeing to meet."

"Not at all. I'm glad to see something being done, now that I can no longer meet with my followers."

"Me too," a voice called from behind them.

Jak turned to see Naem approaching on horseback. Good, he had received her message as well. "I'm always glad to be doing something."

He gave the briefest nod to Seph as he approached. The two didn't know each other well, and Jak was worried that Naem still held feelings of jealousy towards Seph. Completely unfounded feelings of course, but men were strange that way. Naem dismounted and joined their small circle. They stood that way for a few seconds before Jak realized they were all waiting on her.

"Oh, uh... yes. The reason I've called you all here." Naem cracked a smile at her as she blustered on. "I want to rescue the Water Fae from the palace."

Naem and Seph looked at her for a moment. Then Seph slowly began to nod, putting one hand to his chin. Naem, on the other hand, frowned. "Do we really know they need rescuing?"

"Of course, they do. You've seen the queen and the Royal Priest. They don't understand the Fae like we do."

"Well certainly, but that doesn't mean they pose a definite threat. They could just be trying to learn more."

Jak pursed her lips. "You weren't there the other day when I spoke to the Royal Priest. I assure you that he doesn't have their best interests at heart. Plus, they hurt Gabriel and stole the Relic. There's no way their intentions are honorable here."

"Okay, so what exactly do you want us to do?" Naem went on. "We can't exactly march up to the palace gates and ask to be let in. And we can't sneak by, it's one of the most heavily guarded fortresses for hundreds of miles. And then there's the issue of how we get them out. They don't have proper legs, so we'd have to carry them, slowing us down considerably."

"Actually, I believe I can help with that," Seph cut in.

Jak looked at him with surprise, as did Amelia and Naem.

"You see, I lived in the palace for a short while. I learned a few of its secrets while doing my best to stay away from the queen. There's an underground escape passage that leads down the cliffs to the ocean, not far from here. It's cleverly hidden, but I could get us in."

Jak felt her excitement rise. This was more than she hoped. To be honest, she hadn't really thought much about how they were going to get into the palace."

"Where does it lead, specifically?" Naem asked, intrigued.

"To the kitchens. The cooks use part of it as a storage vault, but I found that it continues on for a while until it reaches the cliff bottom. I warn you though, it's a seemingly endless set of stairs."

"Okay, I'm familiar with the kitchens," Naem said. He looked like he was about to go on but caught himself. Lowering his head, he sighed, then looked at Jak. "You're sure you want to do this?"

Jak met his eyes and nodded. There would be no convincing her otherwise, especially not after Seph's revelation. "We need to help the Fae."

Naem pressed his lips together. "Very well. Once we're inside, I think I can find the Water Fae for you." He picked up a stick and began drawing in the sand. "The kitchens are here." He drew a small rectangle within a larger one. "My guess is the Water Fae are being held here." He indicated another area of his makeshift map. "They have a kind of lab there. They took me there for a while to test me for...eh, to see if I was still fit for duty after my journey."

Jak exchanged a knowing glance with Amelia, who had stayed uncharacteristically silent this whole time. Choosing to listen instead.

"Okay, that sounds like a good bet," Jak said. "And if they're not there?"

"Then they're probably in the dungeons, but we'll have no luck getting in there. It's much farther away, and there are three sets of guards we'd have to pass."

"You're a Watcher though," Amelia spoke for the first time. "Couldn't you take out the guards or something like that?" Jak could hear the sub-text under Amelia's question. Now knowing that Naem had multiple brands, she was wondering if that would help him overpower the guards.

"I'm good, but even I wouldn't risk my chances against the guards inside the palace. For one, there are a lot of them, but more importantly, they are some of the best of the best. Even better than most Watchers. The queen would have it no other way."

"Okay, so we just hope that they're in the lab. But we'll have to assume they're heavily guarded." Seph pointed out. "Perhaps even more than the dungeons."

Naem bit his lip and stared at the makeshift map for a while. "That's true. And I'm not sure what we would do if they are. We can't take them all."

Jak blinked at Naem. Why was he so unhelpful all of a sudden? "We can do what we did at Foothold."

"What improvise badly?"

Badly? It had worked, hadn't it? "No, I mean create a distraction. Before, I led Kuldain and his men away while you got my—" She caught herself. "--the Shadow Fae out of the fortress."

"I can do that!" Amelia piped up. "I'm very good at distracting people."

Jak turned to her. She wasn't about to forbid her friend from helping, not after the friction between their relationship up to this point, but she didn't have to like it. "Are you sure? I don't want any of you getting hurt because of this."

"I believe I speak for all of us," Seph chimed in, "when I say that we're all choosing to help you in this. We all have our own reasons for wanting to rescue these Fae. We're ready for the consequences."

Amelia nodded in confirmation. Jak stood still for a moment, feeling a range of emotions that she couldn't quite pinpoint. Part of her felt grateful, but another part seemed overwhelmed with worry for her friends. But she had made this commitment, and she couldn't back out now.

"Okay," she said. "Let's figure out how we're going to do this."

CHAPTER 15

T HEY WAITED A FEW days until the next public execution. Every so often, the queen would burn the worst of the criminals at stake in the public square. Most of them guilty of murder or rape, though some were guilty of treason and the details of their treachery were never clear. But even then, Jak thought it a gruesome scene. Why did everyone seem so interested in watching people die like that? Seriously, people gathered from all over the city to watch. It was disgusting.

Regardless, Naem claimed the palace had less security since many of the guards attended the execution, both to keep the peace and to satiate their own curiosity. So, it was decided. They would sneak in that evening.

As Jak and Amelia quietly left the college and headed down to the coast, Jak ran through the plan in her mind. They'd climb the stairs, enter the kitchens, then Amelia would run off to the bathhouses to make her diversion. Jak had taught Amelia how to do the "faulty" Flamedancer branding trick. Jak didn't even consider it a failed brand anymore, it was quite useful under the right circumstances.

Amelia would use the brand to create an explosion in the bathhouse, one of the queen's favorite luxuries, according to Seph. That should get everyone's attention.

Then it was a simple matter of taking out what guards remained, locating the Water Fae, carrying them back down the secret passage, all without anyone raising the alarm. Simple, right?

Jak had also wanted to search for the Relic but eventually agreed with Naem and Seph that, while the Relic was important, the Water Fae took priority. If they found the Relic with the Fae, great. If not, they would have to leave it for now.

Jak drew up short, realizing they were already at the base of the cliffs. Two torches held in the distance told her that Naem and Seph had already arrived.

"Glad you made it," Naem said as they approached.

Jak dispensed with the greetings, turning to Seph. "Are you ready?"

Seph nodded. "The entrance isn't far from here."

"But first," Naem held a small bundle of what looked like pieces of cloth out in front of him. "We should put these on."

Jak grabbed one of the rags and felt a moment of trepidation. These were masks like those worn by caravan robbers and other thieves. Of course, she knew they were all doing this for the good of the Fae, but she didn't like the feeling of doing something illegal, even for the right reasons.

She couldn't think about that now. Doing so could distract her and ruin the mission. Without another thought, she tied the cloth around her face, obscuring her mouth and nose, leaving only her green eyes exposed. Lastly, she raised her hood and tucked her hair behind it. The red streak in her otherwise raven hair was as much of an identifier as anything. Best to keep as much of her body as concealed as possible.

Once they were all prepared, Seph began to lead them up a small incline only a few meters from where they met. A part of the cliff had crumbled and left a small hill next to the beach. They climbed it, and it was only then that Jak noticed a small cave entrance in the side of the cliff, positioned in such a way that she would have never seen it from the beach.

"Oh, I see it!" Amelia squealed as they approached. "It was right there all along!"

Jak looked up to see the Palace perched at the top of the cliffs. This was likely to be a long climb.

"We'll have to go single file from here on out," Seph said. "I'll lead."

He approached the cave entrance and stepped sideways to better fit through the opening. It wasn't too small of a hole, but definitely small enough so that two people couldn't enter side by side. And it didn't open up immediately either. It almost felt like the walls were closing in on Jak as she walked for nearly a minute before the passage opened up into a larger space.

Jak made out some stairs directly ahead, illuminated by Seph's torch. Amelia entered the cavern after Jak, with Naem taking up the rear.

"Oh, wow!" Amelia's eyes bulged out of her head. "It's really here. I love secret passages." Her voice echoed loudly through the cavern.

Seph winced. "You'll need to keep your voice down in here. This cavern extends all the way up to the kitchens and sound carries."

"Oh, sorry!" Amelia said in a slightly hushed tone that still carried more than Jak was comfortable with.

"Best if none of us say anything," Naem said from behind Jak.

That was asking a lot from Amelia, but once they began the climb, even she seemed to forget about conversation. The climb was a long one, and the steps were steep and narrow, carved into the solid rock that zigzagged up the cavern wall, with only a small length of rope strung along the way to keep them from falling if they slipped.

Only Naem seemed unwinded by the climb, probably thanks to his healing power or Grace, or a combination of the two allowing him to climb the steps with little effort. Seph breathed heavy, but still not as much as Amelia and Jak, who were having to take deep, gagging breathes after a while. Surely their breathing alone would be enough to wake the whole palace. And that was without Amelia's occasional whimpers when she ignored everyone's advice and looked down to see how far they had come.

They stopped once to catch their breath, but it surprised Jak how quickly they reached the top. The chamber carved out of the rock was much larger now and filled with storage containers and random junk. Seph waited for everyone to finish climbing and join him on the large ledge.

"Okay," he whispered. "The kitchens are right ahead through that trap door." He pointed at a small wooden square in the ceiling with a ladder standing next to it. "They always keep it uncovered in case the queen needs to make a quick getaway, though most just assume it's nothing more than a kitchen pantry."

Which it was, Jak realized as she looked around. Many of the boxes held meats, fruits, and other perishables. *You'd have to go all the way to the back to even discover the doorway that led to the massive stone staircase.*

Seph put out his torch, and Naem followed suit. Now the only source of light came from cracks in the trap door.

"I'll go first," Naem whispered. "There may still be people left cleaning the dishes or something."

Jak couldn't hear any signs of movement above them, but she agree that Naem was the best option to go first. He climbed the ladder and gently raised the door. His head went first, and Naem paused to look around. Then he climbed the rest of the way out of the trap door, and Jak could feel Amelia bobbing on the balls of her feet in anticipation, echoing how Jak felt.

Naem's head reappeared as he knelt over the trap door. "All clear."

Jak let out a breath she didn't know she had been holding and followed Seph and Amelia up the ladder to join Naem.

The kitchens were enormous. The queen must entertain a lot of people to warrant having three stoves, five wash basins, and an inordinate amount of table space. Jak was honestly surprised there wasn't at least one person working in the kitchen at all times. They'd need a lot of manpower just to keep the place clean, let alone cook.

"The bathhouses are down the hall on the left, then make a right and another left," Seph instructed Amelia. "If you run into anyone, you can just pretend to be one of the queen's ladies in waiting."

Amelia took the scarf from her face. "So, was there any reason for me to wear this?" She tucked it under her belt and walked out of the kitchens, giving Jak an excited wink as she left.

Naem peeked outside the door as Amelia left, "The coast is clear for now, I say we move."

Jak could feel her heart pumping in her neck as they tip-toed around the palace, expecting to run headlong into a guard or worse, the queen herself, around any corner. It was amazing how few people inhabited such a big space. Even when Jak had visited the palace the first time, she hadn't seen many people. And now, with everyone at the execution, it seemed almost abandoned. But that didn't stop Jak from worrying.

Seph took the lead, but Naem was close behind, ready to defend Seph and Jak if needed. He was, after all, far more accomplished in combat than anyone else Jak knew.

Suddenly, Seph stopped to peak around a corner. Jak waited, and Seph stepped back to regard her. "The lab is around the corner. There's no mistaking it. Your friends are in there."

"How can you tell?" asked Naem.

"Because I count ten guards," Seph said, coolly.

Naem cursed and peaked around the corner to see for himself, then turned again to Jak. "I'm not sure I can take ten of them."

Jak was about to point out that she wasn't exactly use-less when it came to combat when a massive thundercrack rattled the stone around them. That must be Amelia's distraction! It was far stronger than Jak had anticipated, nearly knocking Seph to the ground. Jak peaked around the corner to see the guards for herself, hoping against hope that most if not all of them would run to see what happened.

Sure enough, at a motion from one of the guards, six of them ran off in the direction of the noise, away from Jak and company. She looked at Naem. "There's only four of them now. We can take that many."

Naem grinned, "We?"

"Of course?" She made sure her mask was firmly in place. "You didn't think I was going to let you have all the fun."

And with that, she rounded the corner and dashed as fast as she could towards the guards. It took a few seconds for them to realize what was happening, but it took that long for Jak to close the distance between them. She lashed out with the butt of her spear, landing it squarely on the side of a guard's head. Normally, a blow that strong would have broken the spear, but this spear had Toughness and Healing. So instead, it was the guard who crumbled and fell.

The guards were ready now, their weapons raised, regarding Jak. One reached out his hand, and Jak felt invisible bonds surround her, pinning her arms to her sides. The man was a Telekinetic! But a split second later Naem was beside her, doing a fancy Grace-ladden spin as he lept. His Grace allowed him to penetrate their defenses with little difficulty, and within moments, the Telekinetic was down. Jak felt her arms respond again, and she took advantage of the moment to push ahead at the remaining two guards, one who appeared to have Strength, and the other who had Grace. Both kept their attention on Naem and didn't see Jak coming until it was too late. She landed a blow on the Strength guard and distracted the one with Grace just long enough that Naem stabbed him in the side. The guard yelled but was cut off as Naem brought his spear smashing down on his head.

"I thought we were going to avoid lethal wounds?" Jak whispered.

"He'll live," Naem said without looking at her and began searching through the bodies for keys. Seph joined them, looking down at the bodies with a mixture of surprise and disgust. Clearly he wasn't used to seeing people fight like Jak and Naem.

Jak ignored Seph and frowned at Naem. "You know, you've been awfully grumpy lately."

"So, have you," he said. "I saw how you retreated away from everyone when your little friends were taken. Glad you figured that out."

"What do you mean?"

"Well, you're always a lot happier when you're doing something. I, on the other hand, get grumpy as you call it."

Jak's eyebrows furrowed. "Why?"

He looked up from his searching the guards and grinned at her. "Because whenever you decide to do something crazy, I usually end up doing most of the work. Ow!" he said as she wacked his rear with her spear.

Finally, Naem recovered a ring of keys from one of the unconscious guards, and it didn't take long before they found one that opened the door with a satisfying click. It creaked as it slowly opened.

CHAPTER 16

T HE FIRST THING JAK noticed was the stench. It smelled like the Watchers after marching for two weeks without a bath. For once, Jak was glad they were all wearing masks. But as more light entered the room, she forgot all about the smell. The room held three separate stone tables and on each one lay a body with a human torso, but a long fish's tail instead of legs. The Water Fae. Their skin was wrinkled, and dry skin and scales flaked off their bodies. Dried blood coated portions of the stone tables, and none of them were moving. On the wall were various tools and instruments that Jak could not identify, but none of them looked friendly.

Jak rushed to the nearest Fae, recognizing her as Cerai, the one who had done most of the talking when they first met. Jak felt the girl's neck, and nearly cried out loud with relief when she felt a faint pulse.

"They're still alive."

Cerai groaned, and her eyes fluttered open to look at Jak. "What's... who... I know you."

Jak leaned close. "We're here to get you out." Glancing at Naem and Seph, she waved one hand. "Let's get them up! The other guards will be back here soon."

Naem and Seph didn't argue. They each took one of the two other Fae at the other tables. None protested, barely even conscious as they were lifted up.

Jak followed suit and reached her arms around Cerai to lift her up. The Water Fae felt light, so much lighter than Jak expected. From the look of things, they were extremely dehydrated and needed water soon.

She hefted Cerai's body onto her shoulder and, holding her spear in the other hand, began to make her way outside the room, sparing a glance in each direction before retreating the way they had come. She didn't turn but heard Naem and Seph following behind her.

"Weren't there four of you?" She asked as she half-walked, half-ran back to the kitchens. "And what about Danen, what happened to him?"

"Dead." Cerai croaked from over Jak's shoulder. "They... experimented."

Jak felt her face grow hot, and not just from the exertion of carrying Cerai. What had they been doing to these poor people? Whatever it was, it was worse than Jak had anticipated."

"What about the Relic? Have you seen it?" She asked as they continued.

"Not—" She groaned through the pain as she bounced up and down on Jak's shoulder "—recently. One of them, a priest, tried to use it to reverse what happened, or maybe to make it worse. Then they took it away. I think... they don't understand it."

Jak grit her teeth. Of course, the Royal Priest was involved in this somehow.

"Well, we'll get you out. You won't have to worry about them anymore."

"Thank you." It was a simple statement, but Jak could almost feel the waves of relief radiating off of Cerai.

They were blessed not to run into anyone on their way back to the kitchens. Everyone was likely away at the execution or investigating Amelia's explosion. Speaking of which....

"Do you think Amelia got away?" She asked Naem as they filed into the kitchens. "She was supposed to meet us here."

Seph set the Water Fae he was carrying down on the stone floor and opened the trap door. "Can we risk going after her?" he said as he climbed. Once down the ladder, he waved his hands, indicating that Naem and Jak should lower the Fae to him.

"I don't know," Naem lifted his Fae and gently lowered him down to Seph, who received him with the same careful attention.

"I can go." Jak volunteered as she began lowering Cerai down to Seph as well.

"I wouldn't recommend that," Seph said. "We all stand to lose the most if you're caught."

"If I'm your prophesied hero, then I won't be," Jak said.

"I'm not sure that's how it works. There's also your Fae. We can't take more than one each."

"It's okay," Naem chimed in. "With Grace, it shouldn't be too hard to take one of them down, then climb up quickly for the other."

They had lowered all three Fae by now, and Naem was beginning to make the climb himself.

"That settles it then," said Jak, shifting her spear from one hand to the other. "I'll go looking for her."

"Okay, but promise me," Seph called up. "If they have her, or you run into any guards or someone worse, you'll come right back."

"I promise," Jak said, and she turned to step out of the kitchens once again.

This time she ran as fast as she dared without making too much noise. Following the path that Seph had prescribed earlier, it didn't take long before Jak heard voices. Slowing, she peaked around the corner.

"I'll handle this lot, the rest of you search the palace, there are intruders here somewhere."

Jak recognized the voice, it was the Royal Priest. She barely had time to register this before the clank of armor and chainmail could be heard approaching her position. Her head spun in every direction, looking for a place to hide. There was one small doorway just behind her, so she wrenched it open. Inside was a small washroom, with a privy and washbasin, probably for the servants, given its modest qualities.

Jak held her breath and heard the sound of armored feet walk past her position, then slowly fade into the distance. She let out a sigh of relief. Thank heavens they weren't searching the small corners of the palace just yet. Now, if she could just...

Something caused Jak to stop in her tracks. A small hum seemed to buzz inside her brain, like the sound of a passing fly, except...warmer, more inviting. And it was more of a feeling than an actual sound. What's more, she recognized it, having felt something similar only a few months prior in the caves of the Hollow Peaks. Back then, the source of the humming had been a Relic, the original copy of the Annals of Adam. It had called to her then.

Something called to her now.

Jak knew what it must be, the Relic that had changed Cerai and the other students into Water Fae, that had given them those large tails and fins. It had to be.

Jak felt it call out, inviting her to draw closer, to take it away from these evil men who were exploiting its power, to give it the purpose it was built for.

Instinctively, she knew where it was, not far from where she now stood. In fact, it may just be in or near the bathhouses where she was going anyway.

Putting one ear to the door, she listened for anyone who stood nearby. Hearing no one, she opened the door a crack and peered in both directions, then slipped out and continued towards the bathhouses. From the conversation she overheard earlier, she could probably expect to find the Royal Priest there, though hopefully, he would be alone.

Tip-toeing around the corner, she felt the warmth and humidity in the air rise. She must be getting close. Finally, she found a doorway flung wide open and the wall beside it partially demolished. That must have been where Amelia set her explosion. Jak could feel the strange hum in her head growing louder. It must be nearby. But right now, Amelia took priority.

Inside she could see steam filling a large room. The walls held intricate mosaics of tile, and marble pillars filled the room. Several large circular pools filled the space.

Standing just ahead, his back to her, was the Royal Priest. He had on his typical black robe, and his stance spoke of authority and triumph. Jak peaked around him to follow his gaze. He was looking at the nearest pool, where Amelia lay clutching at the side, her hair and clothes wet. What had she decided to go for a swim?

"Well, well. Isn't this interesting," the Priest said to Amelia.

Jak wasn't going to let him say anymore. There were no guards, for now at least, making this her best chance to get Amelia out, though she found herself distracted. The buzzing in her head had grown so loud.

She still didn't know what the Priest's brand was, so she decided not to take any chance. She snuck up behind the Priest, raised her spear, and delivered a blow to the man's head that left her spear vibrating. He instantly crumpled to the floor.

"Amelia, what are you doing? We need to get out of here!" She paused as she caught the expression on her friend's face.

Instead of the usual cheery look, Amelia's face was awash with panic. Her hands gripped the edge of the pool so tightly that Jak could see the whites of her knuckles.

"Amelia? What's wrong." Jak stood still for a moment, and the room was silent, leaving only the strange hum in her head.

"I... can't." Amelia's face was pale. What could be the matter?

Jak drew closer, not daring to believe her suspicion. Tears began to stream down Amelia's face. "You need to get out of here."

"I'm not leaving without you," Jak said, closing the distance.

"You need to get out of here!" Amelia shouted the words, and there was a great splash in the pool. Bits of water splashed onto the floor and Jak's face. That was when she saw it.

Amelia's legs were gone. Instead, she had a long, silver tale that was the source of the splash. Without the use of her legs, Amelia relied on her arms to keep her fixed to the edge of the pool. Jak's heart plummeted. Amelia had become a Water Fae.

"How?" was the only word she could summon.

Amelia pointed upward. Hanging above the pool was a gold object. Jak recognized it immediately from the descriptions she had heard. It was the Relic, with two gold rings and a circle in the center, looking like ripples in a lake, the pieces somehow magically held together.

"I came in here to make the explosion, and I did it, but then lost all strength in my legs," Amelia explained. Tears were continuing to stream down her face, and her breath came in short, panicked bursts. "And I knew I needed water, so I came here. Then I saw them..."

Amelia swept her hand around the room. Jak had been so focused on Amelia's she hadn't bothered to look anywhere else. She did so now, and her hand rose to her mouth.

The other baths were full of people, some of them looking at her, some appearing to be asleep or dead. There were several of them, perhaps two dozen. And from what she could tell, every one of them was a Water Fae.

Amelia went on. "They've been making more Fae, Jak. They're trying to see how it works! I... I don't know why."

At that moment, Jak heard the clank of armor again. Someone was approaching. Without a second thought, she raised her spear high enough to sever the string that held the Relic above her. It fell to the ground, and Jak hastened to pick it up and shove it into her pouch.

"Come on," she extended a hand to Amelia as she heard the footsteps grow louder. Whoever was coming, there were a lot of them.

"I told you, I can't go with you!" Amelia yelled. "You'll never get away if you're carrying me."

"We came all this way to get the others out, and we carried them. I can get you out too."

"Oh, I would say your friend has it about right," a woman's voice said from behind Jak.

She spun to see the queen standing at the entrance, surrounded by guards. These men and women had a different kind of armor and looked far more dangerous than the others. These were likely the queen's personal guard.

"Well, well," said the queen, glancing down at her Royal Priest who still lay unconscious on the floor. "I admit, I didn't expect anyone to actually try and break into the palace. I see you've already taken possession of the Relic. How did you get in? Actually, never mind that. We'll have all the answers from you eventually. Guards!"

The soldiers on either side of the queen stepped in, surrounding Jak. She began to panic. How was she going to get out of this one? She was surrounded, her friend couldn't help, and there was no way she could fight her way out. To add to the trouble, she felt her arms snap involuntarily to her sides, and her spear fell out of her hands. There was a telekinetic in the group. Jak closed her eyes. She was caught.

"Hello Telma," said a quiet voice.

Jak's eyes snapped open. Armor groaned as nearly every guard in the room turned to follow Jak's gaze. The queen turned more slowly, but her face was white.

In the doorway stood Seph, his mask uncovered, his hands hanging loosely at his sides. "Seph, my boy," said the queen, her face recovered from its momentary shock. "I should have known you would have been behind this. You always did carry a fascination for Relics."

"Let them go, Telma."

"Silly boy, I'm afraid I can't. One of them has fallen ill, along with the rest of those you see here. She must stay."

"The other then. Let her go without uncovering her face."

"Now why would I ever do that?" The queen's voice had taken on a motherly tone, but it was clear that anger boiled just beneath the service.

Jak had an idea of what was coming. She didn't know Seph's past with the queen, but she knew it wasn't good. *Don't do it, Seph!*

"Because you'll get me, willingly."

Jak let out a breath. The queen surely wouldn't stand for it, but the woman did appear to be considering Seph's proposal. Seph's eyes met Jak's for a moment, and... did he just wink at her?

"You realize, of course, that giving yourself in does nothing," the queen continued. "Nothing is stopping me from taking the girl and the Relic."

Seph drew a few steps closer. The guards tightened their grips on their weapons, but Seph made no sudden moves. "Yes, that thought had occurred to me."

With a sudden jerk, Seph smashed something into the ground. Before Jak could process what he was doing, whatever he threw exploded on the ground. Dust and smoke filled the entire cavern, and gasps sounded from the remaining Water Fae in the room.

"Go, Jak." She heard Amelia's soft voice behind her. "That's your cue."

Jak hesitated only a moment. Turning to look at her friend, but barely seeing her through the smoke, she said, "I'll come back for you!"

Then she ran.

Shouts echoed through the room as guards scrambled to find their bearings and the queen barked orders through the smoke. Jak ran at the noise, slipping by a pair of guards as she did so. She caught only a glimpse of Seph, who was throwing himself at the guards to keep them from moving, saved from the soldiers' weapons by cries from the queen. "Don't kill him, don't kill him!"

In the chaos, Jak found herself outside the bathhouses and running back towards the kitchens. Images of Amelia and Seph's faces haunted her as she went. The more distance she put between her and her friends, the worse it got.

It wasn't long before she heard shouts behind her, and she redoubled her efforts and forced her legs to keep running. The hallways seemed to elongate, and Jak felt like she was in a dream, unable to run fast enough. But the kitchens were just ahead.

She flew into the large space and scrambled down the trap door inside, pulling the door closed behind her. She could still hear shouts, but none of them were in the kitchens yet. Perhaps they hadn't seen her go in?

Not about to take chances, she flew towards the edge of the hidden room that led to the stairs. There was a light ahead!

Naem emerged from the top stairs, just as Jak arrived. He held a torch, and Jak could see Cerai and the Water Fae Seph had been carrying.

"He raced after you once I was partway down," Naem said, his voice strained as though worried Jak would blame him. "Is he with you? Where's Amelia?"

The void in her stomach grew stronger, but Jak pushed it aside. "We don't have time."

Without another word, she bent to pick up Cerai. Naem followed suit by lifting the third Water Fae, Haffi, she thought his name was.

"I already took the other to the ocean. He's safe."

Jak nodded but said nothing as she began to make her way down the steep stairs. Realizing straight away that she couldn't hold Cerai, her spear, and cling to the rope to keep her from falling, she cast her spear down the long cavern. It took several seconds before she heard the faint sound of it hitting the ground below. She counted on the spear's branding to keep it from breaking.

Now she focused all her might on not falling as she stumbled down the stairs with Cerai over one shoulder. Naem led in front of her and made better time than she did.

Thankfully, they heard no sounds of pursuit, though that didn't stop both of them from moving as fast as they could. Eventually, Naem made it to the bottom, set down Haffi and began climbing to give Jak a hand. When Naem reached for Cerai, Jak almost hesitated, but let him have the Fae.

Jak felt no lighter as her burden was lifted. The void in her stomach turned into a weight, which only grew stronger as they reached the ocean and let the Fae go. She only barely felt her lips move to tell the Fae to wait where the Trade river emptied into the ocean, just south of Skyecliff. They had rescued the Fae, and Jak had the Relic, but that meant nothing to her right now. She had lost two dear friends, and worse, Amelia was one of the Fae now. Perhaps the Relic really was dangerous.

She resisted the urge to throw it into the ocean after the Fae that swam away, looking far healthier now that they were in the water. Something grabbed her arm, and she looked down to see Naem's hand there. He spoke something to her. They needed to leave. People were coming.

Jak let him lead her away. Away from her friends, away from her failure.

CHAPTER 17

THERE WOULD BE NO sleep that night, no matter how hard she tried. Naem had taken her home but then left, and she hadn't dared to ask him to stay. Now she was alone, lying in bed with her clothes still on and feeling nothing but the crushing weight of her failure pressing down until she thought she might suffocate.

Why had she ever thought it would work out to break into the palace? What could possibly have possessed her? There had been too many unknowns, too many things that could have gone wrong, and they did. She should have remembered that the Relic might change more than just the students that had discovered it. But she had no reason to think they would take it out of the Void box. Perhaps the queen and her priest were responsible for some of the missing people Jak had heard rumored through the streets. They were using them to experiment. And now they had her friend too.

Broken brands! Jak shot up from lying on her bed. She had carried the Relic with her this whole time and into the college no less! People were in danger!

Everyone was asleep, but she knew this couldn't wait. She grabbed her pouch and ran out the door. She didn't slow to keep her footsteps from echoing through the hallways. She simply ran for all she was worth to Gabriel's quarters.

Arriving, she pounded at the door. When no answer came, she pounded again. Her fist felt a mild tingling from the impact.

"Relics," she heard from the other side. "What in the name of…"

Jak heard several latches click into place and then a creak as the door swung open. Gabriel stood there, still in his night clothes, and wearing a fully irritated expression on his face. That expression changed the moment he saw Jak.

"What's wrong girl?" he said.

Apparently, her face echoed how she felt inside. Where to begin? Tell him the whole story or… she settled for handing him her pouch without saying a word. Gabriel looked inside, and his eyes widened.

"Where did you get this?"

"It's a long story, but you need to contain its magic like you did before. It could change people here. It… it changed…" She couldn't say it. Her throat closed, and nothing came out.

Gabriel looked like he needed to know more but retreated into his room with the Relic. Jak followed and found him placing the Relic in a chest he kept in the corner. Then he shut the lid, secured the latch, and his hand glowed as he branded the chest with a Void brand.

Jak felt herself give a sigh of relief. At least now it couldn't hurt anyone else.

"Now, girl." Gabriel turned, and Jak took a step backward. There was a fire in Gabriel's eyes that she had never seen before. "I assume you went against my advice and did something stupid. Start from the beginning."

Jak hung her head. He was right, she had done something stupid. She began by telling him about Seph, and how he knew of a secret passage leading into the palace. She told him how they snuck in, retrieved the three remaining students, and were about to leave before everything went wrong. It took her a long time before she was ready to go further. Gabriel expressed outward patience, but his eyes bored into her the longer she waited. Eventually, it all came out in flood, about Amelia, about Seph, about the other Water Fae hid in the palace.

"Amelia. That is terrible news." Gabriel's jaw tightened. "I've heard rumors that the Royal Priest likes to experiment with branding. He keeps several Gifters inhouse. Most of the work he does is likely illegal, but when you're the one who makes the rules... Well, I imagine this Relic must have been a treat for him. He'll want it back, surely."

Jak nodded, and they sat in silence for a while. Instead of calming Jak, the silence only magnified the weight of her failure. Finally, Jak couldn't take it anymore. "I'm sorry!" she cried. "I should have known, I'm not a hero. You and Seph, you were both wrong."

Gabriel's eyes flashed. "I know you're dealing with a lot right now, and what I'm about to seem harsh, but you need to listen to me. That kind of talk is the worst thing you can do to yourself right now. Get on your feet and be proactive."

"But I'm not the one..."

"Who cares if heroism is in your destiny or not. Does destiny determine your actions, or do you? You have control over exactly one thing, what you do with yourself. So, make something of that. Yes, you acted rashly over a misguided belief that being a hero made you invincible. Now you have to take responsibility for those actions."

Jak couldn't say anything. She was shocked at Gabriel's harsh tone. He had never spoken to her like this before. "I... I don't know what to do."

Gabriel sniffed. "All I'm saying is that wallowing in self-pity will get you nowhere. Don't react, let your grief and your feelings of failure fuel you. Perhaps you aren't the hero Seph thinks you to be. But even if you aren't, that doesn't mean you can't be a force for good."

"You want me to go back and get Amelia and Seph?"

"Heavens no, child. In fact, until further notice I want you confined to the college. For your safety as well as for everyone else's."

Jak took another step backward, towards the door. She didn't need this, not again. "But you said..."

"I said to be proactive, there are many ways to be so. I'd say start by learning to channel these feelings you have into your own development. Stick to your classes, learn to stop blaming your shortcomings. If you want to help others, start with yourself."

Sounds echoing down the corridors interrupted them. People were shouting. What could be bothering someone at this hour? Jak felt her body go stiff. No, oh please no.

Forgetting about Gabriel, she flew out the door towards the sounds of the commotion. Professor Gona was dragging someone down the hall, towards Gabriel's quarters. She spared a confused look at Jak before addressing Gabriel as he followed Jak out the door.

"Gabriel," She said as she neared. "We have a situation."

The student she was dragging had tears in his eyes and was shaking uncontrollably. Jak took one good look and wanted to turn away. The student's legs were now a gigantic fin, just like the other Water Fae. It seemed they hadn't shut away from the Relic in time after all.

Gabriel strode forward to examine the student. "No one must know of this."

"I'm afraid it's too late for that." said the professor.

Jak glanced down the hall to see several other students, probably drawn out by the noise. Gabriel cursed and stood straight. He glanced at Jak for an instant, and Jak saw exactly what she expected to see. Blame. This was her fault. If she had just left well enough alone.

She ran down the hall, away from it all. Gabriel called to her, but she ignored it, running as fast as she could back to her room.

Slamming the door, she collapsed on her bed and let the tears flow. It was the only thing she could do right now. It was all her fault. Amelia's transformation, Seph's capture, now this poor student who had no choice but to be mutated into a Fae. Perhaps the Royal Priest was right. Maybe the Fae were dangerous, or at least the Relics that turned them into Fae were so.

But then again, her own mother was a Fae, and she didn't seem to mind. They weren't demons, that much was clear, even though people like the Royal Priest would like to implicate as much. It was a traumatic change, and the victims had no choice in the matter. That was the dangerous part.

Still, others would persecute the Fae for no other reason than they were different. Clearly, those that changed did not choose to do so. Why should they suffer for something that just happened?

Jak's thoughts raced, turning from despair to fiery anger. Gabriel was right, she needed to do something proactive.

A bell tolled in the college courtyard. It couldn't be time for classes to begin yet, could they? Had she been up all night?

Slipping out of her bed, still dressed, she patted down her hair and found herself joining several other confused students, some of them looking like they were just getting out of bed. Together they assembled in the courtyard.

It was definitely too early for classes. Semwei stood at one end of the courtyard with Gabriel at one side. Professor Gona and several of the other teachers were there as well. Jak swallowed. Where they going to tell everyone about their classmate? What would they all think when they found out that she had mutated a fellow student?

The air was still dark, almost too dark, but Jak could see some light in the east. Morning was coming. Students continued to fill the courtyard, rubbing their eyes and scowling. Jak also wanted to go back to her room, though for completely separate reasons. She hoped Gabriel would leave her out of this, whatever he and Semwei were planning. The darkness seemed to settle around the teachers. Something bad was about to happen, Jak could feel it.

"Gather round," Semwei called out once there were enough students present. After a pause and a nod at Gabriel, she stepped back to give him the floor.

Gabriel cleared his throat. "We've called you here today because something has happened to one of your classmates, and you need to hear about it from us before rumors begin to circulate."

Jak closed her eyes as she heard concerned mutters run through the crowd. She understood what Gabriel and the teachers were doing, but this would not end well, especially for her.

"Do not worry, he is still alive and well."

"That's not true!" one of the students shouted.

All heads turned to face the speaker. Jak recognized him as one of the students who saw the newly-formed Water Fae earlier.

"I saw him. He's alive, but his legs are gone, replaced with a giant... something. I've never seen magic like it. It must be Gifting gone bad."

That brought more concerned mutters. Gabriel put out his hands to try and calm the crowd. "We do not yet fully understand the nature of the transformation. But it does not come from rogue Gifting. We are in possession of a Relic that has already caused several such transformations, including four of my personal students who found the Relic not far from here. I have contained the Relic, so it cannot do more harm."

Harm, Jak thought. Yes, it might not be on the same level as creating demons, but the Relic was dangerous. If people were turned into something against their will, how was that any different from demons who were forced into their circumstances.

As if reading her thoughts, another student called out. "Are they demons?"

"Of course, they're demons," said the first student before Gabriel could respond. "What else would you call such a dramatic transformation. And I don't know about this Relic, but I think I know who has something to do with it."

Jak put a hand to her head. *Here it comes.*

The boy pointed straight at her. "She's the one. I saw her just a few hours ago talking to the Professor and the student. She didn't look at all scared to see him. Like she had seen the like before!"

"Young Jak has nothing to do with this." Gabriel tried to calm the student. But it was too late.

"It's like the first time she came with us at High Morning." Another student squealed. "She got sick when his Holiness used his Relic. I knew there was something different about her."

Another student joined in. "I heard she experimented on demons over at Foothold."

"I heard she defended the demons and told everyone that they're good."

"She doesn't belong here!"

"Always was too good at Gifting to be a beginner."

The talk continued, with students talking over each other until Jak couldn't make out any more specifics. The teachers, including Gabriel, were shouting as well, trying to get everyone to calm down. Meanwhile, a gap had opened around Jak, leaving her alone with everyone staring.

Just a few days ago, she would have been devastated, and probably run away to her room, gather her things, and leave the city. Something was different now. It was almost as though an invisible hand grasped her shoulder in support, holding her up.

She strode forward to where the teachers stood. She walked past them to the stone wall behind, where a small ledge stood some three or four feet high, enough for her to climb and look out to see everyone.

Some of the students quieted down, but most were still shouting, some at her, some at the teachers, some at other students. It was a mess.

"QUIET!" she yelled, feeling a power in her voice that hadn't been there earlier.

It filled the entire square. Everyone quieted down. A glance at Gabriel showed her the regret in his eyes. Clearly he had imagined this going differently. Semwei had her usual pursed lips, but the remaining teachers eyed her curiously, as did most of the students. They were genuinely interested in what she was about to say.

"You've all heard a lot of rumors about me. All I wanted was to study, so I ignored most of them. I see now that was a mistake. So, allow me to set the record straight." She felt venom enter her voice with that last sentence. "My name is Jak

Draconis. I grew up in a farming and grazing province called Riverbrook. Less than a year ago, it was attacked by demons, and I lost my father, and many of my friends. I joined the Watchers, hoping I could get revenge. Then I discovered a people some of you may have heard of... the Fae."

That provoked a reaction, though no one said anything. Even the one student who had riled up the crowd looked at her expectantly.

"I call them the Shadow Fae." Jak went on. "They too were changed by a Relic, but they were still people. I learned very quickly the differences between them and demons could not have been more pronounced. I've heard it taught that the Fae are merely a new kind of demon. But I've seen them, and it is false."

"How can we believe you!" A student called out. She ignored him.

"What you may not know is that there are several types of Fae. And more are prophesied to come." She didn't tell them that those prophecies were only contained in the original copy of the Annals of Adam and in Seph's little book. They didn't need the details yet. "So far, I've seen three. Fae of Shadow, Light, and most recently, Water. I expect there may be more."

"You're lying!" the troublemaking student said.

"I can confirm everything she's said." Gabriel chimed in. His face was completely passive. "I've even met the same Fae."

"My point is this," said Jak. "Yes, the change has happened unexpectedly, and usually there's a Relic involved.

And I don't yet know why these changes are happening now. But I do know that the Fae are not demons. They are people like you and me, but with different appearances, and different abilities. Think of them as possessing new, undiscovered brands."

"My friend will never walk again!" said the student. So that was why he was so upset. The latest victim had been his friend.

"I'm sorry for your friend." Jak went on, still feeling unusually calm. "This power must be contained, I agree. But all I'm saying is that he's not a demon. None of the Fae are."

She thought she saw some of the students nodding in thought. Perhaps she could get through to some of them.

"Oh, my sweet little girl. I'm afraid you couldn't be more wrong." A voice called from the back of the courtyard.

Every face turned to see who had spoken. Jak, from her vantage point, could see clearly. Into the courtyard stood the Royal Priest in his flowing black cloak. To his side stood Wilva, General of the Watcher armies. Behind them, multiple armor-clad Watchers filed into the open square.

"Gabriel Linaystrome," said Wilva, using the formal name. "And Jak Draconis. You are under arrest."

CHAPTER 18

E VERYONE IN THE COURTYARD sprang into action. Students yelped and moved out of the way of the Watchers. Semwei tried to say, "On what charges?" but was drowned out by the noise of the students. The Watchers moved forward as fast as they could manage while the students made way for them. Was Naem among them? She didn't see him, but there were a lot of them.

Gabriel stood alone, facing down the Royal Priest and General Wilva while the Watchers came for him. He turned to Jak, and shouted two words. "Get out!"

Jak did not need to be told twice. She had escaped Watchers before, she would have to do so again. Stooping to pick up some rocks that had chipped off the wall, she imbued one with an imperfect Flamedancer brand and threw it at the approaching Watchers. They shielded their eyes as the rocks exploded in a shower of dust and grit.

She ran for all she was worth.

This was becoming far too common. There was a single back entrance in the courtyard that led to a series of steep stairs that led to streets below. It was her only option.

"You have allies in the city!" Gabriel continued shouting at her as he threw himself at the Watchers that pursued her. Within moments he was bound and on the ground. "Look for them in the shadows!"

His advice barely registered as she flew through the back door. Several Watchers were right behind her, so close one even reached out as she went through the door. She jumped down the first flight of stairs, feeling her knees nearly buckle as she hit the ground hard. Turning, she launched herself at the second flight of stairs, just missing the Watchers that followed. A good thing none of them was a Telekinetic or this chase would have been over by now.

One of them did a fancy flip and landed in front of her. The elegance of his movements told her this one had Grace. She was going to have to fight, but without her spear and with more soldiers coming through the back door, she had no hope.

Suddenly the Watcher's eyes furrowed in confusion, and he looked all around. "Wh... where did she go?" he said.

Jak looked from him to the Watchers behind her. All of them were staring around in confusion as if they couldn't see her standing right in front of them.

Whatever was happening, she needed to take advantage of it. She pushed past the Watcher blocking her way. He yelped as the somehow unseen force caused him to topple onto the steps. Not very graceful after all.

She didn't stop running until she was far from the college, on the edge of the city near the south gate. Ducking around a corner, she took a moment to catch her breath. What had just happened? One moment the Watchers had been chasing her, and the next it was like she was invisible. How did...

Wait a moment. Jak felt her excitement rise. She knew of some people who could stay invisible. Could one of the Shadow Fae be here?

She glanced around herself, suddenly aware that a Shadow Fae might be right next to her, and she wouldn't even know it. Feeling exposed, she walked a bit further and found an isolated alley next to the city wall. She didn't see anyone around, but was it her imagination or could she feel a pair of eyes watching her?

"Is... is someone there?" She called out into the nothingness. Her eyes scanned the shadows. Had this been what Gabriel meant? Were the Shadow Fae in the city?

"You know!" A voice breathed to the left of her. "You're not a half-bad runner."

Jak's face brightened. She knew that voice! A second later, her mother materialized in front of her. Her dark skin and green eyes seemed to fill the shadows around her, but there was no mistaking that smile.

A thousand emotions suddenly welled up inside Jak, and she threw herself at her mother in the biggest hug she could muster. She felt her eyes begin to burn as tears welled up.

"Mother!"

"I missed you." Karlona returned the embrace, allowing Jak to melt in her arms. It was the best feeling Jak could imagine. For the first time since arriving in Skyecliff, she felt completely safe.

When they finally broke the embrace, Jak couldn't help but stare at her mother. "Why are you here?" she asked. "I thought you were helping Skellig rebuild Foothold?"

Karlona's lips made a line. "We were, but someone from Skyecliff was sent to depose Skellig. She was demoted and had to flee for her life."

"What?" Jak said aghast.

It couldn't be. Skellig was one of the best officers she knew, and the only reason they had been able to successfully fight Kuldain and his demon army.

Her mother nodded. "Apparently the order came from the highest level. She was to be court-martialed for betraying Kuldain."

"But Kuldain was..."

"I know, but that made no difference, it seemed. But Skellig got away. Last we heard she was heading to the Southeast Mountains to investigate some reports we've had of more Fae residing there."

That got Jak's attention. "There are more Shadow Fae in the mountains?"

Karlona shook her head. "Not Shadow Fae as far as we know. But the queen has had a steady supply of armor and weapons coming out of those mountains, and none of it comes from trade. We suspect Fae are the cause."

Jak nodded. She had seen the constant flow of wagons coming and going. And Naem had mentioned guarding some merchants, something a Watcher would rarely be called upon to do.

"What do you think they need it for?"

Karlona shrugged. "It's hard to say, but it almost seems like they're preparing for war."

"So why are you here?" she asked again.

"Well, ever since... well ever since we met you, we've increased our spy network far wider than before. As you can imagine, we make great spies."

Jak smiled, but her mother continued.

"We began to hear strange reports of demon activity in this region. Demons infest the area, yet no one sees them. Even we have trouble spotting them sometimes. But they're there, surrounding the city and the land around it."

Jak frowned. "I haven't seen a single demon since arriving here, and I've been out of the city several times. Why wouldn't they attack?"

"We don't know, but they appear to be restrained, just like the demon army at Foothold. We don't know how, or rather, who is doing it."

"Do you think they're the reason the queen is stockpiling the weapons?"

"Possibly, but we're almost certain they don't know about the demons. Whatever it is, it's big, and so I came here with several of my people to investigate." She put both hands on Jak's shoulders. "And to warn you."

"Thanks, but I think I have other problems at the moment."

"Yes, you have definitely caused a lot of trouble." Karlona grinned at Jak. "But from what I've heard about some of the goings-on in this city, I would have expected nothing less."

Jak smiled for the first time since before she lost her friends. "With your help, we can get the rest of the Water Fae out." She could save her friends.

"Ah yes, Gabriel was telling us a bit about them this morning when I first arrived." Karlona leaned against the stone wall and crossed her arms. "What can you tell me about them. Are they anything like us?"

"Well, not really." Jak scrunched up her face in thought. "They're like a cross between a man and some kind of large fish. But they do have some things in common. Their abilities are elementary, and they were transformed by a Relic."

Then she proceeded to fill her mother in, starting from the very beginning when Gabriel had taken her to see the first of the transformed students. She told her mother about how the queen had taken them, and the Relic, and how she had gone to rescue them just hours ago, only to find that the Relic had transformed several dozen more, including Amelia.

As she finished the story, she smacked her forehead. "And I just remembered I promised to meet the few we saved outside the city."

"Well, you're probably safest away from here anyway." said her mother. "Why don't you let me keep an eye on the situation here, while you go find your friends."

Jak felt her eyes moisten again. She wasn't sure why. It was stupid to cry when your mother tells you what to do. But having someone else to rely on, to work with, it was more of a relief than Jak thought possible.

"Okay, I told them I'd meet them at the head of the Trade river. If you need to find me, that's where I'll be."

Karlona nodded. "I'll send someone."

In the blink of an eye, she disappeared completely from view. Jak was glad that she hadn't transformed into a Fae, but there were sometimes she envied their gifts.

It was only then that she realized she had little or nothing to travel with. She had a few coins in her belt pouch, but nothing else to help her find food and drink. And worst of all, she didn't have her spear, having left it in her room. Hopefully, she wouldn't need it while searching for the Water Fae, but she still felt naked without it.

She walked alongside the wall until it led to the south gate. It would probably be best to find a departing carriage or merchant to walk alongside to avoid suspicion. Though she'd want to avoid anything that could be one of those merchant trains owned by the queen and guarded by Watchers. Whatever they were carrying to and from the Southeast mountains had to be important. But she couldn't worry about that now. Not yet.

She quickly found a carriage for some rich person leaving the city, probably to some nearby estate. Doing her best not to be seen, she hopped onto the back of the carriage and let it carry her outside the gate. To her great relief, the carriage continued in the right direction for at least a mile, saving Jak the walk. But eventually it turned the wrong way at a split in the road, and Jak was forced to hop off and begin her trek towards where the Trade River met the sea.

The roads were full of people, now that the sun was high in the sky. Most were merchants who were taking their wares to and from the docks at the Trade River. The river connected nearby Skyecliff with Tradehall, many miles to the west. Most merchants used the river to deliver their wares, either to the dock that lay straight ahead, or by sailing out to the ocean, following the coast north, and eventually arriving at Skyecliff directly.

But Jak wasn't heading to the docks, she had told the Water Fae to meet her where the river met the sea. Hopefully, they were still there.

It wasn't until she had walked a mile or two that she realized just how tired she was. So far, she hadn't slept a wink the night before, and the whole ordeal in the castle, not to mention the steep climb up and down the secret stairs, had exhausted her. Perhaps she could find a place to lie down and rest once she arrived at the river's outlet. It was only a few more miles away, right?

However far away it was, it felt so much farther. The hours dragged on, and soon it was all she could do to put one foot in front of the other. She was off the main road now, heading away from the docks towards the outlet. Only a faint trail marked the way, as most people didn't come this way on foot.

But was that the ocean ahead of her? Yes, it was! With immense relief and a small burst of newfound energy, she rushed towards the coast. She could hear the waves crashing into the beach. They only made her more tired. Cresting a hill, she marveled at how beautiful the river was as it emptied into the sea. It covered a much larger area than she expected, fanning out in every direction. Perhaps she should have been more specific when choosing a place to meet up.

Other than one or two ships in the distance, she couldn't see anyone nearby. So she took a moment to walk along the coast.

"Cerai!" she called out. "Haffi, Nigem! Anyone there?"

When she heard no response, she felt her exhaustion even more. Perhaps they hadn't arrived yet? There was a nice bed of sand over near a nearby tree that looked wonderful. She could always get a little rest and check back later. And maybe the Fae would see her and call to her. It sounded like a reasonable idea.

Turning back, she curled up in the shade of the tree, the roots of which made a small overhang that would keep her hidden from the road, but visible from the sea. It was the perfect spot. Lying down, she was asleep in seconds.

After what seemed like barely a moment, her eyes opened. She could hear approaching hooves. Scrambling to her feet, she reached for her spear before realizing it wasn't there. Cursing, she hid in the slight overhang of the tree's roots.

Voices joined the sound of hooves. Was it just a passing sight-seer, or was it something more serious? Surely the Watchers had people looking for her everywhere, but would they think to come this far out?

"--always was suspicious of her. Even her father kept a tight leash on her growing up, hardly let her do anything."

Jak almost groaned aloud. That voice was Estel's. Somehow the girl had followed her or guessed where she was going.

Peeking over the top of her nook, she saw Estel and a handful of other Watchers rise to the top of the hill. Relics, how was she going to get out of this one? She was hidden for now but couldn't move in any direction without exposing herself to their line of sight.

For now, she remained frozen, not daring to breathe. She must have slept for an hour or so because the sun was lowering behind Estel and the Watchers. Hopefully, the dim light would work to her advantage.

"I used to feel bad for her, living the sheltered life that her father imposed on her, but I eventually learned that she was just as bad. Always had her nose in that journal of hers, thinking she was so much better than the rest of us."

Jak shrugged off Estel's comments. The girl's attitude towards Jak was nothing new.

The sound of the horses grew louder, then muffled as they stepped into the sand. Jak held her breath.

Estel's snide comments continued but stayed on the opposite side of her tree, moving from one side to the other. Did she dare hope they would pass by on the other side?

Estel stopped talking for once, and Jak resisted the temptation to look up and see what they were doing.

Then Estel continued her voice further away now. "Keep an eye out on the oceans too. We might find those water demons while we're out here."

Jak breathed a sigh of relief. They were moving away from her now. The light was dimming, perhaps if she could just sneak in the opposite direction...

"Pst, Jak!" Jak's heart nearly leaped out of her chest as she spun to face whoever had spoken.

Lying on the beach, not twenty paces away, was Cerai. She was perched on her stomach just beyond the waves, looking like she had pulled herself there with her arms. Her large fin flopped around behind her. Jak ran to her.

"Cerai!" she said in a hoarse whisper as she approached. "They could have seen you."

"They're obviously not looking very hard," Cerai replied. "They didn't see either of us."

Suddenly water flowed around Cerai from the beach, but instead of falling back as it usually would, it gathered around Cerai and pulled her up so that she sat in a column of water.

"Woah!" Jak said, her mouth hanging open.

"We discovered recently that we have some control over the water around us," Cerai said, looking down to see the water supporting her.

"That sounds useful," Jak said. "You might be able to use that the next time someone tries to take you away. Hopefully, you won't have to."

"Indeed." Cerai shivered.

"Where are the others?" Jak asked.

"They're just offshore. We tried waving to you before, but you didn't see us."

"I'm sorry, but you're looking much better." And it was true. Cerai's face no longer looked wrinkled and pale. Color had returned to her cheeks, and she almost looked like she had gained weight, even though she had only left the palace a day earlier.

"The water does some good. I feel better than ever! Even in salt water. We weren't sure how the salt would affect us."

Jak smiled. "I'm glad you're feeling better."

"Us too. So what is the plan now?"

Jak felt her face fall. "I honestly don't know. There are Shadow Fae in the city now, meaning we have more allies than before, but at this point, I would suggest you get as far away from the city as you can."

Cerai shook her head but looked curiously at Jak. "Shadow Fae are here? I would love to meet some of them. But we can't leave now. Not when others of our kind are still at the Palace."

Jak frowned. "Your kind? They were just mutated by the Relic like you. Did you even know them?"

"No, but I think you don't quite understand what it's like to be one of us." Cerai searched for the right words. "We're...whole. Yes, at first it was a shock to see our legs go and to turn into something completely foreign. We thought we were turning into demons."

Jak nodded. "That's what most other people seem to think too."

"Yes, but it's not like that. It's almost as if we were meant to become these...Water Fae." She wrinkled her nose. "We're going to have to come up with a better name than that."

Jak felt a smile grow on her face. "That's what my...what the Shadow Fae say as well. But the problem I see is that people don't seem to have a choice. They mutate into a Fae, or they don't, with no say in the matter."

"And I understand how that will be difficult for some to acknowledge. But since we've been Water Fae the longest, we can tell you that we don't feel like it was random."

"What do you mean?"

"I mean that we think we were meant to turn and that others are too. We feel like there's something big coming. I can't explain how it's almost instinct. But whatever it is, we're sure we have a part to play in the years ahead. Maybe even months."

Jak nodded. She wanted to believe that, but she still found it difficult to believe that the Relic was anything but a danger to her friends. Perhaps Cerai was right though. At that moment she wished more than ever that Amelia was there. She always had a knack for looking at the bright side. She could use more of that now.

"So if you're not leaving, then what will you do?"

Cerai met Jak's eyes. "There isn't much we can do in our current circumstances." She glanced down at her tail. "I... I hate to ask this of you, Jak. But you're our only hope to get our brothers and sisters out."

There it was again. If the situation hadn't been so serious, Jak would have rolled her eyes. She wasn't a hero, so why did everyone expect her to be? She could barely take care of herself, the Watchers were looking for her, everyone at the college hated her, and she had lost most of her allies. Once again, she found herself thinking about Naem. What had become of him? Had he been arrested like Gabriel? Wherever he was, she was alone now. What gave anyone the impression that she could solve all of that *and* rescue dozens of people from the most highly-guarded building in the city?

"I don't know, Cerai. I'm not..."

She broke off as they heard voices. Turning, Jak cursed herself for being careless. Estel and her small band of Watchers were returning the way they came.

"I could have sworn I heard something over here," Estel said.

They were staring straight in Jak's direction. Why didn't they see her? She was standing right in their line of sight! The light wasn't that dim. She glanced at Cerai, who looked equally confused.

"I don't see anything." Said one of the other Watchers. Jak recognized him. He had been there when they whipped Seph, and he hadn't seemed too pleased at the time. Now he just looked annoyed. "You can't hide on this beach."

"I'm telling you, I heard voices." Estel insisted.

Suddenly, it dawned on Jak what must be happening. Instinctively, she scanned the area around them. But of course, that was foolish. If Estel and the Watchers couldn't see them, there was no way...

"Ow!" Estel yelled. "Who did that?"

She clutched the side of her head, where a large lump of what looked like wet sand stuck to the side of her face. If Jak hadn't been doing her best not to utter a sound, she would have laughed.

"No one, sir. We only..."

But the Watcher cut off as Estel yelled. Another lump of wet sand hit her in the chest. And another hit one of the other Watchers. Their horses began to look skittish, and one Watcher had to hold on as his mount lifted itself on its hind legs.

Estel had gone silent, looking this way and that. "Fan out!" she ordered. "Find whoever's doing this."

"I... I can't really see anything." Said another Watcher. He was clinging to his horse for dear life.

"Me too!" said one of the soldiers next to Estel. "Did the sun go down already?"

Estel was looking paler. "Follow me!" She said and heeled her horse forward, taking the path that led away from Jak's position and back towards the city. The other Watchers must have been able to see their commander well enough, as they reigned in their horses to follow.

When they were safely away, Cerai whispered. "What just happened? I thought we were caught for sure."

Jak was feeling much better. Now she understood why Estel hadn't seen them earlier. "You can come out now," she said to the open air. "Or are you going to leave us as confused as those Watchers?"

The air shimmered off to one side, and Jak turned to see a dark figure emerge from the shadows. In the dim light, she vaguely recognized the Fae's stance. "Vander?"

"Hello, Jak." It *was* Vander. Jak ran forward to embrace him. Vander had been the first Shadow Fae she had met, though he hadn't said much at the time. He returned the embrace with a warmth that nearly matched that of her mother.

"Vander, this is Cerai, she's a Water Fae. Or at least, that's what we're calling them now."

Vander inclined his head. "It's an honor. I've only met one other race of Fae before today."

"The honor is mine." Cerai stared at Vander with a mixture of awe and apprehension. "The others will want to meet you."

She whistled, and Jak turned to the ocean. The other two Water Fae, Haffi, and Nigem, could be seen in the distance, which they closed with surprising speed. *Those giant tails must be pretty powerful in the water.*

The two Fae rose out of the water in the same way as Cerai, the water holding them in place, and Vander introduced himself to them too. Done with the formalities, Vander turned to Jak.

"There are many patrols like that. You're lucky one didn't find you before I did."

"I assume m... Karlona sent you?" Jak asked.

Vander nodded. "We're holed up not far from the city. It will be safer for you there."

Jak turned to Cerai and the others. "Will you be okay on your own?"

All three of them nodded. "Of course. They can't catch us in the ocean." Cerai said. She was looking expectantly at Jak. "About what I said."

"I know." Jak sighed. "I'll do my best to get your...people out."

And with that, they parted ways. Jak accompanied Vander, while the Water Fae swam out to sea.

CHAPTER 19

WHEN SHE FINALLY ARRIVED at the Shadow Fae's encampment, she was too tired to marvel at how it seemed to simply appear in front of her eyes. The Shadow Fae kept it hidden with their magic until Vander took her inside their protective bubble.

But before she could greet anyone there, or even ask if her mother was around, she asked Vander for a spare tent, and within moments she was sleeping soundly. If her mind was full of disturbing dreams, Jak didn't know it. She was far past that level of exhaustion. Sleep simply pushed all worries aside and gave her a much needed break from her troubles.

Though there was something that bothered her. A voice that kept calling her name. She could see it as some dark void beyond her peripheral vision. "Jak... Jak," it called to her, and in more than a name. She wanted to go to it, there was power there. "Jak... Jak..."

"Jak!" The voice suddenly became one familiar to her. It wasn't a void, it wasn't power, it was her friend. Naem had one arm on her, rustling to wake her.

Startled and disoriented, she flailed about until she realized where she was. Naem nearly fell backward at her sudden reaction. "Woah there, it's me."

"I... where am I? I'm with the Shadow Fae. Naem? How are you here?" Questions popped up in her mind faster than she could answer them. How long had she been asleep?

"Your mother found me. I was looking for you."

Jak snorted. "You and every other Watcher in town. Where did they assign you to look for me? Or did they suspect you too?"

Naem shrugged. "Wilva didn't give me a search assignment. Asked me to keep guard on the camp. I guess she suspected something, even though there was no proof I was there, helping you get the Water Fae out. But that's not why I came looking for you."

"Why didn't you come for me? You could have stopped them from taking Gabriel."

"I... what? Of course, I couldn't."

"Yeah, but you could have done something. Not just waiting at your camp to see what happens."

"That's not what I did."

"Well then, what did you do?"

"That's what I'm trying to tell you!"

Jak bit her lip. She was still tired, disoriented. Of course, Naem couldn't have done anything to save Gabriel, not the way Wilva and the Royal Priest had shown up with a small army. Besides, defying his general would have only created more problems for Naem, and for her.

Jak calmed herself, waiting for Naem to say what had come here to say, but he said nothing, seemingly daydreaming about something. She spread her hands out as if to say. "Why then?" which seemed to jolt him out of his thoughts.

"Oh, right. Um...I think you'd better come to see this for yourself."

Naem rose and exited the small tent. Okay, so apparently that meant she was supposed to follow. She rose, feeling her muscles protest. Wow, how long *had* she been lying on that hard ground? It must have been hours. It hadn't felt like more than a few minutes. Yet her mind felt far more alert than before, so that was something.

Testing her sore feet gingerly, she pulled open the flap and exited the tent. Once outside, she froze.

Dozens of people, men, and woman stood staring back at her. Naem stood to one side, one hand holding his spear, staring at the crowd, then back at Jak again. Several Shadow Fae also stood surrounding the people, not in a threatening way, but keeping an eye out.

Jak was suddenly aware of how matted and wild her hair was. She casually did her best to smooth it back, tucking the long red streak behind one ear. Who were all these people?

One woman stepped forward, and Jak realized suddenly that she knew the person. She had been the one to help Seph right after the Watchers had whipped him. Come to think of it, she recognized several others from that day too. These were members of Seph's congregation!

The thought hit her just as the woman opened her mouth to speak. "Hello, Jak. My name is Elva." She brought her hand to her chest in greeting.

Jak marked the Sleeplessness brand there. Still in a bit of shock, she returned the greeting.

"We've been looking for you." Elva continued.

"Why?" Jak asked. Though she dreaded the answer, she thought was coming.

"Seph instructed us that if we ever lost him, that we were to seek you out, and follow you."

Jak closed her eyes. Not this. She didn't need this on top of everything else. "Why me?"

"He didn't say."

Jak let out a breath. Well, that was something at least. Seph hadn't told them that she was the prophesied Oren spoken about in his book. But still, now these people looked to her for help. How was she to know if she could provide it?

"But..." Elva went on. "We have suspicions..."

"I don't know what to tell you." She said to the audience at large. "Seph and I were friends, but I'm no preacher. I don't know the Book of Illadar like he does, or like many of you do."

"You're not the One?" Elva looked into Jak's eyes, and she saw hope there. Desperate hope. The dangerous kind.

"Why do you ask?" Jak said. This was not a question she wanted to answer. But with every eye on her, she had to say something.

"Because of the position you hold. You are friends with Fae, you have Seph's trust, but most of all, you have the Gift to give multiple brands."

Jak froze. "Why would you think that?" No one knew about her ability, no one except Amelia and Naem.

She looked at Naem, and everyone's eyes followed. He responded by tossing his spear at Jak. She caught it gingerly. It was only then that she realized it wasn't Naem's spear. It was hers. The two brands of Toughness and Healing stood out plainly in the morning light.

"I managed to smuggle it away from the Watchers after they raided the college," he said.

"That spear is yours, correct?" said Elva.

Jak sighed. "Yes, it's mine."

"And you branded it?"

Jak let her head bow. There was nothing she could say now that would convince them that she wasn't their hero. "Yes, I branded it."

A chorus of excited murmurs ran through the crowd. Even some of the Shadow Fae seemed taken aback.

"Well then, that is why Seph wanted you to be our leader. You can brand us, make us into warriors like nothing this Earth has seen. We can lead the Fae, and everyone who will listen to a new and better home."

"Now wait a minute." Jak felt her frustration boil. "I'm not the hero you're looking for. I don't even know if I can brand people like that. I might kill you, or worse, turn you into a demon."

"Jak." It was Naem, and he looked troubled. His arms hung at his sides, and he looked like he was having a hard time deciding. "Before you turn them away. There's something you should know."

A few of the others dropped their heads as well.

"What?" Jak asked, fearing the worst. "What is it?"

Elva and Naem exchanged glances before Naem continued. "Your friends, Seph, Gabriel, Amelia, and several of the other Water Fae. They're all scheduled to be executed tomorrow."

"No." It was all Jak could say.

They couldn't execute her friends. Not after everything. But that was foolish, of course, they could. The Royal Priest would love nothing better than to make a public example of the Fae and their supporters. Besides, there was likely another reason they picked now to have an execution.

"They're setting a trap for me."

Naem nodded. "Probably. But Elva is right, Jak. They may be setting a trap, but they don't know what to expect. They don't know about the Shadow Fae here in the city. They don't know about what you can do." He rolled up his sleeve. Jak eyes widened as she realized what he was about to do.

Almost triumphantly, Naem raised an arm high into the air. Gasps erupted from all around them as everyone saw the marks on his left arm. There were three brands there. Grace, Toughness, and Healing.

"You gave me these gifts," Naem said. "You can do it again."

Jak closed her eyes. This was all out of hand. Silence settled in as everyone waited to see what she would say.

Jak didn't want this. She didn't want to be a hero. But her friends were in danger, and that took precedence right now.

Whether she was a hero or not, she would get them out if it killed her.

"Okay," she said, finally. She held out a hand to cut off the excited murmuring. "But I'm not branding anyone. I've never tested it on a human, and I don't know if I can replicate what I did to Naem. I was... kind of unaware of what I was doing when I gave those to him."

There were a few slumped shoulders and disappointed frowns, but Elva nodded her head as if she understood.

"So, Jak." Elva took a step forward and put her hands on her hips. "What do you want us to do?"

CHAPTER 20

T HEY SPENT THE NEXT day immersed in planning. Karlona returned, and Jak filled her in as fast as she could. Just like Jak hoped, her mother agreed to lend a hand, and the hand of the Shadow Fae. Of the three forms of Fae, Jak had encountered, the Shadow Fae was by far the best warriors, with their ability to move around unseen. They would be invaluable.

The first step was to assemble some weapons. Karlona immediately sent some of her spies to fetch some, though they already had a small stockpile that they had pulled from the caravans from the south-east mountains. When Jak examined them, she was surprised to see the quality of the craftsmanship. They were some of the best spears, swords, and armor plating that she had ever seen, though she admittedly didn't have a trained eye for that sort of thing.

Regardless, she set to work branding what came in. She had refused to brand people, but the least she could do was to brand the weapons with multiple brands, giving them that much of an advantage.

She got through a dozen or so weapons and several suits of armor before fatigue set in. That much branding could drain a Gifter of energy. It would have to do.

Next, she gathered Karlona, Vander, Elva, and Naem to discuss their next steps. It was already late in the night, which meant they had approximately twenty-four hours before the execution.

"What kind of execution is it?" she asked Naem once they were all gathered. She had seen more than one form of execution since she had arrived.

"Burning at stake," Naem said.

Made sense. That kind of execution was reserved for heretics and rogue Gifters. The Royal Priest would clearly classify it that way.

"Okay, well those typically get a lot of attention, and we can expect it to happen at sundown like most executions. We need to act quickly if we want to be prepared by this time tomorrow."

Everyone nodded at that, but they all continued to stare at her as if waiting for Jak to continue. Jak couldn't help but feel a bit foolish, standing there talking like she was in charge. And it was probably foolish of them to listen. But even her mother waited on her next words.

"Okay then." She went on after a short silence. "Here's what I was thinking, and please speak up if you think of something better."

Everyone nodded, so she began.

"Our worst threat is the Watchers," Jak said. "We need to distract them or find a way to get rid of most of them before any rescue begins. Naem and I can infiltrate their camp and perhaps set their command building and barracks on fire. That should distract them for a while."

Naem nodded, one hand to his chin. "That should work."

"Our second threat is the Royal Priest. He will most likely be at the execution. Now, while I don't have definitive proof, I'm more than certain that he is a demon like Kuldain."

Karlona nodded. "That would make sense. Demons are hiding around the city, but they remain immobilized. We suspected a demon like Kuldain was hiding in the city, controlling them."

That brought up another problem. "We'd have to keep him from sending the demons into the city," Jak said.

"And we couldn't kill him, as that would likely have the same effect."

"Then we stall him, keep him occupied. But if he lets the demons loose, we'll have to be prepared for that. How many are there?" she asked her mother.

Karlona shrugged. "It's hard to say. Less than at Foothold, but at least a thousand. Maybe more.

"Okay, well with these weapons, and your Shadow Fae, that shouldn't be a huge problem. Besides, the city has its own defenses that are much stronger than at Foothold. Better they fight demons then us."

Jak turned to Elva and continued. "Your people will be responsible for getting Seph and the others out. We'll need plenty of people to help carry the Water Fae. Once Naem and I return from distracting the Watchers, I'll lead you into the town square, and we'll extract everyone from the pires." She turned to her mother. "The Shadow Fae will need to keep enemy soldiers from interfering, clearing a path for us. But try not to kill anybody," she added with a grimace. She didn't like even the idea of attacking good people.

Karlona nodded. "We'll do what we must."

They spent the rest of the hour hammering out the details before it was time to rest for the night. Everyone, they agreed, needed plenty of rest, especially Jak.

Not like she was going to be able to sleep on a night like this. It felt odd like when they were preparing for the demon attack in Foothold. She hadn't slept much then, and of course, she wouldn't be able to sleep now. If only there were some kind of sleep Relic. Oh well.

Nearing the tent, she heard someone call to her from behind.

"Hey, Jak!" It was Naem.

A smile formed on Jak's lips. "Yes? Did I miss something?"

"No, I just wanted to talk to you in private for a bit. Do you have a minute?"

"Oh, yeah sure." When Naem didn't immediately say anything, she broke the awkward silence. "Thanks for what you said earlier. I mean, I don't think it was very wise showing off your brands like that, but—"

"Oh, ah, those people eat that sort of thing up. If I'm not mistaken, they're some of the few who don't view the Fae, and your powers, as heretical. That's why I thought you should keep them close. They could help you."

"They do seem to follow my lead without question."

"Your friend Seph really rounded up the perfect followers for you, even if he didn't know it at the time."

The mention of Seph brought a tension with it. Was he still angry about that? She didn't think of Seph that way, or at least she didn't think she did. Though he could be very charismatic at times, could really pull you in.

"Look," Naem glanced at the ground, and there was something like worry in his eyes. No, resolve maybe? "Your plan is great, but if something goes wrong. I just wanted to talk about, you know, about what we had."

So, he did want to talk about that. To her surprise, Jak found she didn't mind as much as before. She had found other things to preoccupy her mind. That almost made her feel guilty. After all, her friend Marek had died, and she'd all but forgotten about him with everything that happened to her in Skyecliff. But Naem had been there the whole time, never questioning her. Well, except once, but never after she made her feelings clear.

When she didn't speak, Naem went on in a rushed tone. "I mean, I know you lost your friend, and that's...I should never have expected anything when... I mean you were dealing with a lot and... I know you just didn't want me to get hurt because you've lost a lot, and you were right, you know, your friends that we lost in the palace. People can get hurt, and I guess I'm just trying to say I'm sorry if... if more people get hurt and..."

"It's okay," she interrupted.

Then leaning forward, she grabbed the back of his neck and kissed him hard. After a moment of shock, he leaned into the kiss, returning her affection with his own hungry, forceful lips.

When they broke, Jak was glad it was dark, so no one could see the color in her cheeks. "When all this is over. We can talk I think," she said with a smile. "Right now, I hope you'll understand. It's... it's all a bit much right now."

"Of course, I get it," he said. "We'll get through this. I know it."

"You're not just saying that?"

"No, I mean it. And I meant what I said earlier. You may not know it yet, but you're a hero, and I'm sure you can handle whatever they throw at you, even if things don't go according to plan. You'll make it work because that's what you do."

Her face reddened further. "I'm sure you say that to every girl you've kissed."

He tilted her chin and kissed her again. "The other girls I've kissed never gave me extra brands."

She pushed him away playfully. "So, you're saying you're only interested in me for my abilities."

"What? No. I'm just saying you're special. I know that, and soon everyone in Skyecliff will know it too."

Jak took a deep breath and let it out slowly. "I hope you're right."

He winked at her. "Of course, I am! But anyway, I'll let you get to sleep. We have a long day ahead of us tomorrow.

He kissed her one final time, and she found herself not ready to let him go, but he left anyway. Retreating to her tent, she readied herself for bed.

She didn't even have the presence of mind to be surprised when sleep came more easily than expected.

In the morning, she arose early and started to make preparations for the battle ahead. That mostly meant branding more weapons, which they distributed to Seph's followers and a few to the Shadow Fae. The effort of branding so many items left her more tired than she would have liked, but after a large meal, she felt ready to get back on her feet.

That didn't stop the worries from running through her mind, though. If anything, her conversation with Naem the night before only increased her concern. She didn't want to lose him too. They hadn't spoken yet today, but she'd seen him giving general fighting advice to Seph's followers, in case they needed it. He'd winked at her then and continued his instructions.

After branding a few sets of armor, she rose to take a small break and found herself looking over the hill at the city that lay just ahead. She stood there for a long while.

There were a lot of people in there, innocent as well as guilty. Queens and priests, but also merchants, beggars, and fishermen. How would this affect all of them?

"It's a new feeling isn't it, holding the fate of others in your hand." It was her mother, stepping silently alongside Jak.

Jak didn't have a reply at first, allowing silence to close in on them as they watched the sun pear through the giant pillars of the city.

"I don't know if I can bear it," she said finally. "Everyone is counting on me. And I... I'm not..."

Her eyes burned. She would not cry in front of her mother and who-knows-what-else might be listening. She would not! A hand on her shoulder soothed everything, and the tears disappeared. Her mother wrapped both arms around her. For a moment Jak worried that others might see and guess that she had some relation to Karlona. But honestly, she didn't care about that at this point. She hugged her mother back.

"The burden is not yours alone to bear," Karlona said. "Let us take some of it from you. That is why we are all here."

"But Elva and Seph's people. They came to me."

"They didn't come just so you could help them. They came to help you too."

Jak swallowed. "I don't want to get anyone else killed or ...or turned into..." she broke off, realizing too late who she was talking to.

"Turned into a Fae, you mean?" Her mother broke the hug.

"That's not what I meant."

"It's okay, we didn't ask for this either. But it's something most of us grew to embrace eventually."

"That's what Cerai said."

"Who?"

"Oh, Cerai. She was one of the first Water Fae I met. We lost my friends in the palace trying to rescue her."

"And you're worried you'll lose more friends trying to rescue these friends?"

Jak nodded, feeling her face growing hot with...was it anger, or shame?

"Jak," her mother grabbed her shoulders and turned her so that they were facing. "This may be hard for you to hear, but if anyone dies, it's not your fault. We're choosing to follow you and your plans. No one is forced to do so."

Jak frowned, "I know, but—"

"No buts, Jak." Her mother cut her off. "If we die, we choose to die."

"But I don't want anyone to die."

"Well, we live in a world of tough choices. But between you and me, I think we may have this one covered." She nudged Jak in the arm. "I'm very proud of you. Your plan, it's not bad. And we Fae have a knack for survival. I think everything will be fine."

Inexplicably, Jak found herself feeling much better. Perhaps it was her mother's approval.

Taking a deep breath, she turned away from the city, towards the small army of men, women, and Fae beginning to gather around them. Karlona was right. They weren't forcing any of these people to fight for her. They were doing it because they believed in something. Whether that was her, or Seph, or something else, she did not know.

But whatever it was, they were going to make something out of it.

CHAPTER 21

THAT AFTERNOON, EVERYONE GATHERED together. The sun was setting, and it was time to enter the city. Jak ran through everyone's roles one last time, explaining it as plainly as she could for the group. A few asked questions, but most held their peace, only nodding when their role was mentioned. But as Jak finished explaining the details, she noticed everyone still waited, as if expecting more from her.

Oh dear, were they expecting a speech or something? She hadn't thought of that. What could she say?

"Um… I just want to thank all of you for being here. I know I'm not Seph, and you're choosing to follow me based only on what he's said. But you're doing the right thing. Seph, Gabriel, the Water Fae, these are good people, and they don't deserve the false accusations that the Priest has levied against them. Perhaps, someday, others will come around to your way of thinking, but for now, you will lead the charge in their liberation!"

She felt her voice growing stronger as she spoke. A quick glance at Naem, who was standing next to Karlona, told her they were both approving of her words.

"I know many of you are worried. You're worried that you might not make it through the night. And it's possible that some of us may not. But I will do everything I can to see you all through this. I don't know if I'm this Oren that Seph speaks of and is mentioned in your Book of Illadar. I don't know that. But I do know this: if no one else will do what is necessary to save innocent lives, then I will. And each of you is a force for good in your own right. I'm proud to fight beside you."

Jak felt a rush of exultation as she finally said out loud what she had been thinking for the past few days. Maybe she wasn't their hero, but she could be *a* hero. Everyone else seemed to feel the same motivating feelings she had, for they cheered and began to clap. Even some of the Shadow Fae seemed impressed.

Jak grabbed her spear from where it lay nearby and held it high in the air. That seemed the appropriate thing to do.

"Let's go!" she yelled and began her march away from the camp and down the hill.

Everyone followed close behind.

They paused when they were closer to the city wall. Everyone would wait while Jak and Naem went on ahead to sabotage the Watcher camp. Then the smoke from that fire would act as the signal for Seph's followers to enter the city from the west gate. The Shadow Fae, with their ability to blend in, would enter the city first and get into position. That way they could cause chaos among the soldiers while Elva and the others came in to take Seph and the other prisoners away.

Jak went with Naem, and the two of them followed a merchant wagon inside, doing their best not to be seen. Surely the guards knew about Jak by now and would be looking for her. Thankfully, they managed to slip away as the guards were busy inspecting the wagon. Jak paused just long enough to see what they were inspecting. It was a bunch of armor, and she wondered if that wagon had come from the southeast mountains like her mother had mentioned.

From there, the trip to the Watcher camp remained uneventful. They passed a few soldiers, but none of them looked twice at Jak when they saw her accompanying a Watcher. Though she did pull her hood up over her head to be sure.

Naem was unusually silent as they walked. He seemed lost in thought. Could it have been the kiss they had shared the night before? Neither had talked about that since, and it must be weighing on his mind as much as it was hers. But they couldn't let that compromise the mission right now. Afterward, they could talk. Jak found herself looking forward to it.

Up ahead, she could see two Watchers guarding the gate. Here was the first tricky part. These men would certainly not let her in without verifying her identity.

"Hey there, Lial, Jerum." Naem strode forward and waved one arm at the two. He took one peek inside the camp. "Not many around today."

"There's some kind of high-profile execution today." One of them said, Lial. "The General wanted as many of us in the main square as a backup."

Jak winced. They had expected that, of course. Naem seemed to think that they'd all come running the moment they saw smoke. Hopefully, that was true. Though on the bright side, fewer Watchers inside the camp would make it easier to sneak around.

"Who is your friend?" Lial asked, noticing Jak for the first time. "Hey, isn't she..."

He had no time to finish his sentence. In the blink of an eye, Naem lashed out at both of them, catching each of them hard on the head with one end of his spear. They both fell before either had a chance to react. Even Jak had not had time to blink. She wished she was that fast. Grace had to be one of the most underrated brands. It easily stood at the top of the most powerful brands, right up there with Telekinesis and Flamedancing.

"Come on," Naem waved at her.

Caught in her thoughts, she shook them away and helped Naem carry the limp bodies of the two Watchers just inside the gate. Someone would eventually notice no one was guarding the gates. But that was less suspicious than seeing two bodies lying there.

"Keep your hood up and act natural," Naem said as they walked further in. "Just pretend you belong with me, and everything will be fine."

Jak nodded, falling into step behind Naem, keeping her hood up but holding herself with confidence, like she had every right to be there as the other Watchers.

As they had guessed earlier, there weren't too many Watchers in the camp. Most were on guard duty or preparing to leave. The training grounds were empty.

Crossing the training grounds, they passed the command building and eventually arrived at the barracks. This would be their first target, and then hopefully they'd have time to set the Command building on fire on their way out.

"Okay," Jak whispered as they approached the first barracks. "You stand watch while I brand the wooden supports."

"Oh, I'm afraid he won't be able to do that," a voice from inside the barracks said.

Suddenly, dozens of Watchers exited the barracks, forming a circle around them. What was going on? She whirled around, trying to find an opening. Somewhere to escape and regroup. How did they...?

The Royal Priest exited the barracks last, accompanied by General Wilva. Somehow, they had known about their arrival.

"Jak," the Royal Priest said with a sad smile on his lips. "I really did hope for more from you."

Jak said nothing, only pressed her lips together in defiance. "We will not be intimidated."

"Child, we intimidated that one month ago." He pointed a finger at Naem. "And as far as you are concerned, well we have other plans."

"What do you..." A cold realization hit her. They had intimidated Naem months ago? Almost afraid of what she might see, she turned to look at Naem. "Naem, what is he talking about."

He didn't meet her gaze. "I'm sorry Jak. They knew about my brands, they said they would turn me into a demon and let me loose in the city starting at the college."

"You, you knew about this!" She couldn't believe what she was hearing. "You told them we were coming."

It all began to fall into place, his "scouting" from the night before, his unusual silence on the way here. The fact that he had been moody and demanding for months now. It was because the Royal Priest had him on a string.

He looked at her now, his gaze intense. "All those things I said at the camp, I meant every word. I thought leading you into a trap would ultimately backfire on them, because... well you have abilities I haven't seen, and a destiny far beyond these events today and now."

Jak's mouth hung open. She had kissed him, actually *kissed* him! "I trusted you."

"Seize them," Wilva said from beside the Royal Priest.

Wilva's face was unreadable, a complete mask of duty. Watchers grabbed her from behind, and she saw them doing the same to Naem. Her spear fell to the ground.

"You can save us!" Naem yelled as they bound his hands.

"And get that one out of here. We'll deal with him eventually," said the Royal Priest.

"Jak! I believe in you. You can get out of this, just believe in yourself!" Naem's voice grew fainter as four Watchers dragged him away.

General Wilva and the Royal Priest turned to regard her.

"Now, to deal with you." The Priest's face split into a toothy grin.

Anger suddenly boiled up inside Jak. Anger like she had never felt before. This man had taken her friends and now had manipulated Naem too. He was going to pay. He deserved to die.

Without thinking, she branded a piece of plate armor that rested on the arm of the Watcher that held her. The faulty Flamedancer brand instantly caused the metal to melt. The Watcher cried out in pain as the hot metal burned his flesh.

But Jak had already turned her attention elsewhere. Ignoring Wilva, ignoring all the Watchers, she dove for the Royal Priest. Taking a step back, he reached out one hand in defense of himself. The hand caught her own as it came flying down, ready to brand him and set him aflame! Feeling a fire in her own eyes, she summoned her magic!

And nothing came.

She gasped, feeling something go out of her. She felt, suddenly very cold and...empty. Only then did she finally see the Royal Priest's brand, the one that he kept hidden, but now plainly showed on the hand that held her.

It was a Void brand. The brand to negate other forms of magic. That must be what had stopped her from using her magic.

"Your friend was a fool." The Royal Priest whispered in her ear. His grip was like a vice. "You know it took almost no effort at all to convince him to work for us. I suppose he held onto some notion that you could handle yourself even without his help. But he was wrong, of course. You're nothing special."

Jak heard a grating sound behind her and turned her head to see two Watchers pulling a small cage perched on top of a board with wheels. Like something you might see a small, but dangerous, animal in. One of the Watchers opened the door, and that was when Jak noticed the brand on the metal of the cage. It was another Void brand. It was a cage for people with powers.

"You, you can't do this. Don't you realize that the people you're going to kill today are good people? They won't hurt anyone."

"Throw too much weight on the boat, and eventually it will sink. We humans, have our best hope of survival if we stick together. Your Fae, as you call them, they're too much baggage. They spark controversy, they divide the people in a way that will be our downfall."

"You provoke them!" Jak struggled against his grip, but two Watchers came up on either side to restrain her. And the Priest's hand would not budge. Slowly, the Watchers began removing her armor and picked up her fallen spear on the ground.

He smiled at her response. "Well, it seems we've both made our beds. But as you can see, more people agree with me." He waved his free hand around him to indicate Wilva and the Watchers and likely implying the queen herself.

"Only because you brainwash them with that Relic of yours."

"Yes, I admit that one was a treasured find. But here's the thing, though. You see, I don't need that Relic except to reinforce beliefs that were already there. It's troublemakers like you and that foreign boy that make the Relic necessary. And that is why you will be made an example of."

She couldn't let this happen. She couldn't let them ruin the plan and likely kill everyone involved. "Please don't kill my friends." Jak's eyes were stinging out of desperation. "Take me if you have to, but not them. They haven't done anything."

"Nobility. Not unexpected. We will, of course, make an example of you. But you're fooling yourself if you think you are the only problem. I hope this will be a lesson to everyone that heresy and false magic will not be tolerated."

"You underestimate the goodness of ordinary people." Jak hissed. "And you underestimate me."

The Royal Priest shoved her backward, keeping his vice-like grip on her arm. "Not at all, child. In fact, it's the very fact that I don't underestimate you that prompts me to do this."

In one smooth motion, he grabbed a knife from his belt and plunged it into her side, just below the rib cage. Jak gasped, seemingly unable to draw breath for a moment as the searing pain stabbed into her. Looking down, she saw a dark stain begin to spread from where the knife's hilt lay embedded in her side. The world began to spin.

The Royal Priest leaned in close. "I will ensure you die tonight. I'd prefer it to be public, but I'm not taking chances on some fool trying to rescue you. It wouldn't be the first time you've slipped from my grasp. So, I'm taking precautions to ensure you die, even if you escape."

With that, he threw her into the cage and locked the entrance. Released from his grip, she tried, desperately to use her magic. But nothing came.

"You four, bring her along with us," said Wilva, pointing to four of the Watchers. "The rest of you come with me to round up the rest of the dissidents outside the city."

Jak groaned as she lay curled up in the cage, holding her side. Naem had told them about Seph's followers, and now they too were about to be ambushed and taken away, possibly killed.

As the four Watchers began rolling the cage forward, causing a jolt of pain in her side with every bump, Jak held onto one thing. Her one last desperate hope.

No one had mentioned the Shadow Fae yet.

CHAPTER 22

"**M**Y MY, YOU HAVE found yourself in a pickle haven't you, Jak."

She raised her head. Everything swam in her vision as blood continued to seep out of her side. For a moment, she didn't see anything, but then a face appeared. It belonged to a man, who almost seemed to be in the same cage with her. But that was impossible, it wasn't large enough.

"To think, a little girl like you could cause such trouble."

She blinked. Didn't she know this man? He had golden-blonde hair and solid muscles, the kind most middle-aged women would fawn over. He had on a loose-fitting tunic that exposed his chest hair. And he had a sick grin on his face.

A heartbeat later and clarity sunk in. She *did* know this man. He was the blacksmith that she had seen in Foothold. The one who temporarily mentored Marek. What had been his name? Doran? Yes, that was it. What on Earth was he doing here?

"How are you here?" She managed to croak out. "Am I...?"

"Oh, you're not dead, well not yet."

The man grinned again, and Jak felt a sort of pressure come at her from all sides. A pressure and darkness.

"My servants serve me without question, and all goes to plan." Now, when Jak looked at Doran, it was as if she saw him near, but also a great distance away. Darkness radiated from him.

"Who are you? Why are you here?" In her current circumstances, Jak could think of nothing else to ask.

"Oh, I'm not actually here, or I would kill you myself. I have other concerns to the south. And you don't need to know who I am. You'll be dead soon enough anyway. Think of this as a token of my respect. You've already been a thorn in my side, and you're barely coming to realize who you are. Thankfully, you won't live to recognize your potential. My servants will see to that."

So, I am important. The thought came unbidden to her mind and surprised her so much she said it aloud.

"Oh, of course not a girl. If you were, we wouldn't be having this conversation."

Jak curled into a fetal position. She wasn't sure if she was having some sort of hallucination from her blood loss, or if this man, whoever he was, was actually real. But the darkness only pressed in harder around her. She recognized it. It was the same feeling she'd had on the morning before her branding, the morning before her father died. A voice had spoken to her out of that darkness as well.

"Are you him?" Jak asked, the thought swimming through the haze in her mind.

The blonde blacksmith seemed surprised by the question. "Am I who?"

"My father, before he died. He said that someone fears me. Is that you?"

"Does it look like I fear you? Your father is dead. People say strange things before they die. Just as you are about to find out."

The darkness almost seemed to lift for a moment, and Jak felt that one shred of hope once more. No one had mentioned the Shadow Fae, not even this man. Perhaps no one knew they were here. Perhaps they could still help.

"There there, it won't hurt for long before the nothingness takes you. Though how would I know. I've never died." The blacksmith's face broke into a maniacal grin once more. "I'm just glad I could be the last thing you saw before utter despair. Enjoy your final moments."

And in what felt like rising out of a dark lake, he was gone. Jak gasped for air. Her head still spun, and the pain in her side continued to drain her, literally. But the pressing darkness no longer stifled her. It was only then that Jak realized the air was still dark around her. But it wasn't the pressure of...w hoever that blacksmith really was. It was more comforting. Like being at home sleeping under the comfort of her warm blankets. Was it night already, or was she truly losing her sense of sight?

A few stifled yells and Jak's stomach lurched as the wheels under her cage came to a halt. Something was happening, but she still couldn't see a thing.

A creak of metal as the door to her cage opened, and warm fingers caressed her face.

"Jak, oh my dear, sweet Jak." It was her mother's voice. Soft, warm, loving.

Jak felt a smile come to her lips. "I knew they wouldn't find you."

"Shh. Don't talk. We need to get you to a healer. Surely someone here has the brand.

A healer? Suddenly, Jak's eyes widened as a thought came to her mind. Clarity bathed her brain as for the first time since being captured, she knew what she needed to do. Perhaps this had been what she was destined for all along.

"No, mother. I don't need a healer."

"But your body is already dangerously low on blood. We can't...Jak, what are you doing?!"

She propped herself on one elbow and felt her head swim. She must really be low on blood if that was all it took to make her dizzy. Yet she had to stay awake. Forcing herself to mental clarity with a quivering scream, she grasped at her wound with one hand, skin touching skin. She would not die today!

The brand on her left hand flared to life! An image, as clear as day formed in her mind. The image of a Healing brand. Using the skills she had practiced over and over on the weapons used by Seph's followers, and on her own spear, she willed the Healing brand to become part of her. A shock of what felt like cold water covered her from head to foot. She gasped.

When the light of her brand faded, she took in a huge, deep breath. She was still alive. And she was still herself.

"You did it," her mother said, reverently. "My daughter, you actually did it!"

Etched into the side of her right arm, was a new brand. A brand of Healing. Jak could already feel warmth returning to her cheeks, and the pain in her side lessened a bit. But it was still an open wound, and while a Healing brand could help, it wouldn't stop her from bleeding out if she didn't take additional precautions.

She waved a hand at her mother who she could see clearly now. "Don't touch me yet, mother. I'm not done."

Her left hand flared again as she activated her power for the second time. She formed another picture in her mind, but this time she imagined it differently. The brand danced in her mind, waving back and forth. It was the mental picture she needed to form a Flamedancing brand.

This time, as the brand took root, she felt an odd warmth flow through her. Did every brand feel different when it was applied? The lines of the brand formed and etched into her skin with an acute burning sensation. Had the pain of her wound not overshadowed anything she had ever experienced, she would have cried out.

But then her Gifter brand faded, and she was left with a third brand firmly in place on her arm. She blinked. Something inside her was...different somehow. She had a new awareness for something that had not been there before. It felt a lot like the relationship she felt with her Gifter brand. Perhaps it functioned the same way.

As her mind worked, a spurt of flame ignited from her hand. It shot out, nearly catching her mother who side-stepped hurriedly out of the way.

"Oh! I'm sorry!" Jak exclaimed. "I didn't know how this stuff worked."

"Jak, I'm more impressed that you can do anything at all. I knew you had branded that Watcher boy, but this... I've never seen anything like this." There was a look of awe on Karlona's face.

Jak wanted to join in her mother's rejoicing, but she steeled herself for what was coming next, the reason she branded herself with a Flamedancing brand. Trying out her new power once again, she decreased the intensity instinctively so that there was only a small flame covering her hand. Amazing that it didn't burn the flesh of the hand. How much control did she actually have over fire? Could she manipulate fire that already existed? Could she make flame come out of other parts of her body? How...but she shook her head to clear her thoughts. No time to think about those things now.

Bracing herself, using her free hand to lift her shirt to expose the bloody wound in her gut, making sure her clothing was out of the way.

"Oh, Jak." Her mother realized what she was doing. But she did not turn away.

Jak slapped the flame in her palm down on the tender flesh. Throwing her head back, she screamed. *Relics, this hurt.* Oh, it hurt so badly!

This time she did black out for a moment. Stars filled her vision until they cleared to see the concerned glowing green eyes of her mother leaning over her.

Jak looked down at her stomach. The wound had stopped bleeding, though now it looked horrid, a mixture of red and purple boils and skin. She forced herself to look away and winced as she brought her shirt back down on the tender flesh. Hopefully, that Healing brand would kick in soon, and she wouldn't have to put up with all the pain.

She finally took a moment to look around. All four of the Watcher guards that had driven her cage lay dead around them, killed by her mother's dagger that she saw with a small measure of disgust still dripped blood in Karlona's hand. She supposed it had been necessary, but it would be difficult to argue that the Fae were good if the people feared them as killers.

They were on a deserted street, one that led up to the Watcher camp. With all the Watchers called to the main square, she supposed all of them were already there. General Wilva and the Royal Priest had probably gone on ahead. She reached a hand out to her mother. "Help me up."

Her mother obliged, lifting Jak to her feet. But she grabbed Jak by the shoulders as she swayed. She was too dizzy. Her legs barely felt like they had the strength to keep her upright.

Strength. Yes, that was what she needed. It was a simple brand after all. She'd come this far, she might as well...

For the third time, the glow of her Gifter brand illuminated the abandoned road. This time she called up the Strength brand in her mind. This one was a collection of rectangles and was relatively easy to brand. It required a small variation to envision it properly, but instead of imagining a dancing flame for the Flamedancer brand, this one required her to imagine the brand pulsating slightly. She'd successfully practiced it before, for her professors, but this was the first time that she tried it as one of several brands.

Once again, she felt an odd sensation as the brand settled into her. But this time the strange sensation came when it was all over, and the light of her brand faded. She felt...tight. Like she was larger than her skin could comfortably accommodate for. Glancing at her arms, she saw no difference, other than the new brand that lay there. Her muscles didn't look any larger, but there was definitely a difference she could feel. At the very least, she no longer felt like she was about to fall over.

She turned to the metal cage behind her, and Karlona tentatively lets go of her shoulders. Grabbing the metal in two hands, Jak pulled. The metal screeched as it bent inward, twisting and compressing as Jak brought her hands together.

Jak took a step backward. She didn't know what her face looked like at that moment, but inside she felt like cheering. The cage lay a mangled wreck in front of her, and the whole process had taken little to no exertion at all! She could get used to this!

Her mother stared at her, looking like Jak felt. Her mouth was open in a mixture of disbelief and happiness. Taking a quick step forward, she embraced Jak in a tight hug. Jak hugged her back.

"I'm so glad you didn't turn into a demon," Karlona muttered in her ear.

Jak laughed. "I'm a bit relieved myself."

Which was an understatement? She still didn't understand why she, of all people, seemed able to give multiple brands, but she wasn't complaining just now. She had just become the most magically powerful person in the city, probably on the whole planet. Though, who was that man she had talked to earlier, the blacksmith Doran. He said he was communicating with her from the south. How was that even possible unless there were powers that they didn't know about yet. She knew there were some that were forbidden, like Blood-burning, and some that were kept a secret, like the Void brand. Could there be more?

In the distance, she heard something, the sound of a few hundred voices crying out. Jak couldn't tell if they were cheering or shouting. But the sound caused her to break the embrace with her mother.

"We have to get to the city square!" She said and picked up one of the Watcher spears from the ground.

It wasn't as good as her spear, but it would have to do. She didn't have time to go back to the Watcher camp and retrieve her belongings. Though Naem was probably back there still. But no, she wouldn't rescue him. He deserved what he got, and they could easily make do without him.

With her mother following close behind, Jak began to run down the hill, towards the main square, and the execution.

CHAPTER 23

A S THEY NEARED THE square, more people lined the streets. Karlona turned herself invisible at first sight of someone else, but Jak knew she was keeping pace behind her. She ran as fast as she could, still feeling the pain in her gut, but finding new strength from her brands. She could feel their powers inside her, and it was exhilarating. The only thing that kept her from laughing and recklessly displaying her powers was her urgent need to get to the public square, where her friends were about to be executed.

Finally, she rounded a corner and saw them. Seph, Amelia, Gabriel, and what looked like a dozen or so Water Fae were strung up against large wooden pillars, with great piles of wood stacked beneath and between them. From her angle, she couldn't fully see their faces, but she knew who they were.

People filled the square. More people than Jak had ever seen in one place. All the merchant tables and booths were cleared, making room for hundreds to gather and watch the mass execution, probably the largest execution in recent history. Not only that, but the revelation of the Water Fae must have spread throughout the city. It was going to be nearly impossible to get through the crowd in time.

A man stood with a burning torch in one hand, walking back and forth in front of those awaiting execution. Jak's eyebrows furrowed. It was that swine, the Royal Priest. After everything he had done, Jak was sure of one thing. He had to be a shapeshifting demon. It was the only thing that made sense now, especially after that strange visit she'd had from Doran, the blacksmith. He had referred to the Royal Priest as one of his servants. Like Kuldain, the man held an irrational hatred for the Fae. And like Kuldain, he fueled the hatred of others.

"And in just a few moments, I will bring you the rogue Gifter who is responsible for this new race of demon, these so-called Fae."

Jak shook her head. The man was attacking her in more ways than one. Now, even if she did manage to free her friends, most would see her as a heretic. It was clever, and it was infuriating. Damn him!

General Wilva emerged, approaching the Priest and whispering something in his ear. "I've just received word that some of this heretic's followers were just rounded up outside the city. They were preparing to attack the city and everyone in it to rescue those you see behind me."

A murmur ran through the crowd. Jak closed her eyes. So, it was just up to her and the Shadow Fae now. Well, it was too late now. Who cared what they thought? It was time to get her friends out.

But the Priest was still speaking. "It is this rogue Gifter who deceived the hearts of many into thinking she was some kind of a savior. Yet earlier today we found her, we subdued her. She could not even save herself."

Jak ran forward. There was a path that led upward to the palace which also served as the perfect perch to look over the market square. But more importantly, it gave everyone in the square a clear view of her. She stopped and drove the hilt of her spear firmly into the ground. A few onlookers pointed at her, and a new wave of mutters began to fill the square.

"Don't get ahead of yourself, Priest!" She shouted for all to hear. "You won't get rid of me so easily."

"Jak!" someone cried out. It was Amelia, tied to the pire facing away from Jak, but craning her neck to see who had spoken. "I knew it!"

Seph, Gabriel, and many of the other Water Fae were doing their best to get a good look at her. They said nothing, but Seph had that warm smile on his face as their eyes met.

"You! How did—" The Royal Priest was finally at a loss for words.

He looked genuinely scared for the first time since Jak had known him. Oh, but that alone felt so satisfying.

She took a deep breath. "I know many of you trust this man," she pointed at the Priest below her. "But trust me when I say that he is not who you think he is. He would murder innocent people just because he doesn't understand them."

Troubled muttering turned to shouts as the crowd realized who she was. She couldn't make out what any of them were saying, but most of did not look sympathetic. They were yelling at her, not the Priest. No, she had to make them understand.

"You're punishing the wrong people," she said, but it was no use.

While a few people looked like they believed her, most were shouting at her and making way for the Watchers who, at General Wilva's orders, emerged from the crowd and began climbing the path that led to her.

The Priest held her stare with the barest smile on his lips, his confidence restored. Jak licked her lips and looked around her, eyeing the Watchers making their way up the path. Now might be a good time for the Shadow Fae to emerge. It wouldn't do anything to convince the people that she was in the right. In fact, it would likely do the opposite. But she also couldn't save her friends without their help.

The Royal Priest shouted through the commotion. "I told you she believed in heresy. But it will not serve her."

He lowered his torch to the wood pires.

The wood must have been coated with oil, because it lit up instantly, the flames licking at the captives. Several Water Fae screamed, and Jak saw Seph and Gabriel close their eyes.

No, this couldn't be happening. What had possessed her to climb the path. Now she was too high and too far away to get to her friends in time.

But wait a moment, something felt different about this fire. She was aware of it like she hadn't been before. It... called to her somehow, like she was—

Idiot! She had a Flamedancer brand now. She could use it! Stretching her hands in front of her, she called on her new-found magic. The flames from the pires rushed away from its victims and towards Jak, leaving the wood completely devoid of fire. She felt the heat as the flames coalesced between her arms, churning in a bright, chaotic furnace. Then with a thought, she extinguished it.

Silence filled the square. The captives looked around, unsure of what had happened. But all other eyes were on Jak. They had just witnessed the impossible.

Jak held her arms high again, letting everyone see the dark lines of her brands. All four of them. Gifting, Healing, Strength, and Flamedancing. Mouths gaped open in awe as all witnessed something that could not be. Even the Royal Priest looked stunned, though being a shape-shifting demon himself he must know that multiple brands were possible. Kuldain had some, and it was likely that this man did as well.

"See!" he said after a moment to catch his wits. "She perverts our magic, our way of life. None but the demons that live outside our protective walls can…"

But he was drowned out by the tumult of voices that sounded all around them. The shouting had started again, but this time there was more contention. Some appeared to be arguing, while others continued to shout at Jak.

But Jak had other things to worry about now. The Watchers had reached her and were fanning out to block off her escape down the path. She glanced at their brands. One Flamedancer, two with Strength, and one with Grace. She was not going to be able to fight through these soldiers and still rescue her friends. She needed help.

"Now, my friends!" she yelled at the top of her voice.

The message was received. Karlona appeared directly behind the Watcher with Grace and stabbed him in the chest. Screams reached her from all around the market square as Shadow Fae materialized from all sides.

The other Watchers barely realized what had happened when Jak threw her magic at the Flamedancer. Flame gushed from her fingers and enveloped the man, who yelled but quickly took control of the fire and sent it swirling around him and back at Jak. She countered in the same manner and this time sent the flames at the other two remaining Watchers.

But it was then that she realized that those two were already down, crumpled on the ground. A moment later and the Flamedancer Watcher cried out and fell as well. Karlona stood there with blood dripping off the tip of her obsidian dagger. Jak winced inwardly at seeing the Watchers killed like that. But she had no time to speak to her mother about her techniques. She had people to save.

With a final nod at her mother, she sprinted down the path, her Strength enhanced legs quickly covering much more distance than she would have normally expected. More Watchers were climbing the path, but she barreled into them with her spear held high. One fell off the path as soon as she arrived, and others backed away as she hurled fire at them. No Telekinetics. That was good. She still wasn't sure she could do anything about a telekinetic hold.

She could have stayed to fight the Watchers, but that wasn't her goal. Instead, she found herself flying past them, and running straight into the crowds that lay between her and the back of the square where her friends stood trussed to the dry wood.

Thankfully, the crowds did not try to impede her approach like the Watchers had. Instead, they scrambled to get out of her way, probably wanting to avoid the damage they'd seen her inflict on the Watchers. While the crowd was still impossibly thick, it didn't take her long to run through it and close the distance between her and her friends.

But General Wilva was there waiting, along with the Royal Priest standing behind. Wilva held her own spear high, a determined look on her face. Jak hadn't had much contact with the Watcher General, other than their first meeting, but she could see now from the way Wilva held herself, and the expression on her face, that she was not to be messed with. But most of all, Jak noticed the brand clearly displayed on Wilva's left hand as it held the spear. She was a Telekinetic.

Just as Jak noted Wilva's brand, it started to glow, and Jak felt an invisible force close in on her from all sides. She whipped her head this way and that, but all Shadow Fae appeared to be occupied elsewhere. She had to deal with this alone. The Royal Priest grinned as Jak rose in the air by a few inches, but Wilva's face remained carved from stone.

Feeling the newfound strength in her muscles, Jak began to push outward at her invisible cage. Telekinesis worked like any other force, or at least that's what her father had taught her. Push against it with a stronger force, and it would eventually break. Most people did not possess such strength to break a telekinetic hold unless Strength was their brand.

The slight pursing of Wilva's lips was the only indication that her strength was having any effect. Jak felt the force around her tighten to the point where it was almost unbearable. But she kept it up, pushing as hard as she could against Wilva's telekinesis. It had become a contest of wills. But she couldn't keep this up for long. Wilva had years of experience with her brand, and Jak couldn't possibly break her with nothing but pure strength.

But that wasn't the only brand at her disposal.

With a thought, Jak summoned the fire from the Royal Priest's torch, which he still held in his hand. The flame whisked in her direction, catching Wilva squarely in the back. Wilva spun, and Jak could see a glowing spot in the armor covering her back. She felt the force holding her lessen a little.

Jak seized the moment and pushed with all her might. Wilva, distracted as she was trying to pull her hot armor off her, couldn't keep her focus. The barrier burst and Jak fell several inches to the ground, catching herself with one knee and one hand to the ground.

Wilva lashed out with her spear, a practiced and precise move. Only her years of training with her father, and later with Naem, saved her as she sidestepped the move and caught the spear with one hand. Wilva tried to pull it back, but Jak was too strong for her. Placing her other hand on the spear, she brought it down hard onto her knee.

The wood snapped in two and Wilva fell backward in a heap. Reaching out a hand, Wilva attempted to use her telekinesis once again. But as Jak felt the invisible walls closing in on her again, she felt her strength well within her. Wilva was distracted, unused to the kind of magic that Jak wielded. With considerable effort, Jak pushed and once again broke the hold on her.

She didn't wait for Wilva to regain her composure again. Jak leaped forward and with a swift strike, landed a Strength-enhanced punch to Wilva's head. The woman crumpled in a heap.

Jak took one look at the Royal Priest. Would he reveal himself now? Would he turn and fight her?

She was surprised to see the fear in the Priest's eyes. The moment Jak locked gazes with him, he turned and fled. The crowd, many of whom had paused to watch Jak battle their general, made way for the Priest almost as they had for Jak.

Jak took a moment to scan her surroundings. Almost all of the Watchers were engaged fighting a Shadow Fae, and members of the crowd were scattering in all directions to avoid the fights. Jak's battle with Wilva had felt like forever but had probably been only moments. Most of the crowd hadn't even had time to flee the square, though they were certainly trying as fast as they could. Most were screaming of demons and monsters as they laid eyes on the Shadow Fae.

She watched the Priest go and took a step forward to go after him. But no, she had a duty to perform. The reason for her being here.

Turning, she met the eyes of her friends. Amelia was beaming and probably would have been dancing up and down on her feet had she not possessed a giant fin. Gabriel looked almost confused but pleased with what was happening. And Seph flashed her that smile of his. She felt warmth rise to her face, and it wasn't from her fight.

She bent to pick up the head of Wilva's broken spear and began to cut her friends loose, starting with Amelia.

Jak cut the bonds behind her friend, and the girl threw her arms around her. With no feet, Amelia's full weight fell onto Jak once the ropes were cut, but Jak didn't mind. She hugged Amelia back with everything she had. Well...not everything exactly. With her Strength brand, she could have snapped Amelia in two.

"I knew you would come." Amelia sobbed into Jak's ear. "I knew it. The others doubted me, except for Seph. I think he also trusted you to save us."

"I'm sorry I left it to the last minute," Jak cried into Amelia's hair.

"You'll just have to make up for it. I'm counting on you to find the warmest, cleanest, most perfect lake for me to live in," Amelia said.

Jak laughed through her tears and gently set Amelia down so she could release the others. Within moments, everyone was cut loose.

Seph rubbed his wrists, and his eyes sparkled at Jak.

"Where's the queen?" Jak asked before Seph could say anything.

"She was watching from above." Seph glanced at the palace that loomed over them from behind. "I imagine she's rallying her personal guard by now."

Jak glanced in the same direction and saw no one on the palace balcony. But she did see one figure climbing the winding path to reach the palace. The dark robes gave him away as the Royal Priest.

Her eyes narrowed, and she grits her teeth. She wasn't about to let that snake escape. He would do more damage if left free.

"My people have freed the other humans outside the gates," Jak turned to see Karlona walking to meet her. A quick glance told Jak that most of the other Shadow Fae had succeeded in taking down the remaining Watchers.

"Good," Jak said, looking up again at the fleeing Priest. "There's something I have to deal with if you could get the Water Fae down to the coast." She met her mother's eyes, who nodded.

"We'll make sure they're safe."

Jak nodded, then began running towards the path that led to the palace. With an enormous Strength-enhanced leap, she scaled the first switchback and landed nearly twenty feet above the square. With a second leap, she scaled the next switchback, drawing her ever closer to the fleeing Priest. It was time to end this.

CHAPTER 24

J AK CLOSED THE DISTANCE with a speed that surprised even her. The Royal Priest barely had time to turn and look back before she was on him. He screamed and redoubled his pace. He was certainly putting on a good act, but Jak would change that. She would expose him if it were the last thing she did.

With another bound, she scaled the last switchback and barrelled into the Priest. He flew forward by several feet with Jak tumbling on top of him. In an instant, she was back on her feet, raising one arm and activating her Flamedancer brand to light a fire in one hand. She had to be careful though. Best to keep her distance when dealing with someone with a Void brand.

But the Royal Priest looked no more a threat than a Water Fae did. He was scrambling back up the path, his eyes never leaving the flame in Jak's hand. Why did he look so scared? Why didn't he transform and attack her?

"Show yourself," she said to him, letting the flame in her hand grow brighter. "I know what you are."

"I... I don't know what you mean," he stammered.

Jak shot a flame at him close enough to singe his eyebrows. He yelped and scrambled backward again on the stone.

"Come on!" Jak shouted. "Your charade isn't worth your life. Attack me!"

"You're insane!" was the only response she got. "You'll be the death of all of us, all thanks to you and your Fae." He spits on the ground.

"You still blame me!" Jak had had enough. She leaped at the man and struck him in the face with a Strength-enhanced fist. His head jerked back violently, but he remained conscious.

Desperately, he reached a hand to grab hers, activating his brand as she swung again, connecting with his ribs this time. She heard a crack, and the man screamed! The light from his brand faded.

"Turn!" she commanded. "Turn and show everyone the filthy demon you are!"

She hit him again, in the face. Blood spurted from his nose, and his eyes glazed over. Why wasn't he turning? He was clearly a servant of darkness, the mysterious dark force that took the shape of the blacksmith had even said so. Why wasn't he fighting back?

She hit him again, and again. Soon, his body had grown limp. Something or someone grabbed Jak from behind. She resisted, and with her brand of Strength, the assailant could do nothing to stop her. She spun on the culprit, a fist raised, ready to take out anyone who opposed her.

Gabriel raised a hand to ward off her blow. What... what was he doing here? Barely managing to stop her raised fist from connecting, she finally noticed the blood coating it.

"You were killing him," Gabriel said.

Jak glanced back at the Royal Priest, finally seeing what she had blocked out in her rage. The nameless priest lay limp and unconscious, his face a bloody mess. She looked up and found others running up to them, behind Gabriel. Seph was among them. He looked from the Priest, to Jak, and back again. His face expressed... horror.

No, this wasn't right. This wasn't how it was supposed to be. Why hadn't the Priest turned!?

"I... I thought he was a demon." The words sounded hollow as she spoke them. She had no excuse for this.

"Not every bad person is a demon, Jak." Gabriel held his hands at his sides, calm but sober as he looked directly into Jak's eyes. "Sometimes people are just... bad."

"But the things he's said, the people he's hurt. He's done nothing but work against us."

"One does not have to be in league with the forces of darkness to serve them."

He continued to say something, but suddenly, something pierced her head. Pain stabbed at her head in a splitting headache. But unlike an ordinary headache, this one was accompanied by an emotion. Someone somewhere was furious.

"RELEASE!" a voice pounded in her ears.

Someone grabbed her, it was Gabriel, holding her upright, and a new look of concern on his face. Others among the group that had joined them took steps forward to help. Jak regained her footing and waved them away.

"Did you hear that?" she turned to Gabriel. "The voice?"

Gabriel looked at her with a concerned look. "We heard nothing, Jak. Are you okay?"

A few of the onlookers took a few steps away from her now. All save Gabriel and Seph. Did they think she was somehow touched now that she had multiple brands? Did they think she would turn into a demon? She wouldn't blame them. After all, she had just beat their religious leader senseless. But she didn't have time to worry about what they thought. Something worse was coming, she knew.

As if confirming her thoughts, several terrifying shrieks sounded from below. Everyone whirled about and stared. The very thing Jak had feared began to play out before her eyes.

Demons were entering via the main gate, which was open and relatively unguarded thanks to the commotion that Jak had started. To her horror, Jak saw them fall upon innocent civilians the moment they entered. Shouting, Watchers and other city guards scrambled to close the main gate and fight the oncoming wave of demons. But it was already too late. Demons poured in through the gate so fast that no one could get close.

Jak's jaw hung slack. Had this been the plan all along? Had whatever controlled these demons simply been waiting for them to weaken the city's defenses in their rescue attempt? Or had the Royal Priest been controlling them and some-how lost control when Jak knocked him unconscious. She spared a glance back at the battered priest. No, something else had happened. Jak had somehow witnessed the order given to the demons. Someone was behind this, but it wasn't the Royal Priest. Even now, staring at the man's unconscious form on the ground, she still struggled to believe that he was not behind all of this. Could he really be just an ordinary man with such bias?

Seph's brought her out of her thoughts. "We have to get down there."

Jak's eyes widened. What had she been waiting for? Ignoring everyone else who stood around her, she sped down the path in the direction of the fighting. It was already her fault that the Watchers and city guards were scattered. She had to make up for that fact by killing as many demons as she could.

The first demon to reach her met its end in a blaze of fire that shot from Jak's hands. Jak leapt over its screaming form to meet the next demon. Now in the market square, she was able to get a good look at the situation. Dozens of people lay dead in the streets, and the rest were either running away or engaging the demons head-on. Jak winced as she saw not just humans on the ground, but Shadow Fae as well. She looked around for her mother but did not see her.

Just then, another demon came at her, snarling out of its all-too-human face. Picking up a spear from a fallen Watcher, she hurled it at the demon, using the javelin throwing techniques that Naem had taught her months earlier. She banished the thought of Naem from her mind. None of this would have gone wrong if it hadn't been for him.

She pulled the spear out of the dead demon's corpse and went looking for her next victim. One by one, demons died at her hand. She was a whirlwind of fire and spear tip. Every attack met its mark. Dozens, hundreds of demons met their end that night.

Jak heard a familiar shout and turned to see Naem enter the battle. He ran at the demons from the direction of the Watcher High Command, wielding his own spear and taking out as many demons as came his way. Biting her lip, Jak barely pushed away from the impulse to attack Naem herself, but no, he was fighting demons. For now, at least, they were on the same side. But she would have words to say later.

More screams sounded around Jak, and she realized that for all the demons she'd killed, dozens more kept pouring through the gate. Civilians and others were helpless against them. If they were going to save any of them, she was going to have to change up her strategy. They could try to close the main gate, but that might not do any good. There were several other gates into the city, and she couldn't guarantee that they weren't all overrun by now. They'd have to close all of them. But perhaps there was another way.

"Follow me," she yelled for anyone who could hear her. "There's a secondary gate that leads to the ocean. Help me get everyone to safety."

Shadow Fae, Watchers and guardsmen alike looked to her. She repeated her command, and many took up the call. Naem, she saw, took a moment to meet her eyes, then he started to repeat her words, killing demons as he went, but herding the nearest villagers to the second gate.

But so many could not make it, as gray-skinned, formally human monstrosities leaped on their retreating backs. Jak caught one as it was about to bite down on a woman's neck from behind. The woman turned to face Jak. She had a spear in one hand, a branded spear. It was Elva! The commotion around them stirred up too much noise for Jak to say anything to Seph's follower, but they both nodded at each other, a silent 'thank you,' and 'you're welcome' passing between them. Then they both continued, killing demons as they rushed to the lower gate.

The path grew narrower as they approached the lower levels of the city. This both solved and created more problems. On the one hand, the narrower opening made it easier for Jak and the Shadow Fae to protect the city dwellers from approaching demons. They only had to worry about protecting one side, the back. On the other hand, it also meant everyone moved more slowly.

Jak brandished her spear as more demons hurtled at her, the Fae, and a few other Watchers and guards that stood with her. Just moments before those warriors had fought to kill her and the Shadow Fae, not to mention Seph, Gabriel, and her Water Fae friends. Now they were united against a clear enemy. There had been far too many deaths tonight. But at least something good might come of it. Yet the price left a bitter taste in Jak's mouth.

Naem stood a few feet away from Jak, holding his spear forward in a stance he had taught Jak several months earlier. Relics, it felt so much longer now. They had been far more innocent then. She was grateful for Naem's help. He was, after all, the most powerful human alive besides Jak herself, considering the three brands he held. Yet his aid did little to comfort her. If he hadn't betrayed Jak, perhaps all of this might have ended differently. But no time to think about that now. The demons were funneling themselves down the narrower streets, coming at them with spittle flying from their snarling fangs, and terror in their human eyes.

Jak slashed at one, taking it down with a swift jab of her spear that might have left her feeling proud of her skills if the situation hadn't been so ominous. Others of the Fae and the Watchers held the line, though, with the massive oncoming force of the demons, not everyone managed to stay alive. The civilians behind them kept screaming and pushing forward towards the lower gate faster than before, yet slower than Jak liked.

"Back up," Jak yelled to the warriors around her.

They obliged, not daring to question her authority at the moment, not even the Watchers or city guards. Killing demons as they went, they each took careful steps backward, staying as close to the crowds as they could. Jak said a silent prayer of thanks to the fathers that demons still showed little strategy in battle. It was the only thing saving them at that moment.

Suddenly, she looked up to see the great archway of a stone gate. They had made it! Now to close it behind them. With one last burst of magic, she sent a giant flame spewing at the demons, who shielded their eyes and cowered in fear. Then she ran at one of the enormous doors and pulled. A

Watcher, probably with a brand of Strength, grabbed the other door, and together they began to pull them shut.

But the demons recovered quickly from her flaming onslaught. Seeing the two of them exposed, they scrambled forward, their teeth gnashing as though preparing to gnaw on flesh. They never made it to Jak and the other Watcher, however. With a roar, half a dozen Shadow Fae intercepted, protecting Jak as she heaved the doors closed. The great iron-banded doors shut with a heavy crunch. Thankfully all of the Fae made it inside before it shut. Only a handful of demons made it inside, and the remaining warriors made short work of them. This gate had spikes along the top and the opposite side of the door, just like the walls of Skycliff. The demons weren't scaling it anytime soon. And they were close to the shore now, so perhaps they could find a way to get out along the coast.

Dull thuds sounded on the other side of the gate. A lot of them. The demons were throwing themselves on the spikes! More thuds sounded, and loud human-like cries accompanied them as the demons died on the spikes. Jak backed away with the rest of the onlookers as they listened. Were the death cries coming from higher up the gate now?

This wasn't good, Jak finally realized what must be happening. The demons were climbing on the backs of other dead demons. They were creating their own cushion against the spikes using their own dead bodies. As if confirming her thoughts, a demon crested the top of the wall and quickly impaled itself on the top spikes. Civilians screamed and fled further down the path, but Jak knew it was too late.

The demons had already scaled the supposedly demon proof walls in a matter of minutes. These defenses were never meant to hold back so many demons. They almost never attacked in groups this large. How was anyone to know? Discouragement washed over Jak, and her spear hung loosely at her side as more demons crested the gate, the first of them dying on the spikes, but the rest jumping over the corpses of their dead companions and landing on the other side of the gate.

Shadow Fae and others held their weapons high, preparing for the incoming attack. But Jak knew it was no use. Unless they could kill all the demons in the city, there was no place they could take the remaining city dwellers where they would be safe.

A rushing sound came from behind. A huge, massive churning noise, like the crashing of a wave on the ocean, but far, far louder. The people screamed, causing Jak and the other warriors to turn, even though demons were nearly on them. Jak eyes widened in shock as a huge wave swept upward through the street engulfing the people that stood there. How had it come up so high through the city? Jak didn't have time for another thought at the wave barreled into her. She dropped the spear in her hand and felt salty water enter her mouth. What was happening, was this how she was going to die? Not at the teeth of a demon, but at a freak wave?

Suddenly, her face emerged from the water, and she gasped for air. The wave was still moving, but somehow she managed to stay afloat on top of it! Looking around, she saw other heads bob to the surface! She hadn't been around the ocean long enough to understand everything there was to know, but she was pretty sure water didn't usually behave this way.

The wave began to flow back towards the ocean, with Jak and now hundreds of others floating at a sort of watery plateau at the top of the wave. Eyes still wide in astonishment, Jak let the wave carry her away.

CHAPTER 25

A FACE ROSE FROM the waters beside Jak, water dripping off the hair that clung to her face. The hair was darker than Jak was used to, because of the water, but she knew this person. Amelia smiled at the look on Jak's face. "For once, it's my turn to save you for a change."

In a moment of clarity, Jak knew what must have happened. The Water Fae had somehow brought the wave that swept up the remaining survivors. With almost a sob, she threw her arms around Amelia, both still partially submerged in the strange wave.

When they broke the embrace, Jak stared at her friend, then at the wave, then back at Amelia. "How are you doing this?"

Amelia grinned. "Oh Jak, you have no idea how wonderful it is now that I'm in the ocean. I can feel the water all around me. It's like it's part of my body. Some of the Shadow Fae brought us to the water, and we met the first Water Fae, the students from the excavation. They've already taught us how to use our abilities to make the water move. So, we all teamed up to save you guys! Isn't that amazing?"

Jak wiped a tear from her eye. Relics, it felt so good to hear her friend talking like her old self again, as in non-stop. Indeed, Amelia showed no signs of stopping.

"These powers are amazing! Much better than being a Gifter, to be honest. Oh, speaking of which, my brand is gone!" She raised her left arm, and Jak took a good look. Just like Amelia said, the brand had disappeared.

Jak nodded. "The same thing happened to the Shadow and Bright Fae. They lost their old abilities but those were replaced with new ones."

"It's so cool!" Amelia said. "Watch this."

She suddenly dove back beneath the tidal wave that must have still connected to the ocean and was still moving steadily away from the city and towards the coast, carrying each of the survivors with it.

Jak waited. What was Amelia up to? Then with a suddenness that would have sent Jak stumbling backward had she not been submerged, Amelia came flying out of the water. The force of her tail propelled her skyward, where she did a full backflip and landed gracefully head-first into the wave. Onlookers gasped in awe, and Jak put a hand to her mouth.

"Wasn't that awesome!" Amelia said as she emerged once more.

"That was pretty amazing," Jak said, laughing through her tears. Her friend was alive and more than well. Even as a Water Fae, she was thriving. Jak could hardly breathe for feelings of joy and relief.

"We're almost there," Amelia said. Moments later, the wave subsided and rejoined the ocean, leaving all the occupants wet but safe on the sandy beach. Most rose to their feet shakily at first, and some of them scratching their heads as if still unsure that they weren't dreaming. Others who had previously arrived at the beach, ran up to meet them.

"Jak!" a voice called to her.

She turned, and her spirits soared as Seph and Karlona approached. She ran forward and embraced her mother first.

"I'm so glad you're both still alive." She said as she broke the embrace and hugged Seph as well.

"My time is not yet here," Seph said mysteriously, cracking a small smile at Jak.

"What happened up there?" Karlona asked. "We brought several of the Water Fae to the coast, and they insisted they stay. Then some of them summoned this huge wave which swept up into the city."

"We managed to get everyone past the inner gate, but the demons climbed over it anyway. The wave saved us and brought us here, as you just saw."

Seph's face lost its cheer. "You mean, this is it? There must be no more than three hundred people here."

"There are a few more." Said a voice behind Jak. She spun to see Cerai, immersed in a pillar of water that rose from the beach to meet them. Jak didn't think she'd ever grow used to seeing a sight like that: a half human, half fish person, partially submerged in a pillar of water.

"We're sending waves into the city to drown the rest of the demons and bring back any of the survivors."

Only then did Jak notice the tendrils of ocean water extending from the ocean further down and reaching into the city itself. "Cerai, that's amazing. I had no idea you could do that!"

"Neither did we until recently. But the longer we stay in this form, the more intuitive our abilities have become."

Jak nodded. "That matches what Yewin told me at Foothold. The Bright Fae managed to discover new powers as well."

Cerai nodded then continued. "Anyway, we think there are a few hundred more in the city that barricaded themselves in their houses or the like. Though we still have no idea about the Royal Palace. There may be dozens more holed up there, but no demon can enter the palace if it's locked down. We can't get in either."

Jak scowled, wondering what had happened to the Royal Priest. Had he retreated back to the Palace? Was he, even now, consorting with the queen on what to do next while the Water Fae did all the work? Or had he died where she left him?

Karlona brought her out of her thoughts. "So, what do we do now?"

Cerai pursed her lips thoughtfully, the pillar of water still flowing around her. "Well most of the civilians and soldiers can go back to their homes once we clear the demons out. Though they'll have some work ahead of them since some of their homes will be... er... flooded."

That sounded good to Jak, but it still left a larger problem. "What about you, and the rest of the Fae?" she asked. "Plus

Seph, his followers, myself, and probably most of the college. We're not welcome here anymore after what's happened."

"I actually had an idea on that front." Seph volunteered.

Everyone turned to face him, so he continued.

"It's clear after what's happened here that the Fae face many dangers from the rest of humanity. I think there will be many who will have a change of heart after tonight, but that won't convince everyone."

Jak agreed. The Fae weren't safe here. "So, what do you propose?"

Seph smiled at her. "I suggest we band together, find a place where we can all live in harmony with those of us who won't persecute the Fae for what they are."

"Like your Illadar?" Jak offered. "Your world of peace?"

"Possibly, but even I don't exactly know what form Illadar will take. A simple refuge will do for now."

They all stood there for a moment, taking in the idea. "It would have to be near water," Cerai said. "We can't travel far on land."

"I agree," said Seph. "So might I suggest the province of Riverbrook."

Jak brought her head up so fast that she felt her neck crack. "What? Why?"

"It's relatively uninhabited, especially after your town was evacuated. The river connects with the ocean, so the Water Fae could travel with us. There's plenty of room. Plus, it's defensible with a split in the river on two sides, and a mountain passes behind. So, we could defend it and retreat if necessary. We could even start our own farms for food if we stay long enough."

Wow, he had really thought that through. But... River-brook. Could she really go back there? After everything that had happened...

"I don't know," she said.

"I kind of like the idea," offered Karlona. "Besides, he's right about us needing to band together. We've had too many of us die at the hands of hateful people or demons. We need safety in numbers."

"It sounds like a reasonable plan to me," said Cerai. "Though I don't speak for all of us."

Jak's pursed her lips. "Very well, we'll explain the situation to everyone here, then put it to a vote. If everyone is in favor, the Fae and anyone else who wishes to join may do so."

Seph clapped his hands together. "I'll round everyone up."

A few minutes later and everyone had gathered together on the beach. The Water Fae continued to bring in a few stragglers from the city, all of whom looked completely flustered and thoroughly confused about what had just happened. But they quickly joined the growing crowd, looking at Seph who stood in front of them. Jak saw Naem among them, and her heart soured. At least he hadn't tried to talk to her since he arrived.

"My friends," Seph called out to them. He sounded like he was beginning one of his sermons. "We have witnessed a lot of horror tonight. Demons invaded a city we thought safe from their influence. Yet we were saved by the blessing of the Fae." he swept his hand towards the Shadow Fae who had congregated on one side, then the Water Fae who all listened from the ocean.

Jak watched the crowd closely. Most, she noticed with satisfaction, were listening intently to what Seph had to say, or staring around in wonder at the Fae. There wasn't much hostility in their gazes anymore. Not like she had seen from some at the execution. Though a few still eyed the Fae with suspicion evident on their faces.

"We have determined," Seph continued, "that it is not safe for the Fae to stay here, nor is it safe for them to remain scattered throughout the land. We propose establishing a sanctuary of sorts, where Fae and humans who wish to accompany us, may live in harmony together."

Jak saw a few faces perk up at that. She recognized some of those faces as being members of Seph's congregation. Yes, they knew what that sounded like. Illadar, the promised land of peace. She glanced at Naem, who had one hand to his chin in thought.

As if reading their minds, Seph went on. "You all know Jak by now," he waved a hand in her direction.

No please, the last thing she wanted was for Seph to bring her into this.

"She has learned how to give the gift of multiple brands, branding herself, and many of the weapons that some of us used today. I propose that we visit her homeland of Riverbrook to establish our little paradise. Fae will be welcome. Humans will be welcome."

He went on to explain the other benefits of Riverbrook, its space, defensibility, and the possibility of farmland. Even

Jak had to admit, Seph made it sound good. Jak watched the reactions from the crowd. Most of the Fae looked intrigued. The human crowd, however, seemed divided. Jak didn't miss some of the ugly stares that many threw at her. Clearly they did not trust a Gifter who gave multiple brands, even if she had managed to do it without breaking down her own mind. But others looked at her with an expression that scared her even more. They looked...worshipful.

She needed to get out of here. So much had happened, and she didn't know what to do next. All she had wanted was to live a normal life.

But she wasn't normal. That much was clear. No matter how she wanted to avoid it, she had the abilities and knowledge that others didn't. And she couldn't just stand back as others suffered, especially the Fae, who had done nothing to deserve their persecution.

Yes, she wanted a normal life, but now she was in a position of power. And when given abilities that could help others, she couldn't stand idly by and not use her position to lift them up.

Seph finally called for a vote. The show of hands was nearly unanimous among the Fae, and many of the human hands shot up as well. Jak's gaze met Naem's, as he too raised his hand. She wasn't sure how she felt about that.

Well that settled it, there was a clear majority. Jak took a deep breath. They were going to Riverbrook.

CHAPTER 26

T HEY STAYED THE NIGHT on the beach, huddling together for warmth. But the next day, the Water Fae claimed that the city had been completely cleared of demons, and they had brought all the surviving humans to the beach. There were hundreds of them now, perhaps even a thousand, though not nearly as many as a city the size of Skyecliff should hold.

Cerai confessed, however, that they had not managed to get into the palace. It was locked down tight, and no one could get in or out until that changed. Well at least everyone in the palace was safe from the demons. Jak thought back to the ladies in waiting that had helped her bathe and dress the first time she visited the palace. She hoped they were alright. And the Lord Chamberlain too, he had been nice to her. It was the queen and the Royal Priest who concerned her. She had left the Priest outside the palace, but he had never arrived in one of the Fae's strange waves. Neither had General Wilva or a handful of others. That meant they were either dead or had found their way inside the palace before it went on lockdown.

Upon returning to their homes, the people set about repairing some of the water damage and collecting the bodies of the dead for burial. The bodies of the demons they heaped in a pile outside the city's western gate, where they were burned.

Many came up to Jak, asking her how she managed to stick more than one brand, asking if they could learn, or receive more brands for themselves. Jak quickly shrugged them all off. She wasn't about to give another brand to any other human being. She would not risk it on anyone but herself, and she had only branded herself because of the desperate circumstances. She would have died otherwise.

Instead, she returned to the college and set about collecting her things. She couldn't find her spear, journal, or Seph's Book of Illadar anywhere though. Those must have been confiscated by the Watchers when they failed to arrest her. Of course, they would take her most treasured possessions away from her.

There was still no word from the palace. Not yet, anyway. Though they didn't present much of a danger. Jak was sure that the queen's guards were probably in there, but most of the surviving Watchers were on the outside, and none of them was lifting a finger towards Jak. Not since the execution. Regardless, Jak had to get out of the city, and soon. This was no longer her home, and she had other things to do before she joined the others at Riverbrook.

The night after the execution, she put what she could in her pack. She would leave tonight, while it was dark. No one would see her leave. But before she did that, she had one last person to visit.

She knocked on Gabriel's door. He was home, and awake it seemed, as the light came from underneath the door. Someone moved on the other side, and soon, the door opened.

Gabriel took one look at her, noting the pack and that she was wearing travel clothes. "You're leaving," he said. He did not look surprised.

"I have to," she replied. "I can't stay here any longer."

"I understand," he said, which surprised her.

He didn't argue, telling her why she needed to stay, or asking her to wait until someone could accompany her. Instead, he looked her in the eye.

"Did you come to say goodbye?"

"Yes, but I also need information. I'm going to the south-eastern mountains."

Surprise flickered on Gabriel's face. "You're going to see what the queen has been up to there?

"Yes," Jak nodded. "But you once told me that a Pillar of Eternity can be found there. I was hoping you could give me any information that might help me find it."

Gabriel looked at her then, really poured into her eyes. Jak almost wanted to look away. "It will be dangerous," he said, finally. "I wanted to go there, but the queen's men wouldn't let me. They certainly won't let you in."

"I can take care of myself," Jak replied with a wink.

Gabriel chuckled. "Yes, that much is true." He wandered over to his wall filled with a giant map and many other clippings and illustrations. Reaching out, he plucked one of them off the wall, returned, and handed it to Jak. "Mt. Harafast," he said, pointing to the clipping. It had an illustration of a large mountain that towered above the others around it. "It's the largest peak in the south-eastern mountain range. And it's volcanic."

Jak looked up at him. She had heard that word before, but few ever talked about them. "Aren't those the mountains that spray hot rock everywhere? I had no idea there was one so close."

"Yes, though it hasn't erupted in hundreds of years by most scientists' reckonings. That is where one of the Pillars of Eternity is rumored to live. And it's where the queen has her men stationed. If I had to guess, I'd say they are looking for the Pillar too."

"What about the armor and weapons that have been coming from the south?" Jak asked. "The queen has sent Watchers to guard those caravans. They must be important."

He nodded. "Indeed, and I'm not sure. Perhaps they also come from the mountain, but I can't see how. Perhaps there is a mountain pass that I don't know about, and they're trading with the nations beyond. But I really can't say."

Jak gently folded up the drawing and stuck it in her pouch. "Do you have any other clues to go on?"

Gabriel shook his head. "I'm afraid not. Nothing that would help you. But that is the best lead we have on a Pillar of

Eternity. If it's not in that mountain, it was either destroyed or stolen."

"Is it even possible to destroy a Relic like the Pillars?" Jak knew even minor Relics were hard to break.

"Perhaps... but you're right, it is unlikely. Still, with the queen's men swarming that mountain, you'd think they might have found it by now. Perhaps we're all looking in the wrong place." He met her eyes once more, seeing the resolve there. At least he didn't try to talk her out of where she was going.

"Thank you, Gabriel," Jak said, adjusting the pack on her back. "I won't forget what you've done for me. And I hope I'll see you again."

"I'd be more surprised if we didn't." Gabriel seemed somber. "Goodbye, child. Best of luck on your journey."

"Tell Seph and my mother that I mean the best. For everyone. I fear they won't understand."

"I'll be sure to mention it. One last thing." He fished in a chest next to his bed and pulled out an old book. As he brought it closer, Jak recognized the inscription on the cover. It was the Book of Illadar. "My own personal copy," he explained. "I'm afraid we couldn't stop them taking the one you had. Or anything else they took. You're going to need it, I think." He stretched out his hand, holding the book in front of her.

Jak accepted the book with some trepidation. But he was right. There was valuable information here, and she never had quite finished it.

Jak left Gabriel's room then, avoiding the gaze of several students on her way out. She knew word would get around quickly that she was leaving. Hopefully, she could get out before running into someone like Seph, or...

She groaned as she approached the exit to the college and saw who was standing there, talking to Semwei. It was Naem, in full armor and a spear in hand. Of all the people she least wanted to see, Naem topped the list. As Jak entered, Semwei inclined her head and pointed. It seemed Naem had arrived to talk to her. He turned, saw her, and began walking her way. She did not stop. Clutching the straps of her pack, she increased her pace towards the college exit. But Naem quickly intercepted.

"Hey! Where are you going?"

"None of your business." Jak shot back. She had no patience for him right now and moved past him.

"Wherever it is, I want to go with you." He took a few quick steps to catch up with her, then kept pace.

Jak couldn't help but laugh, bitterly. "After everything you've done?"

"I was under duress, Jak. They forced me to betray you like that."

They were outside the college now, climbing the hill that led to the western gate. But at Naem's last words, she stopped in her tracks and spun to face him.

"I know that, Naem. That's not the problem."

"What then?" he seemed genuinely confused. Really? How did he not get this?

"Because you lied to me, Naem. You made me think you were on my side. I trusted you! More than I've trusted anyone since my father died. Do you know what it's like to trust someone like that then realize you were wrong?"

"I told you I was under..."

"We could have figured it out together!" Jak was nearly shouting now. People were starting to stare, but Jak didn't care in the slightest. "They weren't watching your every move, were they? You could have told me, and we could have kept you safe!"

"They *were* watching my every move. Of course, they were! You have no idea how long it took me to shake off the spies that night when we broke into the palace. The General was furious!" Naem countered. "Besides, I knew you could handle it."

"I almost died!" Jak shouted.

"But you didn't, did you?" Naem shot back, his own voice much louder than Jak had ever heard before. "You branded yourself, you proved my point!"

This was pointless. Without another word, Jak turned on her heel and marched back towards the gate. Naem didn't follow at first, but a few seconds later, she felt a hand on her shoulder.

"Listen, Jak, just let me come with you, and we can work this..."

Jak grabbed the hand that held her shoulder and spun. With a Strength-enhanced heave, she pushed his hand and arm down and swept his leg. Naem's Grace almost saved him, but surprise and Jak's Strength got the better of him, and he tumbled to the ground. The spear he held clattered as it fell out of his hands. Jak summoned a flame in one hand and held it over him. He didn't get back up, but his eyes moved from the flame to Jak's face and back again.

"Don't you *ever* touch me again!" Jak spit. "Or you will lose the hand that does."

"Jak... I-"

"We're done. Do you hear me? You can go to Riverbrook if you want, or you can stay here. I don't care. But you and me, that isn't happening ever again. Do you understand?"

He looked at her flaming hand again, then finally closed his eyes and nodded. Was that a tear on his face? Good, she hoped he cried his eyes out.

Then she noticed the pattern on his spear. It wasn't his, after all, it was hers. The Healing and Toughness brands were plainly visible. Had he meant to give it to her?

Picking up the spear, she left him on the street while she marched to the city limits. Onlookers made way as she passed, perhaps afraid that she might attack them too. Jak ignored them all. Only once she passed the city gate and was several miles away, did she finally take several deep breaths, and let them out with great, heaving sobs.

EPILOGUE

Q UEEN TELMA WAS A sensible woman. She knew when a battle was lost. After the Royal Priest had reentered the palace, looking like the definition of death, and claiming that there were demons in the city, she had ordered the palace locked down. With their stores of food and nearly air-tight defenses, it would take an army to break in, especially after she'd found and sealed that annoying back passage that Seph and that girl had used to get in. A useful find that probably built many generations ago as a way of getting people out of the palace during a siege. Though she didn't like that the secret had been lost to her.

She stood now with the Royal Priest in his lab, a bleak room with tools that did who knows what hanging on the walls. But she had to admit that the Priest often got results. It had been several days since his... failure. His nose was broken, his ribs cracked, and his face was bruised and swollen almost beyond recognition. But that fire in his eyes was still there, mixed with a hate that was stronger than ever.

"It would appear some of the people are leaving the city," he said, giving her the report from his spy network. "Your step-son Seph is leading them to Riverbrook."

Seph, perhaps the biggest disappointment in her life. A shame. He had been such a beautiful boy, so full of promise. But Riverbrook? Now that was interesting. That was where the troublesome girl was from.

She almost found herself disbelieving some of the reports about that girl, even from the Priest, who had been an eye-witness. She had to learn how this girl did what she did. Giving or receiving multiple brands was unheard of, and completely impossible according to her best scholars. Yet the Royal Priest insisted that she had at least Flamedancing and Strength. The mangle of bruises on his face would certainly confirm the latter. No ordinary girl possessed that kind of strength.

"Should we stop them?" The Priest asked as she kept her silence.

"No, I think not. Let them gather wherever they wish. That will only make it easier to wipe them all out in one blow."

"And if they form an army?"

She waved a hand dismissively. "We still have many who will fight for us. And our assets to the south will give us the advantage."

The Royal Priest nodded in understanding. "Then what of this?"

He indicated the table in front of the queen, where a lone figure squirmed under the ropes that tied her to the table and tried to scream through a cloth gag covering her mouth.

"This one won't give us any trouble anymore. We can spread the word that she died in the battle with the young girl. It might even help rally more Watchers to our cause."

The woman on the table, well not really a woman anymore, was Wilva, formally the General of the queen's Watchers. Members of the Watchers had brought her to the palace after her defeat at the hands of that girl. Upon nearing the palace bathhouses, where the strange Relic now hung again, something had changed in the General, turning her into one of those monstrous Fae mutations.

The former General thrashed about on the table, her long, heretical tail waving about. The Royal Priest grinned the way he did when he was about to work.

"Find out everything you can from her." The queen lifted her skirts and exited the lab. "I want to know why some turn and others do not."

She heard Wilva's muffled screams intensify as the Royal Priest began to cut into her. The screams followed Queen Telma as she walked away.

Author's Note

Wow! So not only have you read the first book, but you've gone and read the second one as well! Seriously, thank you so much. It is a delight to know that you love these crazy ideas coming out of my head enough to read more.

And there is a lot more to come, believe me. Following this book is *Through Fire*, a book where Jak finally confronts that mysterious blacksmith, and we learn just how powerful he is. But I'll refrain from saying more on that front. You'll just have to read it to find out.

Growing Ripples was extremely fun to write. I looked at it as Jak's Harry Potter years, but condensed into a single volume. She learned a lot in this one, and she's now a pretty formidable warrior in her own right. But believe me, that's nothing compared to where she's going. I love this character, and I hope you love her as much as I do. I look forward to taking her in bold directions as she becomes one of the most legendary characters in my little shared universe.

This book introduced the "Water Fae" or as they're more commonly known in modern times: mer-people. They are the third major race to form in this universe, but they will not be the last. You might be able to see what I'm doing with these races so far: essentially creating an origin story for all the mythical beings we see in traditional fantasy.

Once again, thank you for reading, and I look forward to seeing you in the next book, *Roots of Creation Book 3: Through Fire.*

GET THE ROOTS OF CREATION PREQUEL!

A prequel short story to the Roots of Creation Series.

(contains some spoilers for Out of Shadow)

Heroes are never born...they are nurtured.

Before Jak became a hero, a horrible secret surrounded her birth. Witness the beginning of that secret as we follow her father while he searches for his wife, and finds more than he could possibly imagine.

Now he's faced with a choice. Follow orders, or turn against his comrades. What will he do when his wife's safety is on the line?

Get this **(and several more)** short stories for free when you join my fantasy group: https://storytellingdb.com/go/argovale

Cheers!

Jason

SPECIAL PREVIEW OF THROUGH FIRE

The Story Continues In...

Magic in the air. Demons on the hunt. To save the kingdom, one girl must uncover her hidden abilities.

After leaving Skyecliff, Jak finds herself trapped in the endless caverns of Mt. Harafast. And she is not alone. More Fae find themselves enslaved by the misguided Watchers, and their leader is more powerful than anything Jak has seen before.

She must find a way to liberate the innocent captives and escape with her life, but her enemy is more than a match for her. Yet there may still be a chance. Lurking in the depths of the fiery Dragon Lake is an artifact of incredible power. With it, Jak could stand a chance against the forces of evil. But in the wrong hands, it could spell disaster.

Against all odds, Jak races to find a solution. Will she be strong enough to face her greatest enemy yet?

Through Fire is the third book in the captivating YA epic fantasy series. If you like imaginative realms, magical showdowns, and heartfelt coming-of-age stories, then you'll love Jason Hamilton's enchanting tale.

Continue Reading!

And Now a Chapter from Through Fire:

For the first time in weeks, Jak experienced the heat of aggression mixed with a hint of fear. Before her, nearly a mile out but clearly visible to Jak due to its size, was a Watcher caravan. It was the first she had seen since leaving Skyecliff two weeks earlier, after leaving the city in chaos. She had almost wondered if she was going in the right direction. But Gabriel had assured her that the exquisite armor and weapons they'd found in Skyecliff were sourced in the south-eastern mountains near Mt. Harafast. Perhaps in the mountain itself.

No one knew where the Watchers were getting such well-made armor and weapons. But one thing was clear, they were stockpiling it. Or rather, Queen Telma was ordering them to do so. Watchers normally wouldn't be bothered to guard something like a merchant caravan, but something about this smith work made it special, and Jak suspected it was more than just the quality of the craftsmanship.

She was alone now, traveling alone for the first time in… well actually for the first time. She'd run across a few people between here and Skyecliff, some of them even friendly, but most of the time she was alone.

In her younger years, she always had her father with her, which had annoyed her at times, though now she would give anything to have him back again. His wisdom and counsel had carried her through her adventures thus far, not to mention his brand of Telekinesis was one of the most powerful magical abilities one could have. Jak had tried to replicate it on various logs or stones when she camped each night, but was having difficulty figuring it out.

She was a Gifter, a person with the ability to grant brands, or magic powers, to anyone who did not already have one. But something about Jak, she did not know exactly what yet, made her special. She had the unprecedented ability to give more than one brand to people or objects. Assuming she could get them right, of course. Telekinesis still eluded her. But just weeks ago, to save her own life, she had given herself the brand of Healing, Strength, and Flamedancing, the ability to create and control fire.

She was now one of the most magically gifted people in the queen's realm. The only other person who came close was Naem, who was the first and only person she had branded besides herself. He now had Healing and Toughness, in addition to his first brand, Grace, or the ability to perform great feats of acrobatic and fighting skill with ease.

Jak's forehead creased at the thought of Naem. Her experience with that one had not ended well. The traitor had the nerve to befriend her, to claim to love her, only to betray her in the end. She hoped she never saw him again.

She turned her attention back to the caravan. It was closer now, and they'd be able to see her soon. Where could she hide? There wasn't much around in almost any direction. She was on the great plains, plains that continued all the way to her home province of Riverbrook, where her friend Seph was gathering the Fae.

Not far in front of her, she spotted a small incline along the side of the road. It wasn't much, but she could hide behind that small hill and hopefully the Watchers wouldn't see her.

Unless she wanted to be seen of course.

She didn't want to pick a fight with the Watchers. Even with her added brands, many of which were quite powerful. And she'd be hard-pressed to fight them if one or more was a Telekinetic. One Telekinetic she could probably best, but with other Watchers present, she wasn't sure she could handle them too.

Yet it would be nice to get a peek at the equipment they were carrying, or maybe one of the Watchers held some clues on where, specifically, they were coming from.

She reached the other side of the small hillock and lay down, waiting. It took several minutes for the caravan to approach, but the rattle of wheels finally gave them away. Jak peaked over the top of the hill, hoping none of them were looking in her direction.

There were two large wagons and one smaller box on wheels tied to the one in the back. There were...six Watchers in full armor and two other men who looked like nobles of some kind. Probably some of the queen's men sent to watch over whatever they were carrying in those wagons. And she wondered what was behind the wagon in that small box. It wasn't very large.

"Hey, metal-heads, isn't it about time you let me stretch my wee legs?"

Jak barely stopped herself from rising to her knees in shock. The voice had come from the tiny box. There was someone *inside* that thing. But surely no human could fit inside that.

"Quiet," said one of the Watchers, glancing about as if to look for someone who might overhear. "No talking or we'll put you out again."

"You know," the box spoke again. "If you don't want me alerting random passersby that I'm in here, you might start by letting me out, so I can see them coming and hide."

"I've got a better idea," said the Watcher. He waved a hand to the others who brought the horses to a halt. "How about I just put you under again, then we don't have to worry about you making any noise."

"Joke's on you," said the box. "I snore."

What was Jak to do? These Watchers clearly had a prisoner, and a very small one at that. Only a child could fit in that box, yet the voice didn't sound like a child. It was high-pitched and shrill, almost like an old man's, yet not exactly frail in the same way. Definitely a man's voice, but what kind of man would fit inside a box that size. Unless...

Her mother had suspected there were Fae in the south-eastern mountains. Could this be one of them? If so, Jak was left with no other options. Peeking over the side of the hill again, she did her best to spot the Watcher's brands. One looked like he had a Strength brand. She could deal with that. But many of the others either had their left hands covered by their armor, or were simply too far away for Jak to make them out.

The Watcher who spoke was fiddling with the lock on the small box. In his hand he held a vile with a light-blue liquid inside. Probably a potion to put whoever was in the box to sleep.

The lock clicked and the Watcher swung the top of the box open. The other Watchers drew close, surrounding the box to keep the occupant from escaping.

"Here, take this." The first Watcher leaned forward and uncorked the vile.

She couldn't wait any longer. If she wanted to speak to this prisoner alive and lucid, she had to act now. Without another moment's hesitation, she activated her brands.

Flamedancing was her biggest offensive weapon in combat. Her other brands of Healing and Strength were more passive, though the latter was quite useful in close-combat situations. But until she could close the distance between her and the Watchers, she had to rely on her flames.

The Watchers were taken completely by surprise. Many of them not even noticing her flames until they engulfed them. A few screamed as white-hot fire licked at their faces and eyes. Hair withered and burned. Two of the Watchers went down, clutching their faces.

But Jak's surprise advantage didn't last long. Within moments her fire changed direction, coming back at her without her bidding. One of the Watchers had his arms out, redirecting the flames. So they had a Flamedancer too. She could deal with that.

From her back, she swung her father's spear, brandishing it in front of her. It too held several brands, those of Healing and Toughness, meaning it could take a massive beating and not break under the force of her Strength-enhanced blows, any little notches healing themselves.

Ignoring the other Watchers for the moment, she lunged at the Flamedancer, channeling flames through her spear as she went. The Watcher took two steps back from her quick and aggressive onslaught. But Jak knew the best way to take down a Watcher was to do it quickly. The Watcher couldn't get out of the way fast enough, as he was too busy trying to redirect the flames that she sent at him. Her spear connected in his shoulder. He cried out, and Jak pulled the spear-tip out of his flesh and whirled the spear around to connect the wooden end with his head. He dropped instantly, out cold.

That was three Watchers down, including the first two. But just as she turned to face them, she felt an invisible vice-like grip grab hold of her. Great, they did have a Telekinetic after all.

The invisible power spun her around to face the Telekinetic Watcher. He stood with one hand outstretched, but looking completely calm, as did those around him. They thought she was beaten. What they didn't know was that she also possessed the brand of Strength, which just happened to be the only defense against a Telekinetic hold.

Straining, Jak pushed with all her might, willing her arms to rise. The Watcher's face tensed as he felt her physical strength compete against his mental hold. Jak continued to fight against the force holding her, and a look of amazement crossed the Telekinetic's face. He was probably wondering how a small girl could be so strong. It most likely didn't even occur to him that she had multiple brands, hidden under Jak's sleeves. Perhaps they would notice that the brand on her left hand was not a Flamedancer brand. That would confuse them.

Jak redoubled her efforts, pushing as hard as she could. With an audible snap, the Telekinetic's hold broke, and she fell two feet to the ground, catching herself gracefully. Well, as gracefully as she could without the brand of Grace. When Naem dropped to the ground, he probably...

No, she couldn't think about that right now. Looking back at the remaining Watchers with a slight smile, she drew fire around herself and launched it at the Watcher's disbelieving faces. No other Flamedancer was there to protect them this time. They ran screaming as their hair and clothes caught fire. In the chaos, it wasn't hard for Jak to catch each of them soundly with the butt of her spear, knocking them out.

She gathered the fire back to herself, making sure that the unconscious warriors were not seriously damaged. She would kill someone if she had to, but only as a last resort. She didn't even like to kill demons if she could help it, given the fact that they were former humans mutated by magic.

"Seems rather a lot for a little girl," said the strange voice behind her. "What kind of mushrooms did you eat?"

She turned to finally get a good look at whomever had been in that box. And...she tilted her head in wonderment. The man, if he could be called that, stood no more than two feet high! Proportionally he wasn't that much different from a man, though he was a bit plump. His hair was a flaming red color, spiking on top of his head. And his arms were folded as he regarded Jak.

"I...hello," Jak said, trying her best to stop staring.

"Go on, get it over with."

"Uh, get what over with?"

"Your questions. How did I get this short, is this my natural hair color, how do I use the privy. The answers are, I've always been this way, yes it is, and we have the sense to build smaller privies."

"Um, I wasn't going to ask any of that," Jak said, sheepishly. "And aren't you going to say thank you?" She didn't care really, of course she didn't, but a little acknowledgement would have been nice. She had just taken on eight people after all, six of them Watchers.

"Oh, so it's gratitude you want, eh?" He sniffed. "Well I suppose that's better than the other things. Why aren't you surprised to see me?" He narrowed his eyes at her.

"I was." Jak clarified. "But I knew whoever was in that box had to be small."

"Yeah, but you're not freaking out? Why aren't you freaking out?" he almost sounded hurt that she wasn't reacting the way he expected.

"Well, you're a Fae, aren't you?" Jak had figured that out almost the moment she saw him. At two feet high, and with natural hair color like that, there was no way he was an ordinary human. A human once, maybe, like the other Fae. They were all human until some force, often originating from an ancient Relic had turned them into something different. Well, not different exactly, something more.

The small man's face furrowed. "We don't like that name," he growled. "That's what they call us." He pointed at the men lying around them. "Don't call me that."

"Okay," Jak let her eyes rise in thought. None of the other Fae had ever objected to being called by that name, though Amelia, her best friend, hadn't really liked the name Water Fae. So far, Jak knew of three kinds of Fae: Shadow Fae, Bright Fae, and Water Fae. Though she could admit, referring to them by those names would get tedious eventually, especially if more varieties of Fae joined them. "So what should I call you?"

The little man puffed out his chest and stood tall, well, as tall as he could. "I am a gnome. That is what we call ourselves, and what all people will know us by eventually. You may call me Girwirt."

"Girwirt." Jak tested the name on her tongue. It was a strange name, but no stranger than the little man, or the gnome, appeared physically. "Why were the Watchers carrying you in that box, Girwirt."

"They were taking me to their home, so far as I could tell. Skyrock or something like that."

"Skyecliff?" Jak offered.

"That's the one. Didn't really care myself, it was better than being a slave in that mountain."

Jak perked up. "You were in a mountain? Was it Mt. Harafast? Tell me more."

"No, I don't really want to," said the gnome. He was looking around now, taking in the flat land in every direction. "I say, is there anything but grass around here?"

"You won't find anyone close by for fifty miles at the least. Why don't you want to tell me?"

"Because the last place I want to think about is that mountain. I'm free now. I'd better make the best of it."

"Okay," said Jak, going along with his logic for now. "What's your plan?"

"Walk in one direction."

"No, I mean, after that. You'll need food and water eventually, and where are you going?"

"Doesn't matter, so long as it's not here." His arms were folded again, and he was looking side-eyed at Jak.

"So your people are slaves, and you don't want to go back and help them?"

"Not much I can do here. Why, are you offering?"

Jak came clean. "If your people are enslaved, I want to help them. But I'll need a guide to get me inside the mountain. If you will do that, I will do what I can for your people."

Girwirt made a huffing sound. "You're clearly capable, lass, I saw you take out them Watchers, but they were six, and there are hundreds of them in the mountain."

"I won't attack them directly," Jak said. "But you'd be surprised what I can do." Then she rolled up her sleeves and showed him the multiple brands.

He stared at the brands for a long moment, but surprised Jak by...not being surprised at all. He looked up at her, meeting her eyes. "Well, that explains something. Tell me, are you...good?" He said the last word like he couldn't find another to use. "Like a good person?"

"I...like to think so."

"And how can you convince me of that?" His voice was lower now, more sober. Jak had the feeling that a lot would ride on her answer.

"I know other Fae, yes I know you don't like that term, but that's what they call themselves. There are many now, and each type governs some kind of elemental power. Like light, darkness, and water." She wondered for a moment what the gnome's element was, but now was probably not a good time to bring that up. "Also, my mother is a Fae. She changed while pregnant with me. I don't really have any way to prove it, but I've spent the last year doing what I can to help the Fae. I'll do the same for you."

The gnome considered her. "Well, I suppose you did save me from those men, even if you didn't know what I was. At least you were trying to help someone in need." He ran a hand through his spiky red hair. "I don't know. It's risky."

"I'll take the risk," Jak said immediately. "I've been in tight spots before."

"Yeah, I don't really care about you. It's the others that worry me. What will happen to them if you fail? I've spent a lot of time working against your Watcher people in that mountain, and we could not afford even the slightest setback."

"What could be worse than being slaves?" Jak asked.

"Like you know a lot about slavery. You have no idea what it's like."

"I know that if there's anyone who could help you, it's me. But if it makes you feel better, I'll do my best to avoid the Watchers and not cause any disturbances until I have a better idea of how to help your people."

Girwirt kept running his hand through his fiery hair, long enough that Jak wondered if he'd heard her correctly. Finally he spoke again. "Very well, if you'll do what you say you'll do, I'll take you to the mountain. I've got nowhere else to go anyway."

"Thank you, Girwirt!" Jak said. She could have probably made it there on her own, but having the little gnome around could give her a lot of information on what she'd find there, and perhaps how to get in without being seen.

Girwirt strode over to the first wagon and with a great leap pulled himself onto the bottom step. "I'll bet there's some armor in here that would fit a girl like you," he said as he took another jump to get higher up on the wagon.

"Erm, do you want a hand with that?" Jak offered.

"No, of course not, I can make do. Though you tall folk really should make everything a little shorter."

Jak raised her eyebrows but said nothing as Girwirt finally crested the edge of the wagon, and began rummaging through the weapons. One of the Watchers was stirring on the ground, so Jak walked up to him and jammed the butt of her spear into his head to knock him out again.

"We're going to need to do something about that lot," said Girwirt, throwing aside a plate gauntlet and continuing to sort through armor. "Without their wagon they'll probably double back to the mountain and alert everyone there."

"I'm not going to kill them if that's what you're suggesting."

"Do you see another alternative?"

Jak thought it through. There really wasn't much that they could do. They would just have to take their chances that these Watchers didn't alert anyone to their presence in the mountain. Perhaps if they could stay hidden well enough, it wouldn't matter what the Watchers said. They didn't know for sure that Jak and Girwirt were going back to the mountain. And they were too far away from Skyecliff to worry about the Watchers going there. Besides, Jak didn't intend to be in that mountain long enough for the queen to send reinforcements against her.

"I'll tie them up, and we'll leave as much food and water as we can. Then we'll take their wagon. That should give us a solid head start."

Girwirt shrugged, throwing another piece of armor over his head.

"Where do they get these anyway?" Jak asked as she too drew near the wagon full of armor and weapons. "They're beautiful." She ran one hand along an arm plate with a large beast etched into it that Jak didn't recognize. It looked like a lizard with wings, and huge jaws, and something that almost looked like fire coming out of them. The embossing was so good, it almost looked like the animal was moving.

"This is our work." said Girwirt. He puffed out his chest as he said it.

"The Gnomes made this?"

Girwirt scratched his head. "Well, I guess you could say that without us it would be impossible. But I suppose the Dwarves helped a bit."

"Dwarves?" Jak's eyes narrowed in confusion. "But...aren't you...I mean." "Dragons and darkness, you're an ignorant one. Don't even know the different between dwarves and gnomes." He was shaking his head.

Jak harrumphed. No one knew the difference between dwarves and gnomes because pretty much no one even knew they existed. But she got the feeling that explanation wouldn't change anything about Girwirt's attitude. So instead she said, "I'm sorry, what is the difference?"

"They're the ones that find the materials, of course," said Girwirt, as if it were the most well-known fact in the world.

"Here, put this on." He lifted up a set of light armor for Jak to look at, grumbling something like "giants" and "impractical" under his breath. Jak tilted her head at the armor. It did look about her size, and wouldn't slow her down too much. Besides, it was beautiful.

"So these dwarves." She said as she set about strapping bits of the armor around herself. "Are they in the mountain too?"

"That's right," said the gnome. "Your giant friends keep us there, building weapons."

"And why don't you try to escape? Or revolt?"

"Dragons and daredevils, it's not that easy, lass. You have any idea what it's like fighting a giant like you? They'd cut us down in seconds."

"But surely you have some...abilities that you could use? The Shadow Fae, they can make themselves unseen, or summon darkness. What can you do?" This was the question she really wanted to ask.

Girwirt paused. "That thing you did, with the fire? Well it's something like that."

"You're like a Flamedancer? But that's a super useful ability."

Girwirt was shaking his head. "It's not the same. We can't throw it around willy nilly like you giants can. We can sense the building blocks of life, and increase their vibration. That's what makes fire."

Jak frowned. How on earth did vibration create fire? That made no sense at all. But she ignored it for the time being. "And the dwarves, do they create fire too?"

"Nonsense, girl. I told you, they find the materials."

"And...what does that mean, exactly?"

Girwirt sighed, as if Jak was a child to whom he had to explain the most basic information. "They're connected to the materials in the mountain, in the Earth, in the ground. Not nearly as useful as what us Gnomes can do," he said proudly, "But they find what we need and together we shape it. Simple."

Jak wouldn't call it simple exactly, but it was definitely interesting. "I'd very much like to meet these dwarves, and the rest of your people."

"Well," Girwirt loosed the harness connecting the horses to the wagon. "Assuming your giant Watchers don't kill us first, or burn us alive, or capture us and send us to the ends of the Earth, I'm sure you'll get that chance."

He waved at Jak, indicating she should take a horse. "Come on, lass, or the beast will leave without you. Does it look like my little legs can get it to move?"

Glad that she had grown up with horses, Jak guided one by the bridle, a beautiful white draft horse. Disconnected now from the wagon, it had no saddle, but Jak could handle that. She thought.

Running a hand on the horse's muzzle and side, she grabbed its mane and swung herself up onto its back. Girwirt jumped off the wagon to land behind her. "I don't much like these things. Naught but dragons should be this big, but it seems everything is backwards with you giants. Nothing the size it should be."

Turning the horse, Jak guided it to a soft canter, and smiled with some amusement as Girwirt clung to her, muttering under his breath.

Well, this was certainly going to be interesting.

About the Author

Jason is a writer of mythic fantasy books. His passion for mythology and history led to him developing the encyclopedic website, StorytellingDB.com, which ties directly into his books based on mythology, Arthurian Legend, and more.

He's currently living the dream within walking distance of the North Carolina beaches with his wife and daughters.

When he's not writing, his favorite hobbies include hiking, reading, playing with his daughter, and developing his websites. See more of his books at StorytellingDB.com as well as some informational articles on Arthurian Legends and Mythology at StorytellingDB.com.

The Site

www.mythhq.com

The Fantasy Group

storytellingdb.com/go/argovale

Twitter

twitter.com/storyhobbit

Instagram

instagram.com/storyhobbit

TikTok

tiktok.com/@storyhobbit

Email

jason@mythhq.com

Also by Jason Hamilton

Roots of Creation

A New Light (short story)

Out of Shadow

Growing Ripples

Through Fire

Into Storm

To World's Above

As Winter Spawns

Seeds of Hope

In Creation's Heart

The Faerie Queen

Path of the Dragon

Lair of the Siren

Rage of the Beast

Strength of the Heroes

Fall of the Faerie

Rise of the Queen

Story Hacker Secrets

10,000 Words an Hour

From Zero to Published

The Plot Module